RUE DES ROSIERS

RUE DES ROSIERS

RHEA TREGEBOV

This book's story and characters are fictitious. However, as the Author's Notes indicate, the attack on Rue des Rosiers is based on an historical event.

Edited by Warren Carriou
Book designed by Tania Craan
Typeset by Susan Buck
Printed and bound in Canada

Library and Archives Canada Cataloguing in Publication

Title: Rue des Rosiers / Rhea Tregebov.
Names: Tregebov, Rhea, 1953- author.
Identifiers: Canadiana (print) 2018906711X | Canadiana (ebook) 20189067128 | ISBN 9781550506990 (softcover) | ISBN 9781550508703 (PDF) | ISBN 9781550508765 (EPUB) | ISBN 9781550508772 (Kindle)
Classification: LCC PS8589.R342 R84 2019 | DDC C813/.54—dc23

10 9 8 7 6 5 4 3 2 1

2517 Victoria Avenue
Regina, Saskatchewan
Canada S4P 0T2
www.coteaubooks.com

Available in Canada from:
Publishers Group Canada
2440 Viking Way
Richmond, British Columbia
Canada V6V 1N2

Coteau Books gratefully acknowledges the financial support of its publishing program by: the Saskatchewan Arts Board, The Canada Council for the Arts, the Government of Saskatchewan through Creative Saskatchewan, the City of Regina. We further acknowledge the [financial] support of the Government of Canada. Nous reconnaissons l'appui [financial] du gouvernement du Canada.

*For Nancy Richler (1957 – 2018),
a great soul.*

TABLE OF CONTENTS

Toronto

LUCKY PENNY

May, 1982

THERE'S A CERTAIN WEIGHT, a light heft, that she likes. Penny in the right front jean pocket, she can slip her hand in any time, turn it with her thumb between index and middle finger, never lose contact. It's another perfect spring evening, like yesterday's, like tomorrow's. When Gail called, Sarah did a quick palm flip, heads or tails. Heads. *Yes.* So she's meeting her sister and a pack of buddies down on Queen Street. Leaving her rooming-house room on Palmerston, the tidy single bed, lopsided dresser, books carefully stacked on the floor, to walk south all the way to Queen, absorbing the city, the evening, the day. Taking the smaller streets, back lanes wherever she can find them, the secret side of the city, raccoon-haunted, private. A scramble of graffiti on garage doors, messages only the writers can read. Roses spilling over broken wooden gates, tin garbage cans rusted into lace.

When she gets down to the wide, raw intersection of Spadina and Queen, it feels too broad. The walk signal to cross to the east side is flashing; she's not sure there's time to cross. That heft in her pocket. Another quick palm flip: *yes.* She hustles across all six lanes, a sedan taking a left heading north leaning on his horn at her. A streetcar shimmies west along Queen, one of the old-fashioned, rusty, red-and-cream models. For a moment she's distracted by a clunky station wagon trying to parallel park, angling awkwardly into a small spot. The driver, an older guy, looks irritated and frustrated. She figures he doesn't need an audience and hurries on past. A scraggly American elm sapling is handcuffed to a post as if it's committed some crime. Poor little

1

elm. The leaves are mostly green, though a few are withered, how often does it get watered? The collar around the trunk is padded to keep it from scarring the bark but the sapling still looks imprisoned, punished –

She hears something, she's not sure of the sequence, an engine or tire squeal and then a thud, a crash, or a crash and then a thud, a dull, flat, hideous sound.

She can't look back. She wants to keep looking at the sad little tree because she knows if she turns around, whatever she sees will stay in her. A leaf sighs, perhaps in the aftershock of whatever it is that has happened behind her.

Someone is screaming and screaming. The strength of that scream allows Sarah to turn around, because no one could call that loudly and be badly hurt.

The big station wagon is straddling the sidewalk. It jumped the curb and someone has been caught between the chrome of the fat rear bumper and the storefront behind her, a shoe store. She can see clothing, a beige cotton sweater entangled somehow with the bumper, and she can see an arm, but somehow she can't resolve the bits she's seeing into the story of what's happened. The driver is leaning forward with his head against the steering wheel. He must have seen what his car did, because his head is resolute against the wheel and she can feel how heavy it is to him.

The woman screaming is not whoever has been caught between the car and the wall. She's a young woman dressed in tight black clothing and her face is whiter than Sarah imagines a face could be and then the woman claps her hand across her mouth to stop the sound and it seems quiet on the sidewalk.

No sound, not a groan, not breath, from the woman caught; Sarah knows now it's a woman, peripheral vision.

A young man pushes his way into the store next door and she hears him say, *Call 911, call 911!* and she sees the clerk reaching for a phone from behind the counter. Sarah can't move, isn't helping, though she's had the sense to step back as others have moved forward. She sees a slim woman about her age in

2

green pyjamas, no, that's not right, green scrubs, she must be a nurse, or a nurse's aide, giving mouth-to-mouth resuscitation, something Sarah never learned, thinking that the emergency would be always someplace else, someone else's.

And now there are sirens, not that much time can have passed but she's been adrift in the moment. It's a fire engine, but almost at the same moment she sees an ambulance pulling carefully beside the station wagon and the attendants are quick but careful as well and she knows there's nothing she can do, nothing for her to do. And she's not a witness, she didn't see it. She lets this thought move through her head and then she steps back and back and turns on her heel and walks the half block to the Rivoli, where her sister is waiting for her. The sirens seem to accumulate in her head and she feels herself slip, move into a no-space. But she keeps walking, goes past the sidewalk tables out front and into the dimness of the restaurant. She sees Gail and her friends at a table in the back.

That heft in her pocket. If she'd waited for the next light, if the penny had said *no*, it could've been her. Her emergency.

Gail's deep in some kind of intense talk but she must sense Sarah – she looks up and waves her over. "So what do you think of the Rivoli? I thought we should try something new, we're always at the Queen Mum… I think you've met Caroline, and this is Sharon and Barb."

"Have a seat," one of the women, a stocky redhead, says.

Sarah can't sit. She doesn't know what to do with her body.

"Sarah," the woman says, "you okay?"

She doesn't have any words.

"Sarah?" Gail turns to her, gets up from the table, moves towards her. And that's when Gail pulls her against her thin chest, because something must be wrong for Sarah to look like that. And Sarah feels herself pulled into Gail, feels herself slip back into herself, pulled through that fine surface of glass that separates them into the halves they have to be without one another, and she knows, her forehead against Gail's cheek, that they're back into the whole they really are, Rorschach inkblots that mean something, anyone can read what they mean. Her sister has her.

❧

The next day the headline in the papers is 'Freak Accident Kills Pedestrian' and there's a picture of the station wagon and police tape but no mention of the woman's name, just her age, 51, and the age of the driver, 71. The next day Sarah will come back to the sidewalk where it happened because she can't help herself. Nothing remarkable, the yellow caution tape is gone and the storefront looks unmarred, but there is a man kneeling at the threshold, something reverent in his bearing. He's fixing the metal doorplate, which must have been injured along with the woman who died.

Laila

My small fist slowly warming the coolness of the iron loop. An oval loop, its stem toothed. The taste of iron when I took it in my mouth, the first thing I knew. I would lean my small head against my mother's chest. My fist holding the key. It opened the door to our house, the old house, the one we lost. My mother's voice low, hoarse, the lullaby slow: *Everyone we love has gone away. When I come to greet the fig tree, no one is there to ask me in. The good nights now are gone. Everyone we love has gone away. But sorrow never lasts forever.* My mother's voice, hoarse and low.

DIRT

"YOU SPEND YOUR WHOLE DAY in the dirt." Gail's fiddling restlessly with the short tufts of her hair.

"I like dirt. I *like* dirt." Dirt is something Sarah understands. It makes her feel real.

Gail has set her hands flat and tense on the rough wooden surface of the table. It's three days since they met at the Rivoli, since Sarah saw but didn't see the accident, the woman who died. When Gail pulled her against her thin chest, Sarah felt herself slip back into herself. But now Gail's separate again, and ticked off. With Sarah, as usual.

"Look, I know how hard you work," her sister is saying. "But what is going on inside your head? Is it some proto-Marxist manual-labour-is-the-only-real-work shit? Or just plain old Protestant-work-ethic shit? Huh?"

Sarah blinks in the sunlight. She can't explain. What she likes about her job is that she can clear away the weeds and garbage, and make a space where something can grow. That's why she likes her job. It's simple. And clear.

She blinks again. There are no curtains, no blinds on the industrial-sized windows in Gail's apartment. Gail has just moved into this raw loft space south of Queen, a corner one-bedroom, 14 foot ceilings, all open, all light. Complete with a colony of mice, Gail has told Sarah gleefully. There's no way anyone can keep a place like this really clean, but it doesn't matter to Gail.

It matters to Sarah. It's why she can't hack roommates. The furnished rooms she stays in are hers only, and they've always been clean, or at least cleanable. Though it did take her three solid days to scrub this last one down. She even went in for a new coat of paint; the place looked like some kind of crime scene, indecipherable splotches all over the walls evidence of god knows what. But the linoleum is in one piece and the other roomers are elderly types too dejected to be loud.

Her sister is drumming her fingers on the table. Gail is perpetually impatient these days, almost as perpetually outraged. At the weather, the patriarchy, the Falklands War, the Middle East, Sarah. Sarah and her preference for the study of dirt over the study of law. No, make that the practice of dirt over the practice of law. Gail's a real lawyer now.

"You are bloody wasting your life. You're twenty-five, for god's sake. Twenty-five, not eighteen."

"I know when my birthday was."

"It's five years since you finished university and you're still living in one crappy room after another, taking one crappy job after another. Pardon me. You never *did* finish university. You're one credit short of graduating and then you go and quit! One lousy course to complete and you'd have had your BA."

One lousy course she couldn't hack. One lousy course that cracked her like an egg. She had to drop it. And anyway, her major was history. What was a BA in history going to do for her?

"God, Sarah, just open your mouth, will you? Can you just say something for once? You know I hate this *silent treatment* shtick. And would you put that goddamn penny away? Just stop it!"

She didn't even know she'd taken the penny out of her pocket, was turning and turning it in her fingers. Nervous habit. She sticks it in her pocket, gets up and goes over to the counter, starts attacking the stack of dishes in the sink to calm herself down. She is not getting into a fight with Gail. And she's not going to start thinking about that damned course again.

"Will you leave my dishes alone? I know I'm a pig. Just leave them." But Gail doesn't get up, instead watches as the stack diminishes beneath Sarah's hands, swift, deft as they always are with anything physical. "Why are you sticking it out in such a dumb job? What are they paying you, anyway? Minimum?"

7

The handsome rent Gail is paying for her bohemian loft is easily covered by the handsome salary from her job at the law firm. Gail, the newly fledged lawyer. Sarah, on the other hand, has never earned anything more than minimum. Gail is right. *Crappy*. That's the adjective. It's been one crappy job after another. Waitressing, tending bar, even a two-week career as a cocktail waitress at the legendary rooftop bar at the Park Plaza. It's 18 months now, including layoffs, that she's been at the City Garden Centre, the longest she's worked at one job since she left university, left Winnipeg for Toronto. It's the usual Sarah job: crummy hours, seasonal lay-offs, unsafe working conditions. She's gotten to the point that she likes the smell of the place: the acid tang of pesticides that mixes with the fumes off-gassing from the plastic hoses and cheap watering cans they sell, which in turn mix with the smell of soil and moss and roots, the spice of nasturtium and geranium transplants.

Gary, her crew manager, calls Sarah 'Mighty Mouse.' She can heft a 64-quart bag of soil if she does it right, and she always does, bending at the knees, spine straight. She just grazes 5 feet and 100 pounds, but she's always been strong and the job has made her stronger.

She's studied up about plants and growing conditions and flowering seasons, and now Gary will send customers to her for recommendations. The rest of the crew isn't interested in looking stuff up, getting to know the plants, but nobody minds getting their hands dirty. Sarah likes that, likes losing herself working with her hands, letting the days melt into her work. She gets to be in her body, that strong little machine that's always willing to take on more work. That's why she's sticking with this particular crappy, minimum wage, dead-end job. At least till the next coin toss. She fingers the penny in her jeans pocket.

Gail picks at the rough edge of the table, sighs. "When's your famous boyfriend back?"

"Michael's back tomorrow."

"So you're not objecting to me calling him your boyfriend today?"

Sarah doesn't answer.

"Lucky dude gets five days in Paris on an expense account. I'm working for the wrong law firm. Has he been there before?"

Never. Sarah shakes her head.

Gail tips her chair back, runs her fingers again through her hair. "I got a call from Rose last night."

Sarah stops doing the dishes, turns around. The room gets smaller. Rose.

"It must have been only 11:00 in Winnipeg, but when the phone rang at midnight, I nearly jumped out of my skin. She wasn't too bad. I mean, there've been times I couldn't even understand what she was trying to say, but last night she was mostly coherent. She went on for a while about her job; she sounded really worried they won't take her back. I get that – she was pretty erratic before David finally convinced her to take sick leave."

The last time Sarah saw their big sister Rose, in Winnipeg, she was just beginning to show. Or at least to show to anyone who knew how willowy Rose usually was – the slight bow to her belly evident only to someone who knew how concave it normally was. When they were little, Sarah would cuddle against her, her head fitting neatly in the inverse pillow of her big sister's stomach, the rise and fall of Rose's breathing a lullaby.

"I called Mom this morning. She was making rhubarb preserves. I had to listen to a lot about the preserves before she'd say anything about Rose. When I finally got her to talk, she told me that David really wants Rose to get onto antidepressants. Now. Their GP is on board, says it's urgent. Even Mom and Dad are pretty much convinced. But Rose is refusing to take anything, she says she doesn't want to be drugged."

Sarah's finished the dishes and now there's nothing for her to do. She sits back down at the table.

"I don't know, Sarah, she just can't seem to get over it." Gail's frowning, picking at the table again.

It. The baby.

Just because Gail doesn't want kids doesn't mean Rose shouldn't.

And Rose did. She and David were always deciding things, planning, and they'd had this pregnancy all figured out. Rose would have three whole months paid maternity leave, thank you Unemployment Insurance. Pat, their mom, empty-nested and eager to jump back into her role as the perfect mother, was set to babysit three days a week when Rose did go back to work. It was all planned out.

They really wanted that baby.

"The GP says she *has* to go on antidepressants." Gail's voice has gone flat. "It's clinical depression, he says, not just her feeling down."

It's the first Sarah's heard of the expression.

Gail puts on her smart-big-sister-to-dumb-little-sister voice. "Clinical depression is the medical term for a depression that isn't just a mood. There's an actual chemical imbalance that impairs brain function. She's sick. Physically. That's why they want to put her on antidepressants."

"Do *you* think she should go on medication?"

"I don't know," Gail says. "She might be getting better. She didn't sound as bad as last time, I don't think. David told Mom that Rose is sleeping a bit better. I don't know… Maybe she *should* try a course of medication, just to help get her over this hump. But she'll get over it. It was just a miscarriage. She can have more kids. The doctor told them it was insignificant in terms of her fertility."

Just a miscarriage. Insignificant. Rose loved that baby already. It was almost full term. And then she had to carry it for weeks, *weeks*, waiting to give birth to a dead baby. How is it possible in the twentieth century that a woman has to carry this dead thing in her for weeks, and modern science can't just take it away, let her bury it, let her bury what she hoped for, what she already loved? "She loved that baby, Gail."

Sarah sees the look on Gail's face, knows she's picked the wrong word, knows what's coming.

"Just what exactly are you saying?" Gail's starting to flush. "Are you saying a foetus is a person? You, of all people?"

Is Gail going to pick a fight? Is she going to start up on a woman's right to choose now? When they're talking about Rose? "No. But I'm saying she loved that baby before it was born. It almost was born."

"It wasn't a *baby*, Sarah! You can't call it a *baby* when it's still in utero!"

There's no point trying to talk this out with Gail, whose face has gone a deep dusky rose, her narrow chest rising hard with each breath.

"For fuck sake, Sarah, where would you be if you hadn't had a safe abortion when you were a teenager? What the hell is wrong with you?"

She should know better than to try talking to her impossible sister. Sarah gets up from the table, starts wiping down Gail's counter, swabbing the rings under the detergent bottle, the crumbs under the toaster. She has to do something. She has to be doing something. She can feel Gail fuming behind her, but she won't turn around, she won't look back.

❧

The abortion's become this cautionary tale Sarah tells herself, told her boyfriend Michael when they met a year and a half ago, two sentences: *when I was sixteen and having sex for the first time I got pregnant. I had a safe abortion at the Morgentaler Clinic in Montreal.* On the Spadina streetcar home from Gail's, she wonders what would have happened if the story had been different, if she hadn't gotten the abortion.

Sarah watches a kid at the back of the streetcar playing air guitar with a buddy. Her highschool boyfriend, Nick, played lead guitar in a band he'd put together. She loved to watch his mouth while he played, he had to hold his mouth just so, really hard and tight, as if he were holding the music back, keeping it inside. Their best song, "Gloria," the one they practised over and over, only had three chords. The chorus spelled out the letters – *gee-el-oh-are-I-ay* – so that they were almost words, almost meant something. Gloria made the boy feel good, *all right*, but what the hell did *she* feel? Gail no doubt would have a lot to say about that omission, about the repression of female sexuality.

At sixteen Sarah knew almost nothing about sex, even the basic mechanics were fuzzy. No real sex-ed in schools in those days. And Pat, her mom, for all her being the perfect cookies-in-the-oven, kitchen-floor-gleaming mom, was too embarrassed to ever give Sarah the birds-and-bees talk. She was too shy to ask Rose, and Gail didn't seem interested in boys. So it was all hit or miss. Sarah tried looking *sex* up in the Encyclopaedia Britannica in the basement, but all she managed to find were a lot of colour diagrams of internal organs.

Nick waged a steady campaign for *going all the way*. He knew Sarah didn't mean to be a cockteaser, but she was leading him on. And he told her about blue balls, how if they just kept fooling around but she didn't let him have sex, this mysterious awful painful thing would happen to him. She'd had no idea boys were so fragile – they were supposed to be the tough ones. Sarah didn't like the pressure. And she *really* didn't want to get pregnant. So part of her thought, *no way. Go find yourself a girl who's easy, Nick.*

But a bigger part wanted to go along.

And it wasn't because of Nick's dumb arguments. It was because before Nick, and his hands, and his mouth, there were times she felt like one of those cheap chocolate Easter eggs, so hollow with loneliness she could break. So finally one day, on the sofa in the rec room, they did it. After, she asked Nick if he shouldn't use a safe next time, he could get a safe, couldn't he? At a drugstore? He said wearing a condom was like washing your feet with your socks on: it wouldn't be any fun for him. So a few days later Sarah went on her own to the Mount Carmel Clinic to get condoms. *Mount Carmel.* It sounded like a candy bar. The Clinic was great. Everybody knew you could get birth-control information and pregnancy tests and condoms there, and they wouldn't tell anyone. But she never did work up the nerve to ask Nick to use them. They used the rhythm method, because what were the odds, Nick said.

Good, as it happened. They must have been having sex for almost a month and the box of condoms still hadn't been opened. And she was late.

She kept thinking she couldn't be pregnant so soon, they'd only had sex five, maybe six times. Then another day and another went by with no period.

How was she going to finish school if she was knocked up? What was she supposed to do with a baby? Sarah remembers the crazy little conversations, bargains she started making in her head: she'd never do it with anyone ever again as long as she got away with it just this once. She'd run away from home, live on the streets, hide in someone's barn. Not tell anyone and give birth in a field, like those women in China, leave the baby on church steps, synagogue steps.

Nothing in her wanted this.

She told Nick she was almost ten days late. She could go back to the Clinic, he told her, she could get a test. And the Clinic could give her a referral for an abortion, if she was pregnant and decided she didn't want it. Abortion was legal in New York. And there was the Morgentaler clinic in Montreal. Sarah knew she was too young, she couldn't have a baby. She couldn't tell her parents, she was too scared. But she could tell her big sister Rose. She'd tell Rose because Rose would know what to do, Rose would tell her what to do.

Which she did. Which was to get an abortion.

The truth is, for all that the story is boiled down now to two tidy sentences, Sarah has this ghost count in her head, how old her kid would be if she hadn't had the abortion. Boy or girl, she doesn't know, could they even tell the sex that early? But she didn't ask.

Eight. The kid would be eight. Briefly her mind flits to a gawky kid, good at baseball, track and field, like her. Good at maths, like her.

She stops herself. The streetcar bumps along the tracks heading north up Spadina. Sarah hauls on the window to open it, she needs the breeze on her face.

Where would she be if she hadn't had access to a safe abortion, what would she be? She sure wouldn't be her sister Gail, who even as a teenager was way too smart to get knocked up. Her sister the crackerjack newly minted lawyer, the success. No. And not Rose either, the perfect sister, who waited until everything was in place – the devoted husband, the stable job – before she got pregnant with the kid she decided to have, wanted to have.

If Sarah hadn't had the abortion, she'd be what she is now, a loser scraping by on minimum wage. And on top of that, she'd be a single mom in some basement dive in Winnipeg.

And how would she feel about the son or daughter who'd kept her from graduating high school?

She can't imagine not loving a kid.

GIFT

PARIS. MICHAEL IS BACK FROM PARIS, his first time in Paris. City of light. City of romance. In fact, Sarah beat him to Paris. She was there once, for four days. Her boyfriend-of-the-month, Reuben, asked her to come backpacking through Europe on $10 a day with a side trip to Israel. The penny said *yes*. Four days in Paris. She remembers how dirty it was, how glorious. The mystery of bidets in the bathroom of the grungy little hotel, *frites* on the street in the Latin Quarter. With French mustard. Reuben got some sort of crotch rot from the dirty sheets, a fungus. The whole place made him nervous. But she loved it. Maybe partly because her French was pretty good even then. And it's better now. She figures she hasn't had much in the way of a vacation since she was twenty and backpacking. Five years.

She's over at Michael's apartment, the sweet two-storey, two-bedroom on Howland he keeps asking her to move into. He's back from Paris and here's his trophy, a gift. The package is wrapped in pale blue tissue paper, a seal of a deeper blue closing the folds. *Un p'tit paquet cadeau.* His grin wide. The salesclerks always offer to gift-wrap stuff. She starts nibbling at the seal with her fingernails. Her nails are always trimmed close for work or she can't keep them clean.

Michael takes the package, opens it for her: a skirt in polished cotton a deep blue, almost indigo, with little slashes of black patterning it. Cotton, but such a fine weave that it feels like silk. The salesclerk thought it would fit: he told the clerk Sarah was *très petite*. He holds it against Sarah's waist, testing for size.

She likes it. Of course she does. But Michael probably paid more for the skirt than she's spent on clothes in a whole year. In the top drawer of the dresser in her rooming-house room, Sarah keeps a spiral-bound notebook to record expenses: newspaper 50¢; subway tokens $8; laundry $2.75; lunch 95¢. Beside it a column of running totals, which she does in her head. *Mene, mene, tekel, upharsin.* She can pay all her bills but it's tight, she needs to keep track. And she always pays her share. She doesn't want to owe him anything.

He pulls her up for a kiss. The skirt was expensive, yes, he tells her. Shockingly, obscenely expensive.

She likes Michael's mouth. A taste of peppermint, a taste of salt. The kiss continues and for moments they both forget about the gift, then she draws away, steps back, looks at it again.

He slides his fingers inside the waistband of her jeans. He wants her to try it on. She unzips the jeans, steps into the skirt. Tugs at the fabric belt, ties a bow at the front. *Très petite.* He steers her to the narrow full-length mirror hung on the closet door.

She's not sure about the woman in the mirror. She looks at her hands – clean, but rough-looking, a bit chewed at the knuckles with nicks and scratches from the job. She looks up again, this slight, graceful woman; the lines of the skirt making her a bit fuller, giving some amplitude to the small self she's used to, the one that doesn't take up too much room.

His hands slip back into the waistband of the skirt. "I missed you." He takes her to sit on the bed, puts his mouth against her neck. "Stay the night this time. The whole night. I don't want you to go home." Now the beautiful skirt is pooled on the hardwood floor. All right. All right. She'll relent this time, stay through to morning, whatever it costs.

⁓

The sisters used to play a game: *if you were a dog, what kind of dog would you be?* Sarah would be a Jack Russell, Gail and Rose agreed instantly. Sarah argued for a border collie because she liked how smart they were, but the other two wouldn't have it, they knew she was the muscle and spunk of a Jack Russell.

And that meant Gail had to be a Jack Russell too. Peas in a pod. People often thought they were twins, despite the twenty months between them. The big debate was about Rose. If she were a redhead, Rose Red, she'd be an Irish setter, but she wasn't a redhead, all three of them were brunettes. The two younger sisters thought Afghan, they wanted lean and elegant and perfect, and wasn't that Rose, even before her growth spurt, before she rose above them, 5' 7" at the least? She wasn't tough in the same way as them, Rose, not interested in softball or track. What she did love was dance, and her long limbs lent themselves easily to it. Back then, Rose was never the centre of a clique but never at the edges either. Not an anxious joiner like Gail, always jockeying for status, and not a loner like Sarah. It was easy for Rose, she was easy in the world, comfortable in her skin. That's how it seemed to Sarah.

Sarah never minded not having much in the way of friends, because Rose and Gail were pretty much all she needed. She remembers the three of them squeezed into the double bed Rose reigned over, the oldest sister getting her own room. The three of them head to toe, toe to head, cuddling each other's feet, which they pretended were wriggling babies. Making sister sandwiches, fighting about who got to be the meat. Squeezed tight against each other, squealing, squished and happy. Rose always supremely in the lead, framing the stories, setting the rules of the games. Winter Sundays, the three of them making grilled cheese sandwiches under the broiler, slices cut from the huge blocks of Bothwell cheddar their father brought home from the factory. Rose in charge, supervising the timing so the cheese was just the perfect melted gold with patches of light brown. The three of them in the long summer evenings of Winnipeg, playing Kick the Can and Hide & Seek in the backyards and alleys, in the rectangles of their neighbourhood. And always being found.

They were all always found.

Now Sarah thinks maybe it's Gail who's the border collie. She's certainly smart enough. But is it Gail or is it Sarah who has that need to herd, keep things together, at least where it comes to the sisters? Sarah, the youngest,

17

who can never let the thread go too far or too loose, or she'll feel herself slip. The thread stretching so far now. Maybe that's what she is, a bulldog. Dog with a bone. Won't ever let anything go.

Not her sister. She is not going to lose Rose. Not if she has to breathe for her; not if she has to make her want to live.

She is never going to lose Rose because without Rose she doesn't know who she is.

❧

Michael's been back from Paris three days now, but they're still hungry for each other. So much so that he's managed to persuade her to stay the night twice in a row. She knows it drives him nuts when she leaves, as she usually does, in the middle of the night. Though he sleeps like the dead, never stirs when she slips out of bed to walk the 15 minutes from his place to hers, he hates waking up without her. She can't explain why she doesn't like to stay, not even to herself. Just knows she'll wake up at 1:00 or 2:00 or 3:00 afraid of that old terror, afraid of being afraid. Just like she used to when she had one of her nightmares, the ones that started when she was just a kid. She'll wake and start to feel herself freezing over, feel it coming over her, and she'll have to get up, get dressed, do something, to keep herself from the dream. Save herself. She'll have to prove to herself that she *can* get up, get dressed, leave the apartment and walk down the street to her own room. She'll walk under the shadows of trees through the dark streets that belong to her, not afraid, fall into her bed and sleep till morning.

She can't talk to Michael about this. Doesn't talk much at all, but tonight, after two nights where she made herself stay with him, where she didn't in fact wake up but slept beside him through the night, she finds herself telling him about the sisters and their games, their dog selves. "You're not a Jack Russell," he says, running a finger along the definition of her ribs, her tight little stomach, following the curve of a bicep. "You're a whippet. Purebred."

"Purebred Jewish," she tells him.

"Purebred Jewess."

"Don't, Michael..."

"What?"

"I hate that word."

"Why?"

"Because it feels full of hate."

He sits up in bed. "Oh for god's sake, Sarah. What now? Why is *Jew* okay but not *Jewess?*"

Jew. The word swells to fill her mouth, the room. *Jew* isn't okay. She can't even say *Jew* to herself without feeling the hate soak through that single syllable, without feeling the word, the hate, obliterate her. And she hates herself for letting that feeling go into her.

"Sarah? Fill me in here; cut me some slack."

Of course he doesn't get it. Michael's a blank slate when it comes to these gradations of hatred, self- and otherwise. He grew up in some WASP hick town in British Columbia and until he got to university, he'd never even met anyone who was Jewish. She's no good with this kind of stuff. Gail's the one who could explain how *the colonized mind internalizes oppressive negative social stereotypes*. But she's not Gail.

"Sarah? Please don't go into your silent routine again."

"I... it's... Look." She takes a breath. "Michael. I have trouble even with *Jew*." He can't stop himself from wincing. "Yeah, it's wrong. But I always hear the slur. Hear all this weight behind the word: history, the war. I can't separate it out. And then that *ess*: Jew*ess*, Neg*ress*. It always seems to mean *less*. And I feel a smirk there. Like the marker for sex is a marker of sexiness." She rubs the heel of her hand against her forehead.

"Okay. I get it."

"Good," she says. *Does* he get it? She may have made a dent or he may just be more confused. No point belabouring it. "So, if I'm a whippet, what are you? A golden retriever?" She touches his fine blond curls, trimmed short for the office. He relaxes back against the pillow, smiles.

19

"I'm a mutt," he says. English, Scottish, Irish, an Icelandic great-grandmother, he's reeled out the Scott family tree for her. His family's butchers, bakers and candlestick makers a match for her Old Country tinkers and tailors. "Purebred nothing. Good breeding stock." Then he curls himself around Sarah and in what seems like seconds, he's asleep.

HISTORY

THE DREAMS GOT WORSE. She remembers the first time; she was little, she must have been four or five. Someone important was visiting from Chicago. Her mother had fussed for days, baking, cooking, tidying the already tidy house. Rose had to sleep on the folding cot between the twin beds in Sarah and Gail's bedroom so the visitor could have Rose's big bed. Sarah remembers playing with the brass catches on the suitcase she found on Rose's bed – they snapped open and shut in such a satisfying way – until her mother told her to stop for goodness' sake. Sarah watched from the doorway as the visitor and her father sat on the living room sofa and talked and talked about something, a river of names, *Chaya, Moishe, Manya, Lev, Basya, Reva, Avramele*. A beautiful lady, her smooth blonde hair carefully framing her face, who would slip into and out of Yiddish, not just names but shreds of stories that unspooled, soaked into the fabric of the room. *Shah*, Sarah's father would say softly, his hand on the visitor's arm, when the English words rose loud, *di kinder*. The children shouldn't hear. Her father, rigid and tender; the visitor's hands pulling at the buttons on the dusty-gold wool sofa till one came off. She held it in her palm, silent, until Sarah's mother came into the room to tell the woman it was all right, it could be sewn right back on. Everything could be fixed.

Who were they, Sarah asked, who were all these people with the funny names? The visitor's hands frozen in her lap. Your family, she said. Aunts and uncles, cousins. My brothers and sister, she said, all lost, all gone. Gone where, Sarah asked. Gone. Dead. Murdered. *Shah*, her father said, *shah*, not now.

Sarah woke that night, both sisters breathing beside her, woke from a dream of someone, something on the other side of the door of the house on Rupertsland, her house, but not her house. Someone at the door of her room that was not her room. She didn't know what house, what room, where she was, someplace far away. Someone or thing at the door coming to take them all. She was awake but wasn't awake. Her eyes were open, but she couldn't move: something at the door, something pressing on her chest so that she couldn't breathe. Something in the room with her that she almost saw, and it wanted to hurt her. To hurt her sisters, breathing beside her. And she couldn't move, couldn't do anything, not to save herself, not to save them.

At last the feeling receded and when she was able to gasp, to make a sound, Rose rolled over sleepily in the cot beside her, patted her hand. *It's all right, it's all right. Go back to sleep.*

That was the first one. The dreams, these waking nightmares, went on, intermittent but repeated, dreams that held her paralyzed, that she would wake from and not be awake. It must have been years before Sarah learned the woman from Chicago, Sosha, was a relative, a second or third cousin of Abe's. That visit was the only time Sarah remembers hearing her family speak directly about the Holocaust, as if there were some sort of holiness around it that wasn't supposed to be put in words. No words beyond the implied, insistent *never again, never forget.* But there were also the second-hand stories from friends at Hebrew school whose parents, like Sosha, weren't lucky, weren't born here like Sarah's parents: *Dad said he hid in a barn.* For the whole war? *I don't know. He doesn't like to talk about it. Months, I think. Maybe years.* Or *they killed my mother's cousin, he was only a baby.* Who killed him? Where? *The Nazis, of course. I think it was in Poland.* Things that happened outside of history, outside of time and place and cause and effect, that happened in the alternate universe of the Holocaust.

There were stories too from Sarah's teachers at Talmud Torah School, many of them survivors. And then, in grade five, from the darkened claustrophobia of the school auditorium, the sour sombre voice of the narrator of the documentary, the film she watched but didn't allow herself to re-member, though she couldn't let go of the wavering images, the naked dead more bones than flesh, strewn like pick-up sticks. The ungainly, abject bodies of middle-aged women, also naked, the broad landscapes of their backs, the soft arcs of the folds of belly, holding on to each other, standing at the edge of a pit. Alive at the moment the photo was taken, but not for long. The lampshade made of human skin, its perverse translucence. Images that were not real, except that they were real. Images of real people and any one of them could have been related to her, any one of them could have been her, if she'd been alive back then, if she'd been there, in that place outside of place, time outside of time.

By the time she started university, the dreams were sparse, almost for-gotten. Spring of her second year at the University of Manitoba, she checked the catalogue for the September course offerings. The course de-scription for a Twentieth Century History class tacked to the bulletin board outside the office read: *Holocaust History. Destruction of the Jews of Europe. Topics include anti-Semitism, the rise of Nazism, treatment of Jews within Germany between 1933 and 1939, plans for the 'final solution' and their execution, life and death within the concentration camps. Lengthy readings, some of them emotionally taxing. Not recommended for freshmen.*

The destruction of the Jews of Europe, this was a story that she wanted to know, one that belonged to her. She wanted to have a way of framing her-self, of claiming more than the four words: *never forget, never again.* More than faded waking nightmares. If she had facts, comprehension, maybe there would be something she could do with them.

☙

The first day of class, September. Among the twenty or so students, a woman who looked to be somewhere in her fifties, sitting at the back of the class. She was a bit heavy, stocky more than fat, and her strong, round face was carefully made up, framed in tidy blonde curls. She was sitting very straight, in a tailored dove-grey pantsuit, her hands quiet in her lap.

The instructor, Prof. Koenig, was a big man, tall and broad-shouldered. His hair was blond, crew-cut, his posture almost military, though there was something immediately gentle about him as well. A hint of an accent but his English was very clear as he welcomed the students to class, congratulated them on their courage for enrolling. Uneasy glances among the students at this, half-stifled laughter. He went on to explain that this was an experimental course, that Judaic Studies in conjunction with the History Department had helped sponsor him to teach it on a trial basis.

"What is a Jew?" Prof. Koenig asked. "This is a question Jewish philosophers and thinkers have been asking themselves over the centuries on behalf of the Jewish people. The answers have been rich, nuanced, and varied. In the context of Nazi anti-Semitism, however, the question was asked to a different purpose. I believe a pertinent opening point for this course would be to examine how, in the early stages of the rise of Nazism, the answer to this question was formulated."

Prof. Koenig put up a colour reproduction on the overhead projector. At first it looked like a diagram of molecules, something from Sarah's grade 12 chemistry textbook: pairs of circles that linked to other circles. Some were open, some had red crosses, some were filled or partially filled with black or grey tones. The heading at the top in German, *Die Nürnberger Gesetze*, The Nuremberg Laws.

The Nuremberg Laws codified the Nazi's anti-Semitic policies. The chart showed the pseudo-scientific method used to identify Jews. Prof. Koenig gently tapped the screen with a wooden pointer. A person who had four German grandparents was considered to be *Deutschblütiger*, of 'German or kindred blood.' A person who had three or four grandparents who were Jewish was considered to be a *Jude*, a Jew. In between were those categorized as *Mischlinge*, mongrels of 'mixed blood.'

False science. False categories. *What is a Jew?*

Criteria were further established to distinguish more finely between Jews and *Mischlinge*: affiliation with a Jewish religious community, marriage to another Jew, whether one's parents were married or one was born outside of wedlock, the dates of marriage and birth. These refinements were necessary to establish racial 'purity.'

If you were a Jew, what kind of Jew would you be? This was what the chart wanted to establish. A true Jew, a full Jew, a half Jew of the first or the second degree? These were categories that subsumed every other thing you were. You were a Jew by blood, not belief; blood was what counted. Converting didn't necessarily save you. Atheism didn't save you. Jewish blood. Were you Jewish to your bones? Were you Jewish in your flesh? Under the Nuremberg laws, back in 1935, before the war had even begun, a Jew wasn't a German citizen, a Jew couldn't marry a non-Jew, a Jewish doctor couldn't treat non-Jews, a Jewish lawyer couldn't practise law. And soon, these gradations of identity would determine not just your civil rights, but whether you lived or died.

"I'd like to continue today's lecture with an introduction to the *final so-lution*, Nazi double-speak for the annihilation of the global Jewish population. In the six years of the war," Prof. Koenig said, "the Nazis in fact did a remarkably effective job of approaching their goal." His voice was tight, dry. Prof. Koenig positioned a new chart on the overhead projector. As he placed it, his hand enlarged, Sarah could see the thick gold wedding ring he wore, the faint blond hair on his knuckles.

"We have all heard the figure, six million. But how do we interpret this

Historic Jewish Population	
1935	16,728,000
1945	11,000,000
1950	11,297,000
1955	11,800,000
1960	12,079,000
1970	12,585,000

loss? Let's start with a statistical evaluation. The approximately six million killed through the programs of the final solution represented almost thirty-six percent of the global Jewish population at the time. How quickly the Nazis were achieving their objective, even though the large Jewish population in North America, which had for decades been a refuge for Jewish immigration, was not directly affected.

"Students should also note that, despite the recovery in the years since the war, a recovery unimpeded by any systematic program of persecution, and despite the existence since 1948 of the State of Israel as a safe haven for Jews, the world Jewish population has not nearly recovered. The figures for 1970 – unfortunately, I don't at the moment have more recent figures – show that the global Jewish population was still four million less than the pre-Holocaust population, putting it at approximately seventy-five percent of its pre-war status after a full twenty-five years of recovery. Numerically speaking, what was done in six years has not been undone in twenty-five."

The numbers started to dazzle Sarah. She couldn't keep herself anchored in the lecture. *Final solution.* She was back in her grade 12 chemistry class, watching solutes swirl into their solvents, salt into water. When the mix was saturated – no, supersaturated – the salt started to precipitate out. Salt and water made tears, didn't they? Or was the problem not a chemistry problem at all, was it mathematics? What were the variables, what was the unknown, what needed to be *solved?*

Now Prof. Koenig was talking about the engine of the destruction of the Jews of the Europe, the concentration camp. More double-speak: *concentration camp.* From the German *Konzentrationslager,* he explained. And Sarah was again in chemistry class: *concentrate,* in the case of a liquid, a substance that had the majority of the solvent removed. Orange juice without its water. A body without its blood? No, that didn't make sense. But what did? *Concentration camp.* Not *murder factory.* Not *annihilation centre.* Prisons for people you meant to kill, people penned up in such numbers you needed to build a city for death. Concentrated butchery.

Prof. Koenig was closing the blinds in the classroom, Sarah could hear the whir of the slide projector and she was pulled out of chemistry class, she was back in the Talmud Torah School auditorium, waiting for the *never again, never forget* images she carried in an album in her head.

"A challenge I am faced with as your instructor is how to take what must remain incomprehensible – the wilful slaughter of millions of civilians – and help you understand the individuality of what was lost. Our method in this class will be to try to put faces to the numbers, to tell specific stories, in addition to the examination of large historical facts, the theories and numbers.

"Many of you will be familiar with these iconic images of atrocity and, much as I don't want to overwhelm students in the first class, we do need a visual reminder."

The class was silent. The lights went off and then the projector bulb turned its brightness on the room.

At first Sarah couldn't resolve what she was seeing into a whole, this intricate pyramidal mountain, piles of bodies like stacks of logs. A heap. Bones barely coated with flesh. A concentration camp liberated too late for everyone in this picture.

There was another brief light in the room, someone had left. Sarah glanced at the door, saw, as the door closed on her, the back of the older woman she'd noticed earlier.

The slide shifted, and there were living people in this photograph. Soldiers regarding the bodies below them. They were smoking cigarettes. They were in uniform and they seemed very tall, very vertical over the horizontal figures of the dead. They were wearing helmets and caps, their guns were in their holsters. It was a quiet moment. Everyone who needed to be dead was dead.

The next photo was barely legible. A grey rectangle in a grey field, it looked like a bit of fallow land, what had grown there harrowed under, until you understood that the crop was bodies. None of them discernable as people, but that was what they must have been. Something that must have been an arm here, a head over there. The bodies were scarcely even bodies, every particle of individual identity taken from the people who died.

Who took these photos? German soldiers, as trophies? As proof, witness? Some of the photos had to have been taken by the liberating Americans or Russians. How did it feel to them to press the shutter, take this moment away with them before it was gone?

The projector continued clicking through its progress. Prof. Koenig said nothing, gave no captions, just kept advancing the slides. Finally paused. "I know that these images are exceptionally difficult to view. Let's take a ten-minute break, and when we come back, I'll go over the reading list as well as the syllabus with you."

Sarah sleep-walked out of the classroom to find the woman who left during the slideshow in the hallway, bent over a water fountain. The woman straightened, wiped her mouth with the back of her hand, a gesture that seemed out of place with the elegance of her outfit.

Sarah went up to her, touched her arm. "Are you all right?"

The woman looked at her with kindness, without smiling. "Of course I am, my darling." Sarah couldn't quite place her accent. "I was just taken a bit by surprise and thought I would give myself a minute. I think our professor is sorting the sheep from the goats."

"I don't understand…"

"I think he wants the students who cannot look at those pictures not to take the class," the woman said, again kindly, again without smiling.

Sarah was still touching the woman's arm. The woman patted her hand. "I'm Helen. Helen Rosenbaum."

"Sarah Levine."

"*Sarah*. A good name, Sarahleh. So, what do you think of our class?"

Sarah shook her head, looked down at the floor.

"And what are you studying here at the university, Sarahleh?"

"History."

"History. Good. Good for you." Helen was fishing around in her purse, took out a toffee in a gold wrapper. "Candy?"

"Yes, thanks."

"I'm a bookkeeper," Helen said. "Tax time I'm busiest. But I figured it out so I would have time to take this one course."

Helen's jacket was a bit long on her compact frame so that her small, manicured hands, a shell-pink polish on the tidy nails, just peeked out of the sleeves.

Helen looked at Sarah looking at her sleeves, then pushed up the fabric first on one arm, then the next, demonstrating two muscled, tanned forearms. "Nothing up my sleeves," she said, turning each arm for a full view. "You were looking, no? I haven't got the tattoo. But I lived through the war, yes."

Helen had been in the war. She was standing right there in front of Sarah, her straight bearing, her strong, tanned arms, alive. She had been in the war. And she was herself, still was who she was.

"I'm sorry," Sarah said.

"You don't need to be sorry." Helen gave each sleeve a tug so the jacket settled into place, then suddenly bent and picked something up. "Lucky penny," she said. "Here, you keep it. For luck."

"Thanks." Sarah slipped the penny into the pocket of her jeans.

"You're wondering why I'm here." Helen's voice made it barely a question.

Sarah couldn't look her in the face.

"You're wondering why you're here," Helen added.

She was.

"Well, Sarah, maybe we'll figure it all out by the end of the course. We can talk more about history some other day. Time to go back into class."

BRUNSWICK

WHY DO ALL BEER HALLS SMELL the same? Spilled beer and cigarettes and old puke and ancient carpet – *why* do they have carpet? – saturated with the above, plus a hint of piss. More than a hint. Gail wanted them to meet up at The Brunswick on Bloor and the coin flip was heads. *Yes.* Even though Sarah doesn't like drinking. Doesn't like cigarette smoke either. Maybe she'd like drinking more if she didn't have to cope with the cigarette smoke. Worth considering.

Can she be drunk? Nobody can be drunk on one beer, but who knows, her threshold is low. Sarah hates beer, that nasty bitter taste in her mouth, but it's the cheapest thing you can order, so beer it is. Gail's several pints ahead and she's holding forth on the situation in the Middle East, Israel's bombing of Palestinian targets in southern Lebanon. The Israeli ambassador in London has been shot and badly wounded by an Arab terrorist group headed by some-one called Abu Nidal. Almost thirty Israelis have already died in PLO attacks.

Thirty Israeli Jews dead in the PLO attacks versus 300 hundred Arabs killed in the Israeli bombing of the West Beirut PLO headquarters. Ten to one. There's a school of thought that would propose that's the right ratio, ten to one. Ten equals one, a Jewish death counts for ten times what a Palestinian or Arab death counts for. Haven't Jews learned anything about counting the dead? This endless hideous ledger of casualties on both, all, sides.

Sarah listens as Gail marshals more facts, General Gail: the PLO are heavily armed with Katyusha rockets, surface-to-air missiles, tanks. It does sound like enough to 'drive the Jews into the sea,' as the PLO have vowed to do. Can Gail be defending Israel? Not likely, but the beer, not to mention

Gail's fervour, is making Sarah fuzzy. Fizzy, too.

The rest of Gail's comrades, it's the same crew as last time at the Rivoli – Caroline and Sharon and Barb, plus a couple of other women who may or may not have been introduced – have fallen into stiff silence as Gail ploughs ahead. This is not their story. Or maybe it is: are any of them Jewish? Sarah doesn't know, can't tell. *What is a Jew?*

The topic has swiftly changed, someone else leading the charge, heady stuff, something about radical feminism, and Sarah is having even more trouble following the tense, intense discussion. She swallows more beer, trying not to make a face at the taste. The other women, Gail included, are way ahead of her, little arrays of empties on the sticky wooden tables in front of them, the circles from their bottles perfect little Venn diagrams of what has and has never been thought before. Now they're talking about someone named Dworkin, and she's afraid to ask Gail who this person is, though she can deduce, through the increasing fog of talk and booze, that she must be an American feminist.

One of the women is leaning into the table and explaining how our concepts of 'woman' and 'man' are caricatures, social constructs. Too reductive. Okay, but only girls get to have abortions. Or miscarriages. Only girls get to be clinically depressed because *no one, no one* can help them when they have to carry their dead baby in their body for weeks, weeks and weeks because science and medicine have failed them.

She must have said this out loud because everyone is looking at her.

"Please don't tell me you're into that Essentialism shit," Caroline – this one with a curly cloud of blonde/grey hair may be Caroline – says. "Have you even read Dworkin?"

Sarah never even heard of her before this evening.

"If you're going to start defending men…"

"That wasn't what Sarah meant," Gail butts in.

"If she's going to start defending men," the woman turns away from Sarah, sets her beer down in front of Gail, "the least she can do is read *Woman Hating*." And then she and Gail are locking horns about the dangers of heterosexuality. The beer has sloshed onto the already soggy table and is starting to edge towards the curly cloud woman's sleeve, but she doesn't seem to notice. Sarah takes a paper napkin from the crummy little tin holder – what genius designed these things? – and starts to dab at the spill but she isn't accomplishing much.

Sarah finds she has a second beer in front of her; someone must have ordered her another. Or is it a third at this point? Possibly. Maybe that's why she was dumb enough to open her mouth. Should've flipped the penny. The penny would've given her the right answer. *No.* Keep your stupid mouth shut.

"Look, Sarah –" this is Gail butting in yet again, "heterosexual women can be seen to be sleeping with the enemy. If you look at it *structurally...*" Gail isn't really talking to Sarah, she's focused on the others. Despite their snippy disagreements, the other women are on the inside and she, very clearly, is out.

Sarah takes another swallow of beer. So she and Rose are sleeping with the enemy. Or are they in fact the enemy? Heterosexual women. Who is Gail sleeping with these days? For all her speech-making, all her *personal is political*, she's been pretty quiet on the personal front. Maybe she's sleeping with Caroline, maybe that's why they're so cosily embattled. Not that she cares if Gail is sleeping with women. But she wishes Gail would just tell her, not imply her superiority on every front, including who she likes to sleep with.

Sarah wants to get up and leave, but now it's Barb talking about the media, about how on the news they'll describe a murder victim as *known to police.* That phrase. How do they know her? What do they know of her? There's an acronym the cops use, NHI, they designate some homicide cases NHI – *no humans involved.* Meaning it was a prostitute or drug dealer who got killed, so no big deal.

Sarah gets up. Barb is okay, but enough is enough. Enough beer, enough feminism, enough Gail.

"Where you going?" Gail asks. "The woman cannot hold her liquor," she says to Barb, who smiles. "Heading for the Ladies?"

Sarah nods a yes.

"Me too." Gail gets up from the table.

Just the two of them, washing their hands in the sink. "You okay?" Gail asks over the roar of the hand dryer.

Sarah rinses her hands, dries them.

"Sarah, would you please answer?"

"It's a bit much," Sarah says.

"What?" Gail bristles again immediately.

"That Caroline woman. I don't know why I opened my mouth. And you. *Sleeping with the enemy.* Come on."

"Sarah." Gail's using her Big Sister voice. She even slows down, to make sure her dumb little sister can follow. "You need to look at these things *systemically.*" Sarah must have twitched or something, because Gail starts to go off again. "Or maybe you're just not that interested. Maybe you don't even call yourself a feminist."

Sarah slumps against the sink. She doesn't know *what* to call herself. Can't she want something, anything? Can't she want Michael? Does she want him? And what about Rose? What about what she wants? Is David the enemy? "What if all Rose wanted was a kid? Was that so bad? Does she have to feel so bad because of what she wanted?"

"What are you talking about, Sarah?"

"Why do you hate David? Why do you have to hate Michael?"

"David? Michael?" Gail leans on the sink, staring at them both in the mirror. "I'm not talking about them. I didn't – Look. Sometimes I don't know what I'm talking about. David is a sweet guy, and even Michael – in spite of the suits and ties and the crease in his pants – Michael Scott is decent through and through. For Pete's sake, I was the one who introduced you two."

She did. Gail met Michael at law school. At first Sarah thought Gail was going out with him, she seemed to like him so much. But she kept inviting Sarah along and soon it was Sarah and Michael dating.

"He might be going back to Paris. For six or eight weeks." Michael's Paris project is taking off. It's some huge office tower in La Défense, the modern suburb that sits just outside the city limits of Paris, which is why they get to build skyscrapers there. His firm is representing the Canadian developers. The negotiations are going to go on for a while, and they might want him to be in on them. If they pick him, he'll get up to two months in Paris on the company dime, starting at the end of June, maybe early July.

"No shit. Lucky ducky. Is he taking you along?"

"He hasn't asked me."

"You worried?"

"About what?"

"Him losing interest. At some point, he's just going to give up on you."

Sarah shakes her head.

"How many times does your dreamboat boyfriend have to ask you to move in before you say yes?"

Sarah turns the penny in her pocket. *Yes. No.* What would Gail say if she knew it was hard for Sarah even to stay the night with Michael?

"The guy's solid, Sarah. At least give him a whirl. Move in before he stops asking. *Toute de suite.* And the tooter the sweeter."

The tooter the sweeter. Their dad Abe's awful old pun. "I don't know…" Sarah says.

"You don't know what?"

Sarah fidgets the penny.

"What? What? Don't give me the mute treatment. Speak!"

They both have to smile at that one.

"Speak! Like this…" Gail barks like a cartoon dog: *arf, arf, arf.* They're both giggling now. A woman comes out of one of the stalls, raises an eyebrow, grins.

Sarah stops giggling, sighs. "I just…I don't do that kind of thing. I don't live with other people. I like being by myself."

"Do you? How come?"

"It's simpler. Besides, I don't deserve to live in a place like that. Not on my salary."

"Oh Jesus, Sarah. *Deserve?* Why do you have to *deserve* anything? The guy's crazy about you, even if you do drive him around the bend." She turns to Sarah, hugs her, whispers into her neck. "C'mon. Stop living this half-life."

"Half-life?"

"Yes. The half-life of Sarah Levine. And yes, even though I wasn't as good at chemistry as you, I know I'm not talking about the time it takes for half of the radioactive atoms to decay. It's a metaphor. Your life. I don't get why you're so stuck. Take a chance. You don't have to mete out your life in teaspoons."

"I couldn't pay my half of the rent on that place. I don't want to owe him anything."

"So work something out that's fair. What's the deal with owing him?"

"*Mene, mene, tekel, upharsin.*" Sarah's muttering into Gail's neck.

Gail holds her at arm's length. "What's that?"

Sarah shakes her head.

"Speak! Good girl!" They start to giggle again.

"You don't remember Hebrew school?"

"Not as well as you."

"*Mene, mene, tekel, upharsin.* From the Book of Daniel. It was the writing on the wall that only Daniel could read: *I have counted and counted, and all has been accounted for, and you have been found wanting.*"

"You remember that shit? Why? Why's it important?" Gail rubs some water on her face. "I think I'm sobering up."

"Me too."

"Tell me how you get drunk on two beers."

"I think it was three."

"Sure. So what's the deal with *mene, mene?*"

"I keep this ledger in my head. Adding everything up, trying to make everything balance out in the end." So she's safe; in control. So the nightmares are tamed. "I wish I didn't have to."

"I wish you didn't have to add everything up either. Too. Maybe I haven't sobered up." Gail scrubs at her face again. "Anyway, quit calculating. Give the guy a chance. Enjoy for a change."

Laila

My father's shirt was a blue flag. When I was a little girl he would sing me songs of our country, though we don't have a country. Songs of lives wasted for no reason, of dreams killed in the messengers' hands, call without response.

But there were songs of weddings, too, of the bridegroom and his beloved, moonlight and doves. His voice a warm rumble: *How beautiful are the doves and how beautiful their children.* Lovely nonsense, my mother would tell us, smoothing the blue shoulder of his shirt. *I come to the house of my beloved, my skin scented with cardamom. I come to the house of my beloved to greet him.* Nonsense, she would say again, but still she would smile.

In our country, he would tell me, you slaughter a lamb for the wedding, you shave the groom with a golden razor in front of all the village, you paint the bride with henna.

His shirt a flag.

We don't have a country.

CALL

SARAH IS CURLED ON HER SIDE, dreaming of the yellow carpet in the living room of her family's house on Rupertsland, when the phone rings. She reaches for it though she's still mostly asleep. "Hello?"

Sobbing on the other end of the line. She's awake. It's not another nightmare. Sarah checks the clock; it's 4:00, which means 3:00 in Winnipeg, if it is Winnipeg. "Rose, is that you?" No answer, just the sobbing. Then her name.

"Sarah?"

"Yes, it's me. Who is it? Rose?"

Choked sounds, more sobbing.

"Rose? Rose?"

More choked sounds. Sarah feels her own throat tighten. Feels herself begin to float outside of herself, tethered only by the phone and its cord.

"Rose?" How many times will she have to say her sister's name before she answers?

Now it's quiet on the other end of line. Could it be a prank call? No, it has to be Rose. The sobs return. "Rose. Please. It's Sarah. I'm right here."

Silence again. Then muttering. She can't understand the words. "Please, Rose. Tell me what's wrong. I'm here."

No words this time, just the sadness of those gasps, swallows. Sarah's standing in the darkness, so little light coming though the blinds from the streetlights outside, even the traffic noise quieted. She feels alone and feels, just now, the tether let go, and she's spinning out into an orbit distant from the surface of the earth. "Please," she says. "Tell me what's wrong. Tell me; let me help."

Now at last Rose has started speaking but the words she chokes out don't make any sense. David's not there; Rose doesn't know where he is. He may be gone. Everything's gone, everyone's gone.

"It doesn't count." Rose's voice is clearer now but she's still not making sense. "That's what they said. But if this doesn't count, what does?"

What's she counting?

"They said not to look back. David's gone. They say it doesn't count."

"Rose, I'm sure David's not gone. And I'm right here."

"You're not. You're not here and I need you."

She's right. They're miles from each other. Half a continent.

"How can it not count? I need to count it."

"Rose, I don't understand you. You need to rest. You're so tired you're not thinking straight."

"That baby counted. How could they say that?" Rose's voice is clear, unshaken.

Then Sarah hears another voice, muffled, in the background. *Please*, he seems to be saying, *please*.

"Rose, is that David? Let me talk to him."

More indistinct noise and then she hears the receiver rattling, then David's voice, sounding groggy. "Sarah?"

"She doesn't sound good, David. She said you weren't there. She was talking about the baby."

"The baby." A silence. David's silence now.

"David, are you there?"

"Yes." His voice comes back. "Sorry. Rose was tossing and turning so much and it's been a couple of days now since I got a good night's sleep. I went to the basement, fell asleep on the old couch down there and then it took me a while to realize she was on the phone." He sounds apologetic, fuzzy.

"What's happening?"

"She just can't seem to sleep. I really want to get her onto antidepressants. She's lost so much weight. I don't know... *Rose, it's okay, I'm just talking to*

Sarah. She's worried. I'll take you right back to bed. I have to go, Sarah. She's having a bad time. Yesterday she couldn't get out of bed; she said she felt para-lyzed – *No, no, you're okay. You're not paralyzed. You just felt that way.* Listen, sorry, Sarah. I got to go. I'll try to call tomorrow if she's doing better."

෴

That evening Gail is sprawled on the comfy sofa in Michael's apartment. She hates Sarah's rooming-house room, has always hated all of them. She's only been to the current one a couple of times, always finagles meeting anyplace else. She came to Michael's bearing *churrasqueira*, roast Portuguese chicken with juicy little potatoes that the three of them hoovered back in about ten minutes. Now Michael's off to the gym and the sisters are on their own.

Gail's taken off her linen jacket – a sophisticated, cream-coloured affair that Sarah is sure she'd ruin in two seconds – and is picking at an invisible spot on her black capris.

"Why so glum, Chum?" Gail asks. Another of Abe's sayings.

Sarah misses her dad. "Glum. Well, yeah."

"Tired too?"

"I didn't get much in the way of sleep. I did think about calling in sick, but I feel better when I'm working."

Gail nods. "Me too. I'd rather be distracted than mope. Is there any scotch?"

Michael keeps the cupboard beside the fridge well stocked. Sarah gets up, goes into the kitchen. Before Gail got to the apartment, Michael and Sarah had been arguing about whether Sarah should go to Winnipeg to help Rose. Gail's been to Winnipeg twice since the miscarriage, two long weekends she carved out of her work week. Although Sarah wants to go – she hasn't been there in almost a year – she was worried about whether she could get the time off at the Centre. That's when Michael hit the roof: the Centre. What exactly did she think she owed them? She was at their beck and call: *come in this weekend, don't come in this weekend. We're busy, we don't need you.* They paid minimum wage, didn't give any decent hours, laid people off whenever things got slow. Her sister was sick. She didn't need the Centre's permission to take some time off.

He hates her job as much as Gail hates her rooming-house room.

He hates fighting too, she knows that, but he left without apologizing. Michael never apologizes, it wouldn't be manly to say he was sorry. Or something like that. Sarah read somewhere that an apology is an act of trust.

Maybe Michael doesn't trust her. Maybe he has no reason to.

Sarah comes back with the bottle of scotch, pours a finger into Gail's glass.

"C'mon." Gail waves her hand in an upwards come-hither. "Don't be a cheapskate."

Sarah adds another half-inch.

"Sarah. Come on." Gail takes the bottle from her, fills half the glass.

"It's Michael's."

"Michael would not *zhaleveh* me his scotch."

True. He wouldn't. She's never seen him stingy about anything. Michael would be happy with the goodly portion Gail has just poured herself. *Zhaleveh*: begrudge; withhold. Spare. Don't spare the single malt.

"Aren't you having any?" Gail asks.

Sarah pours herself a finger, watches Gail sipping reflectively. Sarah prefers scotch, single malt or otherwise, to beer, but it's too expensive a preference to indulge, except on Michael's dime. A portion he would never *zhaleveh*.

Don't zhaleveh *me my worries about work, about Rose, Michael.*

"Sarah?" Gail raps lightly on her sister's forehead. "Anybody home? The scotch hitting you already? Speak. You can do it."

"I'm thinking about Yiddish idioms."

"I can't get a word out of you in English and you're thinking about Yiddish? I doubt it. You're thinking about Rose."

Okay, she is.

"Don't go. To Winnipeg. It'll be okay. I talked to Mom and she said David took Rose to the doctor's first thing. She's agreed to go onto antidepressants.

They say it might take three to five weeks before they can fully stabilize her."

Three to five weeks. How can Rose get through three to five weeks the way she is?

"They think she'll be all right at home, though they did talk about admitting her."

Admitting her.

"She can have herself admitted voluntarily to a psych ward in the hospital. It's not like she's being committed. But they don't think she needs to – she can stay home. David is going to take a few days off work, keep an eye on her. Until the drugs kick in and she's feeling better. Mom can spend more time with her too." Gail takes the untouched scotch from Sarah's hand, sets it on the glass coffee table. "She's going to be okay."

Gail can't know that.

"She will."

Gail finishes off her own scotch, solid gulps now, not sips. "Sarah. Remember how bored we were as kids? Remember how boring everything was?"

Fighting in the back seat of the car as their mom circled and circled the Dominion supermarket parking lot looking for a spot, or dully ploughing through their Talmud Torah homework. Sitting for eons in the women's section of synagogue during High Holidays, being shushed and hushed by the moms and babas, who were in turn shushed by the purple-faced shammes. *(Ladies! This is a place of worship!)*

Gail's leaning back on the sofa, eyes closed. "All that boredom but then, sticking out of that flat everyday landscape, we had those times when everything was all sparkly. Holidays. Treats. *Mom's taking us to the Paddlewheel at the Bay for lunch! Dad caught a fish!* Or those Sundays – *Zaida's taking us for soft ice cream!*

"Treats. We were schooled to expect so little. Because," she opens her eyes, looks at Sarah with a whiskey intensity, "we were supposed to have this ongoing gratefulness: it wasn't the Depression. It wasn't the War. So hooray for boredom." She closes her eyes again.

"I keep thinking of that black-and-white photo of you on the old sofa. You're sitting cross-legged in the red party dress, we had matching party dresses with a border of embroidered cherries. I guess you weren't yet two. Your hair's sticking up all over but you're holding your hands together, arms crossed against your chest in glee. This huge goofy smile across your face. You were like that, Sarah. *We* were. Unadulterated glee. *Soft ice cream. Fishing with Dad.* Where did it go?" She's sitting upright again and has that whiskey stare but something steady, sober, behind it. "Rose was always so solid. What happened to her?"

And suddenly Sarah's crying, quiet but hard. Gail sits there staring at her empty glass.

Sarah can't stop crying. "It's my fault."

"What's that? Here." Gail hands her a paper napkin. Sarah blows her nose, swipes at her eyes. Starts crying again.

"What did you say? It's your fault? Don't be stupid."

Sarah takes another wipe. "It is."

"*Your* fault Rose is sick? What the fuck are you saying?"

"Nothing. Jeez, I'm leaking. I can't stop." They start to laugh a little.

"We're running out of napkins. I'll get toilet paper." Gail gets up, comes back with a wad in her hand. "Here. Blow. Please stop. You never cry."

Sarah crumples the wad in her hand.

"Is it the abortion? You're thinking Rose is somehow paying for your abortion?"

Sarah nods.

"*Mene, mene,* it all gets balanced out like this? Some big daddy in the sky is punishing Rose for your sins?"

She nods again.

"Listen to me, idiot. One has nothing to do with the other. Nothing. That's not how it works. That's not the kind of justice the world works by." She hands another wad of toilet paper to Sarah. "And she'll be okay. Because she's Rose." Gail straightens her jacket, reaches for her purse. "Now that I've drunk three-quarters of Michael's scotch, I better hop on the streetcar home. You okay?"

"Yeah. I'm all right. I'll stay here, spend the night at Michael's."

❧

Where is she? She's not at home. That much she knows. Her body is propped in a special chair, knees apart, and they've given her some kind of drug – she's not fully in the room or in the chair.

A nurse is holding her hand. She can feel the smooth skin on the nurse's hand, lovely soft skin, the bump of her ring. She's watching the ring, blue stones of some sort, sapphires maybe, in a band, set in gold. Beautiful. Not much light caught in it, not much light in her, though the room's bright. It has instruments and cabinets, little horizontal vents in the cabinet doors that remind her of the kitchen on Rupertsland. But she's not at home.

"All right, now," someone is saying, a male voice. "You'll feel some pressure, but no pain. There shouldn't be any pain."

She closes her eyes. What's happening now? Not pain. Something else. Her mind keeps flitting away from what's happening. Which is her being emptied. Flesh being emptied, scraped out, scraped clean. It'll be gone soon, over.

The nurse is stroking her hand, so gentle, but she doesn't want to open her eyes, doesn't want to think about where she is.

She wants to close her legs. She doesn't want to be open like this.

And empty. Hollow. More hollow than she's ever felt before. Lonelier. Nothing to keep her from being this empty. Nothing to keep the thin shell around the hollow from smashing.

"All right, now," the nurse is saying. "Can you tell me your name? Can you tell me where you are?"

She hasn't got a name. She isn't anywhere.

Sarah wakes herself from the dream. And she's fully awake, not in some dreaming-while-waking state – she's in her own rooming-house room on Palmerston, she can hear the traffic along Harbord. When she left Michael's place at 1:00 she almost woke him stumbling against an armchair. So damn stupid. Here she was trying to escape one dream and all she did was fall into another. She checks her watch. 2:30. She has to get back to sleep, her shift starts at 8:30. She goes to the sink, pours herself a glass of water, she's so dry, but the water quiets her throat. The front yard is full of shadows. She doesn't need this damned dream, this dream among all the other damned dreams: she remembers everything. All she has to do is open a door in her head and she's there, sixteen and pregnant. Terrified. Cupped in an orange plastic chair with angled chrome legs in the waiting room at Mount Carmel Clinic, waiting to find out what's going to happen to her, *become of her*. That time when her life was some cheap soap opera.

It was Rose who saved Sarah, Rose who made the appointment at Mount Carmel Clinic for her scared kid sister. Sarah can see herself sitting there in that chair at the Clinic with the news. The news – it wasn't good news/bad news, it was just bad news – and she felt the ceiling opening up above her, she was going to float right through it. That or keel over. The nurse had explained that it was very early, and that was good. The nurse was saying *termination*, not *abortion*. They could get her an appointment for a *termination* at the Morgentaler Clinic in Montreal. And when the nurse said that, a certainty pushed through Sarah's confusion. Her body decided for her: she couldn't have a baby. Because she was still a kid. And it wasn't a baby. It was a clump of cells. Less than a goldfish. It was just something lodged in her body, a part of her body she didn't want.

And at the same time, the very same time, in the same place inside her where she was sure termination was right, she was also sure it was wrong. She was doing harm, preventing a life.

It was wrong and it was also right.

She signed the paper, didn't look back. Even now, she can see the room, the paper with her signature, can see how – before everything broke inside her – Rose came into the room. Rose walking in, spine straight, graceful. Rose picking her up from the Clinic, taking her home.

Everything was going to be okay.

Of course everything wasn't okay. Though the Mount Carmel Clinic did get the appointment in Montreal arranged for her, she needed her parents' consent. And then it was her mother, who never yelled, who was yelling; her mother, who never slammed doors, slamming her bedroom door. And it was her father, always so proud of all of his daughters, telling her he was disappointed in her. Saying they thought she had more sense, better judgement. Hadn't they always trusted her? Was this how she responded to that trust? His big hands wringing themselves, his big strong body pacing the room. And what about this boy she had the hots for. Abe's face heating up, the big hands not knowing what to do. She'd made the decision that *this* was the person she wanted to take these kinds of risks with. *The boy has a responsibility too.* Abe's big voice raised, his big hands clenched.

A few days later, Sarah was flying to Montreal with her mother, Pat's compact self tucked tight into her seat, flipping the pages of a magazine, putting it down, picking it up, closing her eyes to snooze but not snoozing. Together they took a cab straight to the Clinic, an ordinary-looking house in the east end of the city. After the operation, after Sarah remembered her name, where she was, when she came out of the drug mist, there was Pat in the recovery room, taking her arm and folding her into the cab, which seemed to be waiting nervously. Then they were in the hotel room and Sarah was on the bed. And suddenly her mother was her mother again, not silent, not angry, just giving her a glass of water, making her take a pill the doctor prescribed. Pat helping her to the bathroom, and when Sarah started feeling woozy, she called *Mom*, she had that word in her mouth, and there was Pat in the bathroom with her, holding her arm so she didn't fall, swiftly helping her change the pad the nurses gave her, as if she were a little kid again, helping her back to bed.

When she got home from the procedure in Montreal – that's what her mother called the abortion, *the procedure* – all Sarah wanted was to stay in bed. But she couldn't stay in bed, she had to get up, she had exams to study for, her mother wanted her to *get back into a normal routine as quickly as possible.* Sarah couldn't be late for school, no excuses, no reason not to clear her place, not to help with the dishes, not to please put her sweater away, no need to just sit around watching TV all evening, some fresh air would do her good.

Sarah wanted Nick, wanted someone to hold her till it went away. She didn't want to think about what they scraped out of her, what they did with it, a bunch of cells, where they took it. Something that could have become a baby. Her baby. Hers and Nick's.

She called Nick, left messages with his mom a couple of times but he didn't call back. When she finally ran into him at school, he told her her dad had come by his house to give him a talking to, scared the bejeezus out of him. He was really mad, her dad. And then Nick told Sarah he couldn't see her anymore. He didn't want them to be together, didn't want his parents to find out what happened, he wanted it all to go away, like it never happened. His beautiful hands hanging at his sides. She grabbed his shirt, she wouldn't let him do this, he *had* to be with her, especially now. All he did was pull away, pull the shirt from the grip of her hands. He was so much bigger than her; standing in front of her, he was all she saw.

She came home, closed the door to her room. She'd been taken to pieces and emptied out and there was no one to put her back together. She needed something to do, needed to do something, count it all up, account for what she'd done. Figure out the variables. No more Nick, no more Nick plus Sarah. No Nick plus Sarah plus a possible baby. So no Sarah. Maybe it did add up in one way, Euclid's axiom: things that are equal to the same thing are also equal to one another. She didn't want a baby and Nick didn't want her – it added up but the sum was a negative. She was nothing. There was nothing, nothing bad and nothing good. Or was nothing good? Was it bad?

Abe called up to her from the kitchen to come down and eat. She didn't answer, didn't have any words for him. He came upstairs, sat on her bed, his big hands in his lap. Dinner was on the table. Her mom had made tuna casserole. Sarah looked at Abe, expressions she couldn't quite identify flickering across the plane of his face. And then the elements of his face, features, broke into parts that didn't come together. Eyes, bushy eyebrows, nose, mouth, but what had happened to her father? The bits didn't make a face. Was this her good father? She heard footsteps on the stairs, the door to her room opened. Her mother. Sarah looked at Pat's face and the sprinkling of features didn't come into place to be her mother. Her mother and father were saying something to each other that she didn't understand.

They wanted her to try to sleep, and maybe she did sleep, but she kept drifting in and out, the plusses and minuses, equivalencies, moving through her head. There were voices in the hall, Rose, her parents saying something about dehydration, should they call a doctor. The next morning her mother was there again, wanting her to talk, tell her what was wrong; she was angry with Sarah. And then her mother's face, those strange planes and bits of features, changed, and her mother put her head against Sarah's neck and was crying, saying, *Baby, you're my baby, Sarah. I want you to be all right.* She was her mother's baby but she didn't have a baby.

And then her mother was gone and Sarah must have slept again because the light kept changing. She heard steps coming up the stairs again. Rose was sitting on the bed, talking to her. "Have some ginger ale. We know you don't want to eat right now, but you need to drink something." She put her arm around Sarah's shoulders, sat her up. Put the straw to her lips. Rose watched her drink. "You're scaring the hell out of us, Sarah." Sarah finished the glass.

"I'll get you more." The room emptied of Rose, and then she was back, and Sarah took the glass in her hands, drank up.

"Sarah. Nick broke up with you, right? That's what's wrong."

What was wrong. Sarah didn't know what was wrong, or right.

"Gail asked around at school. I'm sorry." Rose's hand on her arm.

Sarah was sorry too, about the abortion. She couldn't ever undo it and no matter what she did, there would never be enough good to make it even out again. There would never be enough good. Maybe Rose understood, because Rose's arms were around her and suddenly Sarah was crying and Rose was holding her, keeping her together.

"Lie down, Sarah. Put your head down and rest. You're wearing yourself out."

And Sarah lay down, and Rose lay alongside her, smoothed her hair. Hummed a song, then started to sing it, her sweet clear soprano washing over Sarah, washing her clear. The lyrics words Sarah knew, the waters troubled, a bridge. And she was feeling small. But she *had* laid herself down and Rose had laid *herself* down beside her so that Rose's body was an edge to her own, a dam, so she wouldn't spill over. A container, so even if her body wasn't a solid, she wouldn't dissolve. Rose's body hemming her in, keeping her in place. Rose rolled over, gently placed her light weight on Sarah, a soft pressure. Her breath in Sarah's ear. Rose's body holding her on the earth. The only thing holding her on the earth.

In the rooming-house room on Palmerston, Sarah sets the glass of water down, wipes her mouth. Fills the glass again, swallows all its water. A car's headlights go by, their light travels across the bed. The clouds have moved off and she can see the moon, almost full, above the street. She needs to go back to bed now, back to the bed empty of Michael, of anyone.

HARDINESS ZONES

WINNIPEG IS ZONE THREE, too cold for any but the hardiest hybrid apples, though the crabs do well. Sarah's never seen cherries grow there, no apricots or peaches either, the soft fruit too tender for Winnipeg. Toronto's zone six. Magnolias dropping saucer-sized blossoms onto the lawns in spring. Gorgeous Bing cherries in people's front yards. Peaches, with some coddling; plums.

Sarah's even heard of expat Italian families growing small fig trees. To winter the trees over, they dig a trench next to the trunk, dig around to loosen the roots and then tip the tree sideways into the trench, bury it in soil. And wait for a resurrection in spring. So much trouble. Such a long dark wait for the tree.

But they shall sit every man under his vine and under his fig tree; and none shall make them afraid.

Where did that come from? *Loh-yissah goy el-goy kherev veloh yilmedu ohd milkhamah*: The song from Passover Seders: *and they shall beat their swords into ploughshares, and their spears into pruning hooks: nation shall not lift up sword against nation; neither shall they learn war any more.* The promise of peace, and a garden, or at least a blossoming field. The verse goes on: *But they shall sit every man under his vine and under his fig tree; and none shall make them afraid.*

Fig trees, grapevines – in the Winnipeg of her childhood they had seemed iconic and impossible, symbols of that unimaginable land of milk and honey. No – not unimaginable, the much-imagined new State of Israel, the promise of the map on the wall in every classroom, a delicate pale yellow country surrounded by delicate pale green. Lopsided little dagger pointing south. *And the desert shall rejoice, and blossom as the rose.*

How much does it cost to grow an exotic fruit in a place it wasn't meant for? And how did anyone ever first think of forcing its growth, then continuing, over years, to cultivate it?

"You look preoccupied, Sarah." Mrs. Margolis is wearing her usual gardening uniform: faded khakis and a white shirt with the sleeves rolled up, both over-sized on her slim self. The shirt could be a cast-off from her husband, though Sarah's sure Mr. Margolis never wears anything remotely rumpled to the bank. He'll wave genially at Sarah as he heads for his BMW, briefcase in hand, always pressed and ready. Maybe that's what Michael will look like in twenty years.

Mrs. Margolis is Sarah's favourite customer, and Mrs. Margolis's backyard in Forest Hill her favourite garden. The front yard of the house is restrained, a well-kept lawn, white impatiens in a ring under the shade of a huge basswood. But the backyard is where Mrs. Margolis makes herself felt. She and Sarah spent weeks setting up a Gertrude Jekyll-style perennial bed in the middle of a sunny spot in the backyard lawn, figuring out the design, which plants would bloom when, at what height, in what colour. Now they're working on plans for a water feature farther back, near the little flagstone patio.

"Well, Sarah? A penny for your thoughts."

Sarah's penny is safe in her front jeans pocket. "I should be turning over this sod for you, but I have fig trees on the brain."

"Fig trees? Not for me, I hope. Too much trouble."

Sarah shakes her head.

"I remember eating the fruit right off the tree in Provence. Teddy and I lived in the south of France for three months... That was ages ago, before the kids were born."

"I saw fig trees in Israel, but I didn't have the nerve to pick them."

"Israel." Mrs. M. shakes her head. "I don't want to think about Israel right now." The bombing in Lebanon hasn't stopped and the count of civilian casualties goes on, more injury, death, to add to the ledger.

"I know," Sarah says. "The TV footage is –"

"Distressing," Mrs. M. says, her face severe. "Did you watch the news yesterday? That clip of a young woman running with her toddler in her arms; the child had on a bright blue party dress. I keep remembering the flag of that dress. The mother was so young. And her face – she could so easily have been a young Jewish mother." She turns to Sarah. "When you read the Jewish press, it's all 'an attempt to obliterate a dangerous enemy.' *Obliterate*. They use a word like that to talk about other human beings. Up till now I've always wanted to stand up for Israel, but this…"

Sarah nods. She's had her own knee-jerk responses about Israel – *after what was done to us during the Holocaust, now the Arabs say they want to push us into the sea!* But now these images, the ugly tally… Now her blameless good guys, the heroes of the kibbutzim who made the desert bloom, the Davids who beat Goliath, they're not Davids anymore. *If you were a Jew, what kind of Jew would you be?* What can a Jew be?

"Oh, look!" Mrs. M. is pointing. "See my feeder? Ruby-throated. They're quite common here, but they still always give me a thrill." Mrs. M. is standing with her head tilted back, hand shading her eyes.

"It's the males, of course, who have that showy red throat. And the hovering, it's actually a kind of sculling motion." Mrs. M. seems to know everything about birds as well as plants. She turns to Sarah. "Sometimes these humming-birds remind me of you. So much concentrated in such a small package."

If you were a bird, what kind of bird would you be?

"Oh don't wrinkle your brow at me, Sarah Levine. They're amazing creatures. To keep their engines running at such a high rate, they have to drink so much nectar so consistently that they're always only a few hours away from starvation. A fine balance. Oh! Look at that." Two birds approach the feeder, but with a drumming whoosh one dive-bombs the other. "Hummingbird dogfight! They're territorial and that one's trying to keep the feeder to itself."

"Mrs. Margolis," Sarah says. "I've got that copy of Jekyll's *Colour Schemes for the Flower Garden* that you lent me in the truck. Should I bring it in?"

"Hang on to it if you're still reading."

"It gives me ideas."

"You've no shortage of ideas, Sarah. Have you had a chance to check into those Ryerson courses on landscape design?"

Sarah doesn't even need to turn the penny in her pocket. *No.* It will say *no.*

"Well, I'm sure there's a lot you know already without going to school, but these kinds of courses will solidify the ideas you do have. Do think about it." And then Mrs. M. is off, brisk strides around the corner of the house.

These feisty, ferocious little birds fighting to keep what's theirs. A miniature war. The feeders are their territory, but so are nests. Paradoxically, they fight less when food is scarce. Living in that economy of starvation, calories in, calories out, they can't afford the energy spent in aggression when the balance gets particularly tough. Such a precise equation, but one they nonetheless seem to have control over. At will. At will they can curb being so territorial.

When Mrs. M. comes back into the garden, where Sarah's busy digging, turning up the worm-rich soil, she's brought two tall glasses of iced tea. They move onto the wrought-iron bench Mrs. M. has set into the shade of some lilac bushes. "I've been wanting to run something by you." Mrs. M. lays her gardening gloves on the bench beside her. "I'm quite serious about this. I'd like you to think about starting your own landscaping company. It would be such a positive change, working for yourself, having more control over design. It's a waste, you doing all this donkey-work for other people. I like the way you think about gardens. If you took a couple of those Ryerson courses first, I think it would build your confidence. And you've got the smarts to make a business work."

Sarah turns the penny inside her pocket. *No.*

"You haven't said anything."

"I...I need to think about it."

"Of course, of course. Here I am, nattering away. Enough nagging for today."

"It's not nagging. It's very kind of you."

They get up from the shade into the dazzle of sun, go over to the plot Sarah's been working on.

"I want a whole bed of bee balm here," Mrs. M. says. "I love the scent. Did you know it's a natural antiseptic?" She looks at Sarah. "I'm dithering again and you've got work to do. How's your sister doing?"

"Rose is having a hard time."

"I'm so sorry. The baby blues aren't easy."

There was no baby. "They've got her on antidepressants now, so we're hoping that will help."

"Once she's feeling a bit better, see if you can get her to go outside. Takes you out of yourself. And exercise. Even if it's just walking." She touches Sarah's shoulder. "She's going to be okay, Sarah. I know you want to help, but you can't necessarily make her well. It's not up to you. She has to make herself well."

But it is. It is up to Sarah.

"You're worried, aren't you?"

Sarah nods.

"She'll be fine. She will."

Everyone's so sure Rose will be fine. How can they know? Every night Sarah waits for the phone to ring, for a call she won't know how to answer. She isn't doing anything.

"And Gail? What's she up to?"

"She has a lot to say about the Lebanon situation."

"I can imagine. And is she working on that feminist collective you mentioned?"

"Several. Fund-raising for a rape-crisis centre. A bunch of her friends are starting a magazine. And she's doing some volunteer work for a feminist press, helping them draft their contracts properly."

"That Gail. She's a firecracker, your sister."

"She makes me tired, Mrs. Margolis. She's just so angry so often."

"Still. I admire the force of Gail's conviction. I missed that boat. Feminism."

Another hummingbird zips by them, wings a blur, that dizzy hum.

Mrs. M. puts her garden gloves on, takes them off. "Here I am, 56, a kept woman with an indulgent banker husband, who amuses herself by playing with garden design. I'm a dabbler." She's playing with the fingers of the gloves. "It's too late for me. But you young women. You could do anything." Mrs. M. stoops to bundle up her garden tools. "Teddy will be home any minute. I should get cleaned up. See you next week." And she's gone.

Sarah has another hour to go and about 50 square feet of sod to turn and soon her mind has been dug clean. She's still bent over the shovel when a van pulls into the driveway. It's Jim, the handyman who washes the windows, clears gutters, shovels snow in winter for the Margolises. He does some rough yard work, mows the lawn, but leaves the real gardening to Sarah.

"Hey, Jim. What's up?"

"Windows." He's hauling his equipment out of the van. Lanky, maybe six foot four, slim but strong. "Mrs. M. loves her windows clean. Other folks get them done once a year at best, but this place, I do 'em March, June, October."

"Must be a million windows..." Sarah says.

"I don't mind. The more the merrier. I like my job, especially this stuff. Things start out dirty and then they get clean." He stops unloading for a moment, looks down at his hands. "I used to be a social worker, did I ever tell you that?"

She shakes her head.

"Yeah. Ten years. Children's Aid. A caseworker. The trenches. I figure, for every thousand people I touched in that job, I helped one. One. Got so I couldn't take it." He starts unloading again. "So now, I wash windows. And when I'm done, everybody's happy. The windows are clean."

❧

There's a short hissing sound as the needle catches its groove and the schmaltzy violins swell. Then this throaty woman's voice comes growling into the living room in Michael's apartment on Howland, singing in French, infiltrating the smoke from Michael's cigarette. He's getting himself ready for Paris. Last week he learned he'd made the cut; the trip is on. Too bad Sarah can't come, her French is so much better than his. She's got a good ear for languages. He's pretty damned excited. The office administrator that he met in Paris, Laura something, a Canadian who's stationed there, even got him a place to stay. A small place, just one big room, really, in the old Jewish quarter, which is also kind of the Arab quarter, lots of Moroccan restaurants, really funky, down to earth. It's called the Maquis or Marois or something, Michael can't remember the name. The Marais, maybe.

The Jewish quarter. Sarah didn't know Paris had a Jewish quarter. And she doesn't know that she wants it to. There can't be a Jewish quarter in Paris because Paris isn't Jewish. The categories are confused. Paris should just be Paris.

Edith Piaf. That's the name of the songstress. Sarah's come straight from Mrs. Margolis's, hasn't washed up yet, but Michael sits her down on the sofa. He's always steering her places, *sit here, listen to this, drink that, like this*. But when he stubs out his cigarette and takes her hand, she softens, tucks her head against his neck. His skin, above the muscle – she's never been with a man with such soft skin. His hair soft, too, baby-fine and blond. Soft Michael.

The *r*'s are trilling like crazy: *Non, rien de rien. Non, je ne regrette rien.* Is that why Michael can't ever say he's sorry, not because he doesn't trust her, but because he regrets nothing? How does anyone do that? A boy or a girl, an eight year old ghost. *Ni le bien qu'on m'a fait. Ni le mal; tout ça m'est bien égal. Piaf* wasn't her real name; it's Parisian slang for sparrow. *Non, rien de rien. Non, je ne regrette rien.*

Michael wants her to translate the lyrics for him. She is good at French, somehow the texts on all those cereal boxes and milk cartons sank into her head. And she took a couple of courses at university. Though, other than her teachers, she'd never even met anyone who actually spoke French till that first trip to Paris. She never figured she'd have the chance to use it. At least she can help Michael with this. The words go something like: *No, nothing at all. No, I regret nothing. Not the good that's been done me. Nor the bad; it's all just the same to me.* Michael's running his finger along her rough knuckles. Sarah closes her eyes. *C'est payé, balayé, oublié. Je me fous du passé.* It's paid for, swept clean, forgotten. I don't give a damn about the past. *Avec mes souvenirs, j'ai allumé le feu.* Memories are matches to light a fire. The orchestra's playing a see-sawing carousel tune in the background of Piaf's voice.

Screw the past. Don't look back.

The Little Sparrow. *If you were a bird....*

"Do you think hummingbirds are anxious?"

"Huh?" Michael's nibbling on her fingertips now, dirt or no dirt.

"D'you think they're anxious? They have to work so hard to stay in one place."

She can feel him straighten beside her. She opens her eyes.

"Hey. You. You feeling stuck?" he asks. "Is it Rose?"

"Yes. But – it's work too." She feels him tighten, start to close against her, the fight rising back up. How much he hates her job. Piaf keeps singing. No regrets. "Look at my hands. I haven't even washed up. Should I go take a shower?"

"No. Tell me what you were starting to say."

She drums her fingers along his knuckles. His hands are so clean, nails trim. Is Mr. Margolis one of those men who get manicures? Would Michael do that? She *can't* tell him about Mrs. Margolis's idea, going back to school, starting a business, because the penny's already decided for her, or she's decided for the penny. *No.* Her running a business. Where would she get the money? She'd need some sort of capital, tools, a truck. She can barely cover the rent on her room.

Michael would help. Michael would love to help. Mr. Fix-It. He'd love to come to her rescue. Save her from herself. Michael the knight in shining armour.

And he does shine. There was that time he saved them from a crash. They were heading back into town on a Sunday evening on a two-lane country road when Sarah saw a car coming towards them in their lane. Head-on. In

56

the sharp shard of a second before they crashed, faster than he could possibly have formed a conscious thought, Michael turned the wheel smoothly and swerved onto the shoulder, braked, his body thinking for him. And they were safe, though they could hear the thud and crash of a collision behind them.

One minute Michael had his hands on the wheel, his clever, clever hands, which had saved them, and the next he was out of the car, shouting to Sarah as he closed the door, *Don't get out of the car!* Then he was gone, running towards the crash. Of course she got out. The first thing she saw was Michael kneeling beside the driver, checking if he was all right. In the end, it wasn't that serious. Sheer luck, but no one was badly hurt. Later, after the sirens and cops, on the slow shaky ride home, she asked Michael why he didn't want her to get out of the car. He was scared, he said, of what he'd see. What she'd see. He didn't want her to see dead bodies, people mangled. He wanted to spare her.

And now he wants to fix her, fix her life with his good advice.

"I wish you'd quit that stupid job," he says now. "Are you going to keep working at the frigging Centre till the end of days?"

The end of days. He's let the usual irritation come into his voice, but she doesn't mind, his body is saying something else. It wouldn't be so bad to spend the end of days like this, her mouth against Michael's neck, his hand pressing lightly against her belly.

"Stay the night," he says. "Don't leave tonight. Stay here."

She closes her eyes again, letting the penny turn in her hand. *Car ma vie, car mes joies. Aujourd'hui, ça commence avec toi.* Because a new, a joyful life starts with you. What kind of life does she have now, what kind of life does she deserve?

"It's crazy," Michael mutters. "It's crazy that you won't stay here with me."

HISTORY

MUCH AS SARAH LIKED PROF. KOENIG, the course was hard. Every Tuesday and Thursday before class she found herself clenched. And the dreams, those waking nightmares, had come back, often. There was fodder for them. The *something* at the door now wore Nazi uniforms. And Sarah seemed to take longer and longer to unfreeze from them. Sleeping Beauty waking slower and slower from the evil spell. It didn't happen every night after class, but many nights.

Sarah couldn't be the only one struggling, because the ranks had thinned: from the twenty-odd students who began the class, there were only about a dozen left. But Helen being there helped, Helen as a barricade on Sarah's side of the door. Helen as proof, Sarah wasn't sure of what.

One day Sarah found Helen's lucky penny in her jeans pocket and kept it in her hand through class, turning and turning it between her fingers. Another barricade, a distraction. That day Prof. Koenig had written *After Auschwitz, writing poetry is barbaric* on the blackboard. A quote from Theodor Adorno. Prof. Koenig wanted the students to compose their own responses to the quote, agreeing or disagreeing or simply expanding upon it, 300 words maximum, due next week.

They were supposed to write 300 words about six words. *Writing poetry is barbaric.* Maybe writing anything about the Holocaust was barbaric.

For now they were reading Primo Levi's memoir about surviving Auschwitz. Levi started writing his book almost immediately after he'd been liberated, words after Auschwitz. But it wasn't until 1958 that he was able to publish it. Until then, none of his words about Auschwitz were wanted.

❧

It was mid-November, only a few more weeks of class before Christmas break. Sarah found Helen in her usual seat at the library. She was wearing moss-green tweed pants and a matching green turtleneck, pearl earrings. She quietly passed Sarah a little paper bag, a present, and Sarah couldn't resist taking a peek – more of Helen's cinnamon *rugelach*. It was hard not to nibble on one right away.

The class was reading Viktor Frankl's memoir: "the story of a man who became a number who became a person," according to the quote on the cover. A man who became a number. Sarah shivered. Frankl's book came out in Austria right after the war, in 1946; it had sold millions of copies. These words were welcome while Levi's weren't. Sarah got through the first few pages when she came to this:

> […] On the average, only those prisoners could keep alive who, after years of trekking from camp to camp, had lost all scruples in their fight for existence; they were prepared to use every means, honest and otherwise, even brutal force, theft, and betrayal of their friends, in order to save themselves. We who have come back, by the aid of many lucky chances or miracles – whatever one may choose to call them – we know: the best of us did not return.

The best of us did not return. What did that mean? Sarah had heard other vague, ugly versions of this idea about the *grineh*, Yiddish for *greenhorns*, the displaced persons who came to Canada after the war. DP – the acronym itself a slur. Those whose alleged success was attributed to their cutthroat natures because, as Frankl put it, they had *lost all scruples in their fight for existence*. *Grineh*. Like so many of her Talmud Torah classmates' parents. Like Helen. Found guilty simply because they survived. But it wasn't fair. Wasn't true.

59

Sarah underlined Frankl's paragraph in pencil. Helen's head was bent over her book. "Helen," Sarah whispered, "can you look at this quote?" Helen pulled the book over to her, read the paragraph quickly, then read again slowly, her finger under the lines.

"*The best of us did not return.*" She gently touched the page again, spread her fingers across it as if to weigh it down. "What are you asking me, Sarahleh?"

Did she think it was true?

Helen sighed. "I know you're wondering. I was never in the camps."

Helen didn't have a number tattooed on her arm, but Sarah knew that not everyone who was in a camp got a number. She'd been afraid to ask.

"I was young and strong enough to run east from Poland and I did. Before the Nazis got there," Helen continued, her voice a whisper in the quiet of the library. "I got to Tajikistan and waited out the war there. It was very hard, very dangerous, we were hungry and cold and afraid, but I was never in a camp.

"Everyone who lived through the war has a different story, Sarah. People ran to the woods, some joined the Partisans. The Partisans weren't always angels. People were hidden, children especially, and pretended they weren't Jews.

"All this you know, you're studying this.

"The people who did go through the camps, that was something separate from everyone else. But whatever people went through, I don't throw everyone into the same bucket." Helen looked out across the room, her gaze scanning the students, their heads bent, intent.

"People who had goodness in them did come back. They walked out of what swallowed them up and still they had goodness in them at the end of it all. I can tell you that every person's story is a different story. And good luck, or chance, or someone else's goodness, even for one moment, turning away or looking ahead, one moment of luck or goodness, or many, that's how people survived."

☙

January, and Sarah was almost used to the dreams, almost every night before class Tuesdays and Thursdays. She tried watching TV till midnight, silly stuff, the old black-and-white movies her mom liked to watch. Sometimes it worked. She told herself she would tough it out. She would prove to herself that she could tough it out, that she was tough enough. The class had one more memoir to read, *Night*, by Elie Wiesel. It had taken Wiesel ten years before he was able to start writing anything about the camps. For ten years Wiesel's words were stopped up. No words after Auschwitz, no words for Auschwitz. *Night* was so small, less than 150 pages, as if Wiesel could just barely get out what he had to say.

Prof. Koenig was showing a slide of a photograph taken during the liberation of Buchenwald. As always, the room darkened and then brightened. Sarah blinked. The photograph was taken on Monday, April 16, 1945, Prof. Koenig explained, five days after troops from the 80th Division of the American Army entered the camp. The photographer was an American private by the name of Miller.

The first thing Sarah noticed in the photo was the man standing on the right, leaning against a wooden post in the bunkhouse. His face was framed by a short black beard. His flesh was tight over his bones, and he was naked, but he was holding a striped shirt in front of himself. For modesty's sake.

Those pyjamas. How ridiculously innocent those striped uniforms were. Pyjamas like her father's, Abe, wandering around the kitchen on Saturday mornings, a cup of coffee in his hand. Wiesel must have been just a few years younger than Abe. She pushed the image of her father away, looked back at the slide.

The standing man was looking upwards, slightly, to the right. Almost everyone else in the photograph was looking directly at the camera.

All right, then. She was going to look herself. She was going to look into each face: *this is a person and this is person and this another person.* They were not *slave labourers,* they were not *survivors.* They were not *about to die,* they were not *those who had just escaped death.* Words would not swallow who they were. They were themselves.

61

There was a young man on the bottom bunk at the far left and he looked both frightened and hopeful, astounded by the salvation that he was being offered. Sarah knew by now that the boy had reason to be afraid, because many people who were liberated still died. Some died from the food the well-meaning liberating soldiers gave them, their starvation so extreme that their bodies went into shock when they ate. Others were just too worn out from malnutrition or typhus or TB to make it through more than a few days, even with the help of the people who'd liberated them.

Only three men were turned away from the camera, two of them, whose heads were raised – there must have been something other than the camera to look at in the room, perhaps the one man who, Sarah now thought, was so bravely able to stand. She saw now the slight smile on the upright man's face. The third of the three turned away from the camera had his head down, only his dark hair visible, a blanket tucked tenderly around his neck. Maybe he was too weak to lift his head.

She saw suddenly that many of the men had something shining with them, a shining metal object set on the surface of the wooden bunk. It was their food bowl, the only possession most prisoners had, a food bowl which they also used as a pillow. A man on the second level of bunks had his arm held protectively over the bowl. He seemed at first to be wearing rimless glasses, but it was just the bags under his eyes and the wise arc of his raised eyebrows. He had something white wrapped around his head, a turban, or bandage. Perhaps he had been wounded. Perhaps he was observant and at last, after liberation, he was allowed to cover his head, and the white fabric was all he had.

Because of the way the photograph had been framed, Sarah was sure that there were men in the top level of the bunks who had been cut off, whose faces were not in the picture. She wanted to imagine their faces too.

"We have detailed information on the contents and origin of this photograph," Prof. Koenig was explaining, "because it is held in the American National Archive, and so the date it was taken, the name of the photographer, are known. We know also that the man at the far right, the far back of the lowest level of the bunks, was Max Hamburger. He did in fact recover, though he was very ill with tuberculosis at the time the photograph was taken. He recovered and became a psychiatrist in the Netherlands.

"And," Prof. Koenig went on, "on the second row of bunks, seventh from left, is Elie Wiesel. He was 16 years old."

The room darkened and then brightened again, and they were shown a close-up of Wiesel's face. He looked frightened and serious and sad at the same time.

That boy's face.

The boy who went on to produce the words she had been reading.

No words after Auschwitz, Prof. Koenig had said. No, it was Adorno who said no poetry. How was Sarah supposed to produce words for her essays? Everything she was feeling and thinking had been thought and felt already, and in a better way. By people who were there. And even for them, words didn't do enough.

❧

February. Sarah was getting a bit more sleep, the dreams weren't quite as often, though they were just as bad, worse maybe. The class had a major essay due next week, and Sarah had her topic. She was writing about "The Erosion of Civil Rights in Pre-War Nazi Germany." She was going to discuss the impact of the Nuremberg Laws and of each step that followed, each regulation and prohibition, a progression that made what was inconceivable reality.

She was turning the penny in her fingers, reading an article about the stamp Jews had to have on their identity cards. Everyone in Germany had to carry an identity card, but in the fall of 1938, a law was passed requiring Jews to have their cards stamped with a red 'J' so that they were immediately identifiable. Who was a Jew, who wasn't – the single red letter told everything. The age-old questioned answered. *What is a Jew?*

Even before the 'J' stamp, she read, in August of 1938, the Nazi authorities said that any Jews who had first names that weren't immediately identifiable as Jewish had to add a new middle name to their identity cards. Men had to take *Israel*. Women had to take *Sarah*.

Her own name. The word that meant her.

If her name was everyone's name, it was no one's.

The Erosion of Civil Rights in Pre-War Nazi Germany. How could she write about this? Words did nothing. How could she put together any words that meant anything? She put down her pen, pushed the journal aside. Started gathering up her books, pushed them into her bag.

She couldn't stand being there. Couldn't stand the library. Helen. Herself. She started pulling on her winter coat, wrapping a scarf around her neck. She couldn't say anything to Helen, couldn't find any words for this. It didn't stop. It wouldn't stop until the names had been erased, and the stories, and the bodies that went with them. She didn't want to dream like this. She didn't want to study the destruction of the Jews of Europe. There were no words that were any good. There was nothing she could do. No good she could do. She wanted to go home.

❧

Sarah was in line at the cafeteria in the Student Union Building two weeks later when she felt a light tap on her shoulder. It was Helen, bundled in her navy winter coat, her cheeks pink with cold.

"Sarah, you haven't been in class. Were you sick? Is something wrong?"

"I'm not coming to class any more, Helen. I've dropped the course."

"Dropped? Why would you do such a thing? You did so much work already. Was it the essay? Sarah, talk to me."

"It was everything."

"What everything? What are you talking about?"

"I kept having these dreams, bad dreams I couldn't wake out of."

"Sarahleh, dreams are just dreams."

"It's more than that, Helen. I don't know how to make arguments about the Holocaust. I don't want to study evil. I don't want to understand it." Because it couldn't be understood. There were no words to frame it. Because there was nothing to be done. Nothing she could do.

"Sarahleh. Listen to me. You don't have to understand evil." Helen's face was ruddier now, not just with the cold. People were looking at them. She pulled Sarah out of line over to a corner. "Sarah. You know what I'm interested in? I'm interested in goodness, the mystery of goodness. Maybe that's what you're interested in too."

No. It wasn't enough. Helen didn't know what she was talking about. Helen didn't know anything and Sarah didn't know anything. If you added one drop of goodness, a tincture of goodness, to all that death, nothing would change. One good act would do nothing. Any good act did nothing.

"Sarah. Listen to me. You can talk to Prof. Koenig. For sure he'll take you back. You're almost finished the work."

No. She didn't want to go back. Nothing she could do or think or write or say would change anything.

She had only done one thing in her life that ever meant anything – she kept a life from happening – and she didn't know whether it was wrong or right. Or maybe she knew that it was both wrong and right.

She couldn't understand, she couldn't do anything now.

"I'm sorry, Helen. I don't want to. I'm sorry."

Helen looked at her, looked down at the floor. "You don't have to be sorry, Sarah." She straightened her bag across her shoulders. "You do what you need to do." The room suddenly brightened, a stray ray of sun lighting up Helen's face. Sarah could see the makeup on her face, the eyeliner, powder, rouge, lipstick, as though Helen had had to make herself a face. "But you call me if you want to talk about this. You have already my number." Helen blinked, the light was too hard on her, then turned to the dark room.

Laila

I have something from home. Something forgotten in my suitcase until now, my mother packed it for me. A package, wrapped in brown paper. I unwrap it, put it to my face, but it doesn't smell like home. Not anymore. A square of black cotton, the fabric embroidered in red, green, blue. Cushion cover. A gift from my mother. To make me feel at home here.

When my mother learned cross-stitch from her grandmother in her village, in our country, she was only seven. And when I was little, I would watch her hands as the designs formed stitch by stich, cross by cross. She'll work without a pattern, holding the whole in her mind as the needle takes each stitch. She learned everything from her grandmother: hem stitch, stem stitch, satin stitch, chain stitch; feather stitch, braid stitch, manajel and sanabel stitches. Each for a different purpose: binding, filling, couching, running, tacking. My mother learned everything, knows everything, can do anything with cotton thread. She works evenings, after she finishes in the orchards. For the neighbours' daughters she makes wedding dresses, spends months on them so that the fabric is thick with colour and pattern. And for us, for the family, gifts: cushions, tablecloths. Into every one she works in symbols for good luck. Good luck, good health. Protection. Peace.

She told me the names of the patterns: Moon of Bethlehem, Moon of Ramallah, Moon with Feathers. Damask Rose, Garden Rose, Rose in Bud. *This is you, Laila*, she told me, when I was little. *Rose in Bud*. Trees too: Hawthorn, Cypress, Tall Palms, Tree with Lions. Apple Tree, False Tree, True Tree, Tree of Scorpions. These are the running border patterns: Eye Wide Open, Dragonfly, Chickpeas & Raisins, Road to Egypt, Frogs in a Pond. Old Man's Teeth, Old Man Upside Down, Bachelor's Cushion, Baker's Wife, Chicken Feet. Key of Hebron. Four Eggs in a Pan.

Good luck. Good health. Protection. She was making a dress for me, she didn't say wedding dress. Didn't want to make bad luck, wishing for me. And a wedding could wait, she said. Till things got better. Till I found a way to get more schooling. She used manajel stitching at the neck opening, the sleeve edges. When she was done, there would be embroidered panels all down the front, down to my ankles: roosters in red with blue and yellow cockscombs, hawthorns, cypress. On the chest panel, thick borders of roses and lyres braided into one another. And inside them, diamonds of roses, red and pink on the white cotton, a rose in bud at each corner, damask rose at the centre. Turn a diamond on its side and it's a square. That was the pattern my mother intended for me. Some kind of order, some kind of beauty I could put myself inside.

I lift the fabric to my face, but it doesn't smell like home.

DANCE

TORONTO IS SUCH AN ORDERLY CITY, *stand right, walk left* on the escalators to the subway station platforms. Tidy queues at the bus stops. And privacy once you sit down. Sarah likes the anonymity, the way people leave you alone. On the busses in Winnipeg, people always start chatting away when they sit beside you; in Toronto you're left in peace. She'll be at the dance venue in about twenty minutes, plenty of time to help get things set up.

Gail has invited Sarah to a women-only dance, a benefit for the first ever rape-crisis centre in Toronto. Zero government funding, so they need to raise money. Plus they want to raise awareness about the whole issue of violence against women. That's the term they're using now for wife-beating, rape, child molestation. Women Against Violence Against Women is another group Gail's involved with. WAVAW. The acronym seems baby-ish, or cry-baby-ish, wah-wah-wah. They have to say *against* twice because they can't be *for* something. Sarah wasn't sure about the whole thing, but the penny said *yes*. And she gets it, she gets that the crisis centre they're raising money for has to use an all-woman staff because so many women are scared off from even reporting a rape to male cops or doctors who don't believe them, or make them feel they *asked for it.*

Nobody ever asks for it.

Gail wants her to come early; Sarah's going to take a couple of shifts selling beer tickets. Not *manning* the table, *staffing* it. Word wars: Gail insists on chair, not chairman, doesn't like *man hours* or even *man-made*, writes memos using *s/he*. How do you even pronounce that? Gail loves slashes. It's exhausting.

At Union Station there's a kid ahead of Sarah, he looks to be about 11, who's hopping right up the stairs, just for the hell of it, energetic little guy. That happy in his body. Sarah passes through the permanent, synthetic smell of cinnamon buns, her mouth watering as it always does, fooled into wanting.

They're holding the dance in a big empty barn of a place. She sees Gail off in a corner, her arms around two women, waves, and Gail cuts across the cavernous room towards her. One of the women, it's Barb, follows. Barb has her red hair tucked under a checked cotton scarf, a couple of curls peeking out. She's wearing denim overalls and Sarah can't help thinking *Rosie the Riveter*. Barb is all business, though, and soon they're counting the float, setting up the cash box, setting out the tickets.

The all-woman band is warming up on stage, tinkering with the drumkit, hooking up their guitars. They're a just-coming-together seven member group called either The Association or The Nihilists, depending on which day you ask them. The lighting crew is fiddling with the set-up, and the erratic switching on and off of banks of lights has colours stuttering across the band members' faces and torsos. Spotlights nose their way across the stage, highlighting the music stands and empty stools rather than the performers.

Barb takes a long swallow of her beer. She looks down at her hands for a minute, then smiles and looks up at Sarah. "So, about three years ago I was living in Kingston and the girls I was sharing a house with left the back door unlocked. I woke up in the middle of the night, and there was a man lying on top of me in the bed." Barb's laughing now. "I'm one of those people who is always crazy-mad if anyone wakes me up. If I fell asleep in front of the TV, my brothers used to have to poke me with a broom to get me up, because I'd automatically flail out at them, slug them in the face if they weren't careful. Twice my size, hockey players, and still they were scared of me. That night, when the weight of the man woke me up, the only thing I was was angry. The guy had his hand near my throat and I grabbed at it, but what I didn't know was that he was holding a knife. So what I grabbed was the guy's knife. Grabbed the blade of his knife with one hand and threw the guy off with the other. Screamed blue murder and my housemates rushed in and the guy ran like hell." Barb laughs again. "I don't want to make a big deal out of it. I scared the guy off, right? Nothing really happened. Well, the cut on my hand, that was bad, I needed stitches. But they let me out of hospital right after they sewed me up, didn't even admit me. My housemates made such a fuss, but it could have been worse. Here." Barbara sticks out her hand. There's a deep scar across her palm. "Good thing it didn't hit an artery. I grabbed hard."

Sarah takes Barb's hand, holds it in her own. Three years ago. The scar looks new, a shiny, tight pink path across Barb's palm.

Women have been seeping in since the doors officially opened but now there's starting to be a real lineup. Barb jokes around with everyone but still works quickly, efficiently, making swift change, tearing off the tickets. During a lull, she gets them each a Coke. She clinks their bottles, Sarah and Barb, a good team.

Once they're done the shift, Barb heads directly for the dancing. Gail hustles over with a big grin on her face, grabs Sarah's hand and pulls her onto the dance floor. She's going to make Sarah have some fun whether she likes it or not. After a couple more dances, Barb comes up to them. Her kerchief has disappeared and her hair's a red shock around her face. The band breaks out into the Beatles' 'She Loves You' and Barb starts hand-jiving with Sarah, something she hasn't done since she was a little kid with her big sister Rose, and Barb's spinning her around and back and forth. Everyone, including Sarah, chimes in loudly, and mostly in tune, to the 'yeah, yeah, yeah' chorus. When the song ends, Barb pulls Sarah into a big hug. "You are *fantastic*," she whispers into Sarah's ear.

Barb has clearly had her fair share of beer.

"All right, *ladies*." The lead singer, a skinny woman in tight black jeans and t-shirt, who looks to be almost six feet tall, draws the word out to about six syllables. The audience erupts in a rumble of elated shrieks. "We'll close down this set with one last *slow* dance," more shouts, "and then we'll be back before you know it!" Cheers and yells.

The singer starts to croon into the mike and the women start pairing up, giggling or intent. Barb and Sarah are standing about two feet apart. They move towards each other, and each raises a left arm to the other's shoulder. They stop and giggle. Sarah looks up; Barb's about a head taller. "You lead," Sarah says. Barb puts her arm around Sarah's waist, then pulls her closer. Sarah's never danced close with another woman, but she likes this. She can't feel the scar on Barb's hand, but it's there.

The music stops. "That was nice, but I really gotta pee." Barb veers towards the washrooms, then veers back to Sarah, pulls her into a corner. "C'mere." She's leaning into Sarah, this huge happy smile on her face. "That was fun. That was really fun, dancing with you. You're a good dancer."

Barb should see Rose. Rose is the dancer in the family.

"You're, you're just a beautiful dancer," Barb says, smiling even more. "Little sister." She puts her hands lightly on Sarah's chest, a palm on each breast. A soft bit of pressure. "And you know what? You've got beautiful little breasts." Sarah doesn't know what to say. Barb kisses her on the mouth, a quick buss, puts her forehead down for a second on top of Sarah's head. "I really gotta pee." And she's gone. That's okay. Maybe Barb's embarrassed. Maybe she isn't. It's okay. Sarah likes how Barb likes her, however Barb likes her.

Sarah goes back to the beer ticket table. The woman who's taken over asks her to count the float and she's bent over the cash box when she feels a kind of murmur in the room, a ripple of unease. There's a bit of a crowd at the door, some voices raised, some sort of commotion. A woman she doesn't know but recognizes as one of the organizers comes marching across the room, red in the face, maybe a bit drunk.

"Hey! You! You Sarah? Gail's sister?" She's almost shouting.

Sarah nods.

"Well, there's a *man* at the door who says he's your *boyfriend* and he has to speak with you and Gail. Some sort of family emergency. This better be good."

Sarah feels the room churn around her, grips the edge of the table. *Rose.* Feels the blood drain from her face. She has to find Gail.

71

The woman is going on about this being a *special* place, they are trying to create a *space* for the women at this dance, when suddenly Gail is at her side, and Barb, and Caroline.

"Shut the fuck up, would you?" Barb says quietly to the angry woman. She takes Sarah's elbow. Gail is already striding to the door where Michael is standing, his face a painful mix of delicacy and sadness and grief.

"Look," he says when they reach him, "I know I'm not supposed to be here." Sarah shakes her head. It doesn't matter.

"I got to my apartment after work and your parents called. They'd tried to reach you at your place too. They'd left me about six messages on the answering machine but they kept calling."

It's Rose it's Rose it's Rose it's Rose.

Gail's holding onto Michael, hugging him, burying her face in his chest. The irate women at the door have altered, are fading away. Barb and Caroline stay with them, a protective arc.

"What is it?" Sarah asks.

"She tried to hurt herself. David took her to Misericordia. Your parents are there."

Hurt herself. Violence against women. Self-violence.

Gail is holding onto Michael, her fists caught in his shirt. "Is she okay? Is she going to be okay?"

"They don't know. I don't know. Your dad was pretty wrought up. We'll call them when we get home."

"Is she in ICU?" It's Caroline, the curly-cloud-hair woman, asking. Is Caroline a nurse? Did Gail say she was in med school?

"No. I don't think so. I think they mentioned a ward number. I wrote some of this down." Michael's hands are tentative in his pockets.

"That's good," Caroline says, touching Gail's shoulder gently. "That's a good sign, Gail." She turns around, looks at Sarah. "Really, it's a good sign."

"We have to go," Sarah says. She walks past Barb, past Caroline, past Gail still gripping Michael's shirt, into the street.

HOME

SHE'S GOING HOME. SNUG IN HER AISLE SEAT, seatbelt fastened, watching a toy Toronto diminish under the wing of the plane, a Tinkertoy CN Tower in the distance, the lake secret this morning, holding itself back, silent and alert. Soon she'll be watching Ontario stream by below, farmland giving way to intricate patterns of forest and lake as soon as they reach the southern tip of Georgian Bay. It's hard to believe in flying, even though the science is clear, lift and thrust. It's just so unlikely that this packet of metal can hold itself suspended, the force moving it forward stronger than the force of gravity. Just over two and a half hours in the air and she'll be in Winnipeg. Toronto–Winnipeg by car is 26 hours hard driving. Ten hours ago Sarah was at the dance with Gail.

They called their parents' house in Winnipeg as soon as they got to Gail's loft, three of them huddled around the phone. Pat's usually firm, bright voice was wavery, thin. Abe was at the hospital with David, they didn't know much. That afternoon Rose had seemed a bit better and David had gone out to do a couple of chores – gas up the car, get a few groceries. He wasn't gone more than an hour, but when he got back he found Rose in the bathroom. Pat didn't say what Rose had done. *Tried to hurt herself,* that's all they had. After they hung up, Gail had gnawed her way through the options with Michael. He'd finally convinced her that Sarah should go, Gail couldn't possibly get away. She was in the middle of a big case, meetings lined up back to back for the next three days.

Michael drove Sarah to the airport first thing in the morning, bought her a ticket on the next available flight. She didn't argue about the money, gave

Michael a stiff hug as she walked to the gate. None of them had slept much, though Sarah knows she must have dozed off and on, curled beside Gail on her bed, Michael cramped on Gail's sofa. They stopped on their way to the airport at Sarah's rooming-house where she threw fresh underwear and socks, jeans and tees into the old brown hard-shell suitcase, flotsam she'd somehow inherited from Sosha, their dad's cousin. The brass hinges snapped shut. Michael would phone the Centre for her, explain that she couldn't come in to work.

Sarah must have slept through the rest of the flight because she's woken by the jolt of the plane's wheels hitting the tarmac. She loves coming down to land in Winnipeg – the shadows of occasional clouds the only irregularity among the tidy green and gold squares of prairie farmland – and now she's missed it. She files down the aisle, through the gate; the sliding doors open and the escalator takes her down. To her *family emergency*. Whatever she's going to find. Every single time she comes home someone is waiting for her at the bottom of this escalator. So often Rose, big sister picking her up, taking her home.

Sarah scans the cheery crowd, eager greetings, hugs, a couple of kids hopping up and down holding a home-made sign, *Welcome Home Grandma*, and there's Abe, all six feet of him, broad-shouldered, head of thick grey hair, beside the baggage carousel, talking with a heavy-set rumpled-looking man. Not looking for her. She calls *Dad* and he looks up, touches the man's arm, moves towards her as she moves towards him.

Abe pulls her into a bear hug and she lays her head against his big strong chest. So solid. Nothing surer than her father's chest. The fresh smell of the plain white shirts he always wears, the light, comforting smell of him beneath it. She can feel Abe swallowing, blinking.

"It's okay, Sarah. Your mom's at the hospital visiting with her. David went home to get a little sleep. The doctors say she's going to be fine."

How can Rose be fine? Nothing is fine anymore; nothing ever will be. Something has slipped in their lives, a crack in what their world is supposed to be. "What did she ... what did she do?"

"Let me get your bag. We'll talk in the car." Abe grabs the bag off the carousel, an easy swipe of his big paw. "You're still using this antique? Sosha would be pleased as punch." Smiling in spite of himself. He always insists on carrying her bags and for once Sarah doesn't protest. They're not saying anything as they walk to the lot, the sunlight a soft weight across their shoulders, no wind. Sky-blue sky, the sky is never this blue in Toronto, this open. He sets the suitcase in the trunk, slams the lid down to make sure it locks and, for a second, rests his hands on the warm metal. They get in and he puts the key in the ignition, then stops, doesn't start the motor. Rests his big hands on the steering wheel.

"She cut herself, cut her wrists. David found her on the bathroom floor."

Sarah's holding onto the door handle, doesn't want to let it go.

"Crosswise just below the palm." His voice is dry, pinched. He clears his throat. "The cuts go – people *know, everyone* knows – the cuts go *lengthwise* if you mean business." Clears his throat again. "There wasn't much…she didn't bleed much."

Sarah has to think of her sister bleeding, blood emptying her out, and the thought expands into an old physics lesson: the three states of matter, solid, liquid and gas, and only a solid has a set shape and volume, a liquid has a set volume but no shape, it takes on the shape of its container. She remembers that it's a gas that expands to fill its container but her thoughts have no container. And Rose? What will happen if Rose is lost to matter?

"She was unconscious when he found her," Abe is saying. "The bathroom door was locked. David said he doesn't even remember how he broke it down." He keeps swallowing, he's having trouble speaking. "Of course he called 911." The emergency right here; their own emergency. Abe touches the ridge of bone above his nose, closes his eyes briefly. "The doctor, this pipsqueak, he can't be older than you, he says it was more a cry for help than a genuine attempt. But I don't know. The door was locked. She lost some blood." Abe turns away from Sarah, turns the key in the ignition and they sit for a minute, the car quietly idling.

Abe reverses, pulls out of the parking lot. Blue sky above them, improbable flight. "The doctor, I mean, I don't hold that much to one doctor's view – was he even a real doctor? he might have been some sort of student doctor – but he was probably right. A cry for help."

You're not here and I need you.

Weren't they enough? Wasn't their love enough, even at a distance?

"So the medication wasn't doing any good?"

Silence. They're pulling out of the parking lot, pulling onto the road. Not another car in sight, the road all theirs.

"Dad?"

"She wasn't taking the pills. She told David she flushed them down the toilet. One a day, so it looked like she was taking them."

Stupid. Just stupid. A cry for help! She had help right there and she didn't use it.

Stupid. Stupid Rose.

She touches Abe's arm. "Can we go straight to the hospital?"

"That's where we're going. Then we'll head home, get you something to eat. Mom has some fresh smoked goldeye in the fridge for you."

❧

Rose is in a locked ward, psych ward. They have to buzz to be let in, and a nurse comes up to the door, her face professional, wordlessly opens for them. Abe leads them around one corner and then another, that awful pale green painted on every wall, then they're at what must be Rose's room. They stand together at the threshold and there's the hummingbird mother, Pat, who puts down her magazine, flits in an instant from the chair beside Rose's bed to Sarah, puts both hands along her face, they're eye to eye. Her small mother, wound up tight, clockwork. "She's all right, Sarah. She'll be fine. I think she's asleep right now."

Sarah goes up to the bed and there Rose is, her beautiful sister, Rose, with her narrow, elegant wrists bandaged. The doctor said he didn't know if there would be scars. Rose, big brown almond eyes closed, thinner than Sarah can ever remember her being, paler, despite the beginnings of her summer tan. Her skin so brown they used to joke that it was like photographic paper, expose it for ten seconds to the sun and she'd go dark. The famous story of Pat scrubbing and scrubbing at the back of Rose's neck when she was a toddler, thinking the instant tan was grime. And now she's paper white, a wraith.

Even with her eyes closed, she looks sad.

And Sarah wants to shake her, shake her awake and shake her back into her life. Why didn't she want her life? Weren't they enough for her? Even without the baby, why weren't they enough for her?

She can't live without her sister. Doesn't Rose know that?

Her mother's touch on her shoulder. Sarah realizes she's been clenching her fists, releases them. She tells Pat she'll sit with Rose, they should go and grab a cup of coffee.

Pat nods, touches her shoulder again, pulls the blanket gently straight on Rose's bed before she and Abe leave. Sarah doesn't want to sit down, doesn't want to open her mother's magazine, doesn't care what the pregnant Princess Diana is wearing or who the real Brooke Shields is. She turns her back to the bed, stares out the window onto the hospital parking lot.

"Sarah?" Rose's voice behind her. Thick, slightly muffled. Sarah doesn't, for a moment, want to turn around. She doesn't know what to say.

"You're here?"

You're not here and I need you.

Sarah turns, touches her sister's cheek. "I just got in."

"You're really here?"

"Yes. Dad drove me from the airport."

"I thought I was dreaming. I had the strangest dream just now. Something about water, you and Gail were with me, and you wanted me to go down to the shore of some lake, maybe it was the ocean." Rose's eyes begin to darken, a shadow passing over them.

"Was it a bad dream?"

"No," Rose says, her eyes fixing on Sarah again. "Something came up out of the water, a log, and then it turned into something else, right in your arms, Sarah." She's looking at Sarah and tears are coming into her eyes. "A little water creature of some sort, an otter maybe. And you gave it to me." Rose blinks away the tears, her face loses focus, goes blank.

"Rose?"

Rose closes her eyes.

"It was a good dream?" Sarah is stroking Rose's arm through the blanket. "You tired?"

Rose opens her eyes again briefly, nods.

"You don't have to talk. I'll just sit with you." She takes Rose's hand, starts humming.

Her eyes closed, Rose asks, "What's that?"

Simon and Garfunkel. 'Bridge Over Troubled Water.' "Nothing. Just humming. Sleep now." And Rose seems to be drifting off again. Sarah hums quietly through the tune. Rose's hand with its bandages is cold, thin, the long elegant fingers have their nails chewed all the way down. Rose used to keep her nails a bit long, always a touch of polish. She'd tease Sarah about her stubby fingernails. Rose lets go of Sarah's hand, turns on her side, asleep. A slip of a girl. A fingernail paring. Crescent of a new moon.

Sarah wants to give her something, a gift. For the dance last night she put on this corny silver puzzle ring she picked up at the Winnipeg Folk Fest years ago, some hippie sold it to her. She takes it carefully off her finger, puts it onto Rose's. The ring fits fine, it holds.

❦

"Sarah?" A light touch at her shoulder.

"Mom?"

Pat is back in the room, a Styrofoam cup of coffee in her hand. "Has she been sleeping?"

Sarah nods. "She saw me for a sec, talked to me for a minute or so about a dream she had."

Pat shivers.

"It wasn't a bad dream. Something about finding an otter in the lake."

Pat rubs at her forehead with the back of her free hand. "That all she said?"

"She's been asleep most of the time. Me too, I guess. Where's Dad?" Sarah stretches, rubs at her eyes, which are gritty.

"I sent him home. We should be getting you home too. David will be back here soon. You need to eat something. Coffee?" Pat offers the cup. "It's awful."

"Thanks – I think."

"It'll help you wake up."

"What do the doctors say?"

Pat nods towards the hallway. "Let's not talk here. We don't want to wake her."

More awful washed-out green on the hallway walls, odd black smudges an indecipherable script, marks from the gurneys, no doubt. A nurse nods as she goes by. Soft squeak of her white shoes. "I don't want Rose to overhear," Pat says. "Not at this stage. Give me a sip." She reaches for the coffee, sips, shudders, hands it back. "My standards aren't high, but really. Ugh." She's biting her lower lip. Pat is wearing cheap little sandals made out of some kind of transparent pink plastic, her toenails painted pink too. Jelly bean pink. Like a kid's. Her mother's feet look like little kid feet.

Pat is explaining that the specialist, the psychiatrist, has confirmed what the GP was saying all along. It's not just the blues, it's clinical depression. But they're diagnosing it as *reactive* – it didn't come from nowhere. Generally that's good. The other kind, *endogenous* – which does come out of nowhere – is harder to treat. So it was reactive in response to losing the baby. At first they didn't want to put Rose on antidepressants, because talk therapy is supposed to do the trick if the depression is reactive. They tried a counsellor, and then a psychologist, but Rose didn't like either of them, and they certainly did sound like morons. Rose just kept getting worse. The psychiatrist explained that people get into a vicious cycle. Rose wasn't feeling well, so she wasn't doing well at work, so she was afraid she'd lose her job, so she started getting even more anxious and down. By the time she finally got the prescription for antidepressants, she just wasn't thinking straight. That's what led to the suicide attempt. Right now, she needs to rest and stabilize for a couple of days, and then they can let her go home. Physically she's all right. David got there soon enough, so the blood loss wasn't significant. The antidepressants take a while to work, they'll have to be patient. And they'll have to keep an eye on her. Pat looks down when she says this.

Keep an eye. Make sure she doesn't try to kill herself again. Doesn't try. Doesn't succeed.

Pat is twirling her wedding ring, a band of small diamonds set in white gold. She bites her lower lip again. "I'm just going to go in again for a minute and then we can head downstairs and get a cab. Rose will probably stay asleep. The medications are making her dopey. She'll be all right for a little while, even if she does wake up and no one's here."

Sarah stands in the hallway, watches her mother's swift hands lightly touching Rose's forehead, straightening the covers, quickly righting the arrangement of the water glass and pitcher on the bedside table. Pat touches Rose's forehead again, a whisper of a blessing.

Riding the elevator down to the lobby, Pat sorts through her purse, offers Sarah a mint. "I'm glad you could come. We really appreciate it. Taking the time off work. And the expense."

"Michael's helping out with the ticket."

"He's a dear." Pat pops a mint into her mouth. "He's a lovely man. I wish you'd give him a chance." She looks at Sarah.

Sarah fidgets with her bag, adjusts the shoulder strap.

"Sometimes it seems like you never did get over that boy Nick. That whole thing. You had such a hard time of it." Pat closes her purse, her mouth. Not wanting to say *abortion.* Not wanting to say *crazy.*

WORK

HER FIRST DAY BACK AT THE JOB, Sarah's stacking bags of peat moss and sheep manure, tackling the backlog from her ten days in Winnipeg, sinking into the work. It's hot out, muggy, the weather's moving into full summer swelter. Sarah's coated in dirt from the bags, sweaty. She keeps seeing Rose's face in the hospital bed. After asking Sarah a couple of questions about Winnipeg that she didn't answer, her crew manager Gary backed off, let her be. She'll put in extra hours to make up the time for as long as they need her to. Sarah's just thinking about taking her lunch break when Gary comes up, clears his throat. She looks up, wipes her hands on the back of her jeans. Gary's frowning, which isn't unusual, but he looks hesitant, which is.

"The boss – Hank wants to see you."

"I'll wash up."

"He's in the office."

"I know." When is Hank ever not in the office? He's certainly not on the lot hefting bags of manure, and she hardly ever even sees him dealing with customers. Hunched over his desk, yes, with a fan trained on him that looks like a prop from a 1940s private-eye movie. The whole office looks a bit like a B-movie set.

She goes into the grotty staff washroom, rinses off her face and hands as best she can. Runs her hands through her hair in a cursory attempt at respectability. When she looks in the crummy little mirror she sees she still has a streak of dirt on her forehead. She rinses it off, stupid though it is to fuss. She's not some school kid ordered into the principal's office.

When she walks in, Hank scowls in the faint breeze the fan is wafting through the stuffy room. Hank is always a bit of a blowhard, playing up his authority, and today he's clearly in a bad mood to boot. "Sarah," he says, without the usual invitation to sit down, "can you tell me exactly why you took ten days off work, with no notice, at the busiest time of the season?"

"My boyfriend called you," she says. "The day I left. I had to go to Winnipeg."

"Yes. Your *boyfriend* did call. And I had Gary call him back a bunch of times while you were gone to see when the heck you'd be back, but your *boyfriend* couldn't say. Tell me, just what exactly was this *family emergency?*"

"It was a family emergency. My family needed me."

"Look, Sarah, you're an employee of this company, and you have certain responsibilities. One of those responsibilities is really quite simple: we need you to show up for work. You get that? Is that too hard to figure out?"

Hank's starting to fidget in his wooden swivel office chair – which really *does* look like a fugitive from a Raymond Chandler movie. Maybe he fancies himself a Philip Marlowe, giving her the third degree. Jerk. She doesn't want to tell Hank about Rose.

"Girls like you don't have the foggiest idea what it really means to put in an honest day's work. We're counting on you here. It's not all fun and games. You need to grow up. Take your job seriously."

"I *do* take my job seriously. But I also have a responsibility to my family."

"Look… Sarah…" His face and neck and ears have started to go red. "What you don't understand is that I myself personally, I did you a favour trying you out for this job. You don't exactly look the part of a landscape crew, do you now? What do you weigh? Ninety pounds? But we wanted to give you the chance to prove yourself. Everybody else here has to pick up the slack for you. I've gone out on a limb hiring a girl and now you go and take all this time off without any explanation. I need you to take responsibility, not just rely on your boyfriend to make excuses for you. And just because you have a lawyer boyfriend who's ready, willing and able to foot the bills for you doesn't mean you don't bother to show up for work."

She doesn't want to be here.

Sarah gets up from her chair, heads to the door.

"Sarah, I'm talking to you. Don't you walk away from this conversation just because you don't like what I'm saying."

She doesn't turn around.

"You walk out of here and you're fired." Hank has raised his voice as the door closes. "Sarah? You hear me? If you can't take criticism, you're fired. Tell Holly to pay you up what we owe you."

She goes into the cubby they call the staff room, grabs her stuff from her dented, pitiful little locker.

"What's up?" Gary's hovering in the doorway.

"I quit."

"Just calm down, Sarah. Let me talk to Hank."

"Actually, I didn't quit. I got fired. You heard him. The whole friggin' block heard him."

"The guy's being a schmuck, Sarah. I'll talk to him."

Schmuck. Gary's got the Yiddish she taught him just right. Schmuck indeed. "I'm going home."

"Okay, okay. Just take it easy. I'll talk to him tomorrow and call you at home. Be reasonable. Okay?"

She walks out the back, her purse slung across her shoulder.

"Sarah!" Gary calls after her. "What about your pay?"

They owe her three weeks. Plus this morning's wages.

Holly can mail it to her.

Outside it's even hotter, the city revving its engines, ready to go full throttle into summer. A bus stops at the corner right beside her, breathing its foul breath in her face. She wants to throw something, hammer her fist through a wall. Guys would do that. But guys wouldn't get told they didn't deserve the job they were good at. *Nobody* has to help her do her job, *nobody* has to pick up any slack for her. She does an honest day's work. She's just as good as any guy on the crew. She's better. She's better than any of them. And twice as smart.

And she's out of a job.

She's out of a job. Because she lost her temper. Because Hank's a schmuck. How's she going to pay Michael back for the airfare to Winnipeg? How's she going to pay her rent? She has two months' rent in the bank, her dad always said make sure your savings come to two months' rent, but that's about it.

What's she going to do, and who the hell is she, without a job?

She's the schmuck. She's the idiot. She can't even hold down a crummy job. She'll have to tell Michael. And Gail. And the family in Winnipeg. Everybody will be disappointed in her and nobody will be surprised.

She doesn't care.

She does.

She wants to hit something.

⁓

The next day Sarah's back at Gail's loft, which has evolved since the first time she visited, a leather club chair, thick luxurious candles along the tops of the bookshelves. Every detail a sign that Gail's settled in, that her life is in order: job, apartment, furniture. A whole, not a half-life. There's a big fig tree drooping in front of one of the windows, *Ficus benjamina.* It looks like the sun may be too intense here: the tree is dropping yellowed leaves on the wooden floor. Sarah sticks a finger in the soil – dry as a bone. She fills a mug with water, empties it into the big pot, fills it again, empties it. Gail's been standing at the window, swallowing what must be her second or third beer since Sarah came.

"Do you have a watering can?"

"There's a pitcher on the table."

Sarah swishes the residue at the bottom. "What is this?"

Gail takes the pitcher from her, sniffs, shrugs. "I dunno."

Iced tea? Dead sangria? She takes the pitcher to the sink, rinses it out, fills it and douses the thirsty soil.

"Do you want me to make us spaghetti? Or I might have some leftover couscous." Gail's shuffling dishes and plastic containers in the fridge, opening lids. "Damn." She's spilled something viscous onto the floor. Maybe three beers, four?

"Why don't we just order in Chinese?" And before Gail can raise an eyebrow, Sarah says, "My treat."

Gail closes the fridge door. "No couscous." She starts to mop up the mess on the floor with a dishrag.

Sarah takes the dishrag from her, rinses it, grabs paper towels to attack the spill. "So let's get Chinese."

"Okay, but let me pay for it."

"No dice, Gail. My treat."

"Your funeral. Spend your last ten bucks on take-out Chinese."

She's got more than ten bucks. She can pay for their dinner. She's not penniless just because she got laid off.

Not laid off. Fired.

She's never ever been fired before. She quit a few jobs, got laid off some, but never got fired.

She hasn't said anything to the Winnipeg family yet. When Gail called to invite Sarah over, eager for the Winnipeg news direct, she had to tell Gail, who didn't say much. Probably biting her tongue. Because it was Sarah's own fault. Mostly. Sarah had to tell Michael too, of course, who almost seemed relieved. No. No *almost* about it. He *was* relieved. He immediately started yakking about how proud he was that she finally told Hank off and walked out on him. Sarah is so much better off not stuck in that crappy job. Why doesn't she give herself a break before the next crappy job, come with him to France? No point looking for another job until she gets back from Paris. The office is arranging Michael's tickets, and they can still book her too, she just has to confirm. There's no job holding her back.

She feels in her pocket for the penny. She must have left it in her room, she puts it on the bedside table when she goes to sleep. Every penny counts. She'll be counting pennies now, all right.

No job to hold her here, but how can she owe Michael for a trip like this? He says there's room in his apartment, it won't cost anything for her to be there, just the ticket and he's happy to pay. She doesn't know and the penny isn't here to tell her. The last few nights have been okay, but can she spend every night for six weeks sleeping beside Michael? Plus how can she leave now, when Rose is still sick? What if they need her in Winnipeg?

"Chinese it is," Gail says. "Your treat." She dials, finishes her beer as she orders. Honey garlic ribs and beef with broccoli in black bean sauce, her standard order. Mu-shu chicken for Sarah. Hangs up the phone, grabs another beer from the fridge. "Twenty minutes. You want a beer while we wait? No, of course not. Soda? Lemonade?"

Sarah nods. At least the pitcher's been washed.

"So tell me more." Gail's pouring her a glass of lemonade directly out of a fresh bottle. Good. Gail's also swallowing back more of the new bottle of beer. Not as good.

There's not much to add to what she told Gail over the phone yesterday, but she knows Gail needs to hear it again, quiz her, ponder, worry it. Needs the beer to process the data Sarah's providing: the cuts were crosswise just below the palm, not lengthwise. They're not sure if they'll scar. The bathroom door was locked, David had to break it down. Rose was unconscious when David found her but probably hadn't been out long. All the evidence they've already gone over, and over, to figure out just how serious it was. Quoting the pipsqueak doctor – *a cry for help, not a genuine attempt*. She's tired of these bits of facts but she knows Gail needs them. What she's not sure about is whether Gail needs that much beer.

The doorbell rings and Gail buzzes the delivery guy up, pays and tips him a buck, then changes her mind, hands him three more ones. On a ten dollar order. Sarah never tips delivery guys anything. She digs out a twenty from her wallet, hands it to Gail, doesn't refuse when Gail gives her ten dollars change. Gail's digging noisily through her cutlery drawer for chopsticks. "So once she got out of hospital, what was she like?"

"I don't know… She stayed in bed a lot. Really quiet. Not herself."

"But did you get a chance to really talk with her, ask her? Why she did it?"

Sarah shakes her head.

"How come you didn't talk?"

"I don't know. The closest we came was right after I got there, when she told me about this dream she had. When I first got there she was pretty drugged up. But even after she got out of hospital, it was like she still wasn't fully there. I'd be saying something completely ordinary, and she'd get all spooked looking. Like what I was saying wasn't what she was hearing. But the last day or two that I was there, she started to seem a bit better, probably because the antidepressants were starting to work. Like she was maybe shaking it off a bit. Maybe."

"And, and when she did it, when she cut her wrists, it was because the meds were making her worse somehow?"

She's told Gail this twice already. "No. She never took the pills. She told David she was taking them, but she flushed them down the toilet. One a day."

Gail takes another long swig of her beer. She hasn't touched her food. "I hate her."

"What?"

"*That.* I hate *that.*"

"You said you hated Rose."

Another long pull on the beer. "I didn't. It was a slip of the tongue."

"You can't hate Rose."

"I don't! I never said that! It should have been me who went to Winnipeg."

"You had a case. You *have* a case."

"Fuck, Sarah, you lost your job! I wouldn't have lost my job because I went to Winnipeg because my sister was in hospital! I have a decent employer!" Gail's picking at her beef with broccoli but she hasn't put anything in her mouth yet.

"The Centre isn't such a bad place to work. It's this one guy, Hank, the boss. He's a jerk."

"How can you defend them? *Why* are you defending people who just fired you?"

Sarah's hands are full of mu-shu pancake. She bites in, the hoisin sauce drips onto her plate. "Don't feel bad."

"*Don't feel bad!* How can I not feel bad when my sister tries to commit suicide?"

It's a funny verb, *commit*. It's usually crimes that are committed. Is suicide still a crime? In French it's a reflexive verb, *se suicider*.

"What is *wrong* with you? How can you sit there musing on French verbs when our sister tried to kill herself?!"

She didn't know she'd said anything out loud. She's so used to talking in her head. "I meant, don't feel bad because you couldn't go."

"Well, I do feel bad. It would have been better if I'd gone."

"Why?" They didn't need a lawyer, they needed a daughter. A sister.

"Why? Because ... Look, Sarah –"

"What?" What's Gail on about? Sarah feels herself starting to go red.

"Never mind."

"Spit it out, Gail."

Now it's Gail who's flushing. "Because they probably spent more time worrying about you than about Rose."

"What do you mean?"

"What do I mean? I mean, *Poor little Sarah, never finished university, what will become of her? And now she's gotten herself fired from another loser job.*"

"Just stop it, Gail."

"You asked." Gail takes another long swig of her beer, looks for a place to set it down. "You – you're never any help. You're hopeless. You can't even look after yourself, much less Rose."

"That's not fair."

"I'm sick of you, Sarah. I'm sick of everything."

Fine. Let her be sick of everything. Sarah picks up her plate, dumps the food in the trash can. The lid bangs. Her purse is on the floor by the armchair. She picks it up. Second day in a row, here she is, walking out again. This time on her sister. "Don't tell Mom about the job. I haven't said anything to them yet."

Gail's still at the table. "You don't have to go. Eat something. You paid for it."

She paid for it all right. Sarah puts the purse over her shoulder.

"Sarah. For Christ's sake, I had too much beer, I didn't mean it."

She walks out, but in the hallway, has to stop, cover her face. *Walk it off.* That's what their softball coach would say when someone got clipped by a ball. She'll walk it off, walk all the way home, let the city repair her.

But she keeps just walking out, walking away from things.

I'm sick of you, Sarah.

That's what Gail really thinks of her.

Screw Gail. Screw everyone. She hates Gail. She hates everything about her life. She takes her purse, hurls it against the stair railing. The strap catches on the newel post and the purse boomerangs back into her face, smacks into her nose. She puts her hand to her face. Her nose is bleeding. The only time in her life she gets into a fight and she punches herself in the face. She is fucking hopeless. Just like Gail said. Even if she did try to take it back. Sort of. She sits down at the top of the stairs, digs a Kleenex out of her purse, two Kleenexes. It's not that bad.

At the curb she hails a taxi, still holding the Kleenex to her nose. When she gets into the backseat, she can't find the seatbelt. The taxi starts, and she feels like a little kid, loose in the enormous back seat.

She punched herself in the face. She wants to laugh and then she doesn't. She can feel the tears coming into her eyes. This sick sense that everything is dropping away from her, everything she needs most: work, her sisters.

"You okay, Miss?" the driver asks. He's a thickset guy about Abe's age.

She nods.

"Somebody hurt you?" In the rear-view mirror she can see the fatherly worry in his eyes. Violence against women. Women against violence against themselves. Somebody hurt her.

Yes, me.

She shakes her head. "It was an accident," she says. "I'm okay."

CALL

"IT'S YOUR CALL," MICHAEL TELLS HER. He's laid it all out for her. It's a simple plan. There's no reason she shouldn't go with him to Paris, there's nothing to tie her down, nothing keeping her here. Her job is a bust. And she can ditch the room on Palmerston without penalty, it's week-to-week. He knows she doesn't want to take any money from him, but she can cover her own airfare to Paris with the money she saves on rent. She doesn't have to split the cost of the apartment in Paris; his firm is paying for it.

He knows she's worried about Rose, but there's just not that much she can do. Rose is in Winnipeg and besides, she has a husband and parents right there to help her through this.

And this way, they can see how things go in Paris. If she doesn't want to move in with him when they get back, if the experiment fails – he actually says this, *if the experiment fails* – it'll be easy enough for her to find herself another room to rent when they get back. Simple.

It's her call.

It's her call, but really it's the penny's.

It feels cold in her hand; she'd picked it up from the bedside table. Such a small weight. She lets it shift in her palm, over and over. The flip side. The flip side of *yes* is *no*. The flip side of Michael is what? No-Michael. The flip side of Paris is Winnipeg. She closes her fist, shakes it back and forth like a pair of dice. *C'mon Lady Luck.* Opens her hand.

What do you want?

She's afraid to want.

She gives the penny a proper toss, catches it in her right hand, flips it down onto the back of her left. What does it say?

The penny says *yes*.

And so does she. Yes, she's going with Michael to Paris. It was her call and the penny called it and so did she. Paris. City of light. City of romance. When Sarah was a teenager, she taped a cheap print of Van Gogh's 'Café Terrace at Night' to the wall by her bed. Cobblestones and round café tables with their empty chairs and the light from buildings brightening the night. The dream of someplace else, someplace not Winnipeg, not the dull place she had to live in.

The flip side of Paris is Winnipeg.

And now it's Winnipeg she needs to call, because she needs to call Rose. Sarah hasn't spoken with her in the ten days since she left Winnipeg. Pat and Abe have telephoned, told her Rose seems steady, maybe a bit better. The meds just take time. Sarah's been afraid to call, but now she needs to talk to her sister. To the sister she still wants to talk to. If Rose weren't sick, Sarah would have told her about the argument with Gail, and Rose would have found a way to fix it. But if Rose weren't sick, Sarah and Gail wouldn't have had the fight.

She needs Rose. Sarah dials, gets through right away; David answers.

"Hey, it's me, Sarah."

"Oh, Sarah, we're just finishing dinner."

"Do you want me to call back?" But he's already set the phone down, is talking in a low voice to Rose. Sarah can picture their kitchen, the big window over the sink that looks out onto their side yard. Rose's quirky tchotchkes lined up along the windowsill: a little ceramic pitcher with stubs of pencils in it, an olive-wood bowl Sarah brought her back from Israel, candlesticks made from antique wooden spools. The shadow box David made from an old printer's tray he found in the garbage mounted on the wall, filled with tiny contact-print photos he'd taken of all of them: Rose and Sarah and Gail, Abe and Pat, David's parents.

"Hey, Sarah." Her voice is thin, not quite Rose.

"Are you eating dinner? Should I call back later?"

"Dinner? No, no. We've … we're finished."

"How are you feeling? Any better?" Water is running in the background. David's probably started the dishes. She can hear the light splash of dishes in the sink.

Silence.

"Rose? Are you there?"

"Sorry, what did you say?"

"I was asking how you were feeling."

"Feeling? I'm okay. I'm taking the pills now. They're supposed to help." The sound of water stops.

"That's good," Sarah says.

"Well, I knew all along I was supposed to be taking them," her voice is wispy, "but I thought it would be better just to get well on my own." A rustle on the end of the line, Rose adjusting the receiver. "That's what I was thinking."

She wasn't thinking right. She wasn't thinking at all. "But you're taking them now?"

"I *said* that, Sarah. I said I was taking them and I am."

"Right. You did. And are you sleeping okay?"

"Up and down. Mom says I need to catch up on my rest. I'm trying."

Sarah can hear David's voice in the background. "Do you have to go?"

"No, no, David's just saying he's going to sit outside on the porch."

"Nice evening?"

"Beautiful." There's some of the old Rose, the real Rose, in the word. "How about there?"

"Beautiful here too." Sarah looks out the window; the leaves on the oak in front of her room still have their fresh spring green. The muggy heat has passed for now, and the last few days have been perfect. "Remember that Japanese quince bush I told you about in front of Michael's apartment? When I was there yesterday I saw the buds opening."

"That's nice." The voice has gone wan again.

"Rose, I was calling because I've got some news. Well, kind of good-news/bad-news. I'm not working at the Centre anymore."

"The pay *was* pretty bad."

"Minimum wage. But they laid me off." She doesn't say *fired*, doesn't want to tell Rose the whole sad story, make her feel bad. Worse.

"Oh, Sarah, that's too bad."

"It's okay. So … since I'm not working anyway, I'm going to take a holiday."

"Holiday?" Rose's voice has gone even flatter, as if she doesn't quite understand the word.

"With Michael. You remember he went on that business trip to Paris?"

"Michael was in Paris?"

"I think I told you. I guess you forgot."

"Maybe you told me and I forgot."

Memory lapses: a side effect of the antidepressants or the sickness itself. Little pieces of Rose gone that they can't get back. Silence. Sarah can't hear anything in the background. "Rose? Are you there?"

"You were saying something about a holiday? Paris?"

Rose has never been to Europe. Never did the back-packing thing because she was always busy with her dancing – the troupe was on tour, they had rehearsals, performances…

Why should Sarah get to go to Paris? It isn't fair.

"It isn't fair."

"What?" Rose's voice asking.

"I'm sorry."

"For what?"

"It's not fair. It's not fair you losing the baby."

She can hear Rose's receiver rustle again. "No," Rose says. "It's not."

Sarah leans her cheek against the window. "Remember that night you called me – you thought David was gone?"

Pause, then, "Yeah. I remember."

"I kept thinking, why is she calling me, how can she think it's me who can help?" The loser with the loser job. The screw-up. The dented floor model. She'd felt oddly honoured. And helpless.

"Sarah."

"What?"

A sigh. "We can help each other, but only so far."

Only so far. But aren't they supposed to look after each other?

"Sarah?"

"Okay. I mean, I'm not sure."

"Hey, Sarah, you know I'm wearing that ring you gave me."

"The puzzle ring?"

"Yeah. It fell apart once. David helped me put it back together. It's not that hard."

"I'm glad."

"You said Michael's going to Paris?"

"He wants me to go with him."

"And?" There's a hint of impatience in Rose's voice.

"And it's not fair that I get to go to Paris and you don't." And it's not fair that Rose's baby died and it's not fair that she wanted to kill herself and leave Sarah all alone.

"Okay. But that doesn't mean you shouldn't go."

"No?"

"No."

꧁

And now Sarah's got her passport, little navy-blue book with its gold-embossed coat of arms, its lion and unicorn, Union Jack and fleur-de-lis, crown. Her passport photo a black-and-white mug shot of her serious formal face, emblem of her official self, some self she doesn't recognize. The woman with no job. No place to live. The woman who gets to go to Paris. The passport means she's claimed for a given state, a given country. Home and native land. *Description of bearer*: sex: F; height: 151 cm; hair: brown; eyes: brown. *This passport is valid for all countries unless otherwise endorsed.* A Canadian passport, the golden ticket that gets you where you want to go, that keeps you safe, immune, when you get there. With a Canadian passport, no one can touch you. And this declaration of innocence and belonging will carry her out of the life in Toronto that's wearing thinner and thinner; it will lift the barriers at the border and wave her into the dream city.

Paris

PARIS

July, 1982

THE TAXI IS PULLING THEM FROM THE AIRPORT, moving through cornfields
and hayfields. Miscellaneous weeds are overtaking the steel barriers on the highway median, a green intrusion. Sarah spots a wild dill plant that must be five
feet tall, tall as her. Her mother puts up mason jars of dill pickles every summer,
the aunts competing for whose are the best. Dill from the garden, one clove of
garlic in each jar, one hot pepper for zip. Bottle them the same day you pick
them, that's the trick to keep them crunchy. Her mouth waters. Winnipeg.

But they're here, in Paris. Almost.

Sarah had pictured the Eiffel Tower planted like a pointy little chess piece
beside the river, but as they were landing the city itself was nowhere to be
seen. She feels thick with jet lag. The airplane was choked with cigarette
smoke, and her head is clogged with smoke, and next to no sleep, and the
time change, six hours. The traffic slows and then speeds up mysteriously.
Flash of a tile-roofed farmhouse, a memory of a time before the highway.
The thickness in her head is making it hard to read the new landscape. *Cédez
le passage* under a red-bordered triangle must mean *yield*. *Chaussée déformée.*
What can that mean? *Something* deformed… The sign is gone before she can
figure it out. Translating is the only job she has now and she can't even get it
right. The taxi is moving them through suburbs now; she can just barely see
low, ordinary-looking buildings above and beyond the concrete scallops of
the barriers enclosing the highway.

Where is she? She touches the penny in her pocket. Lucky penny. Lucky
her. Whether she deserves it or not.

The barriers recede, they've moved off the highway onto the surface roads. The cab stops at a red light and something inside her stops. She sees this woman, a thin young woman standing at the curb in a thin print dress. The woman's right hand is crossed to stroke her left cheek, what seems to be a scar on her cheek. It looks new, raw still. Sarah thinks of Barb, the scar across her palm still new-looking, as if it hadn't really healed. The young woman at the crosswalk and Sarah – they must be about the same age, the same height, weight – briefly exchange glances. The woman's eyes are the same deep brown as Sarah's. Doppelgangers. Strangers mirroring each other. They look for a moment, then look away. The woman hesitates, seems to pick a direction, and turns, walks away from the intersection. There's something both determined and defeated about how she holds herself. Sarah's mirror self. But the woman is someone who belongs in this city, who isn't a stranger in it, a foreigner, like Sarah. Maybe.

They're in the city itself now and more faces slideshow past, vignettes of expression: surprise, amusement, indifference, hauteur, appreciation. People's features are supposed to be shaped by the language they speak. The French have these sharp, fine features, like foxes – canny and wary and smart. All those complicated vowels to get your mouth around. What's going to happen to Sarah's own face here? Will she get to be someone else, someone other than her old useless self, the one the penny let her shuck?

Two boys in their mid-teens walk down a narrow lane that's shadowy in the brightness of the day; they're unselfconsciously holding hands. There, down those side streets, those lanes, people are allowed their private lives, which are both more and less than the official tourist version the city proposes. That thin woman with the scar back at the intersection, her thin print dress, what life or half-life is *she* allowed?

When Sarah finally spots the five- and six-storey buildings with the angled-back roofs that she remembers from her first visit, something in her suddenly tightens in happiness. She's been waiting for this. *Mansard*, she tells Michael, after Mansart, the architect who invented them in the 1600s. How did the *t* turn into a *d?* On those top floors behind the slanted windows are the *chambres de bonne*, maid's rooms, with sloped ceilings cutting into the space – the garrets where artists are supposed to starve. And now they're in the Marais, where their apartment is, the driver announces, speaking slowly and carefully for them. Sarah can tell that his French is heavily accented, he's probably Moroccan or maybe Algerian. Sarah's been reading up on the area a bit. The whole neighbourhood used to be a nasty marshy wasteland: *marais* means *marsh* in French.

The taxi pulls up at their address, and they tumble their bags out onto the sidewalk. While Michael pays the cabbie, counting out his francs, Sarah checks the elaborate handwriting on the cramped chart at the door for the concierge's doorbell, rings. They can hear the chime faintly through the heavy wooden door. It opens, and a roly-poly little woman duly lets them in, chattering away rapidly in a French Sarah can't begin to understand – so much for her French being a big help – *oui, oui, merci,* all she can manage in response. The concierge is a flawless Parisian concierge. She couldn't wear anything but what she's wearing, the worn flowered apron protecting her worn flowered housedress, her sense of propriety, proprietorship. She hands them the impressive, heavy keys with some formal little phrases Sarah doesn't understand either and then waves them on, closing the door to her suite, where they can see laundry hanging off a little wire rack in the middle of the living room. A smell of carrots, beets maybe, boiling. The apartment is on the *deuxième étage*, second floor – second floor in France, which means the third in Canada. The ground floor is called the *rez-de-chaussée*, which accounts for the mystery of the 'RC' on elevator buttons. Sarah thinks, though she's not absolutely sure, that *chaussée* is an old French word for 'road' (that must have been what the highway sign meant, *chaussée déformée*, uneven surface, under construction, something like that) and *rez* means something like 'flat' or 'level.' So it's like *street level.* And 'SS' on elevator buttons, that's for *sous-sol*, which means basement. So much to figure out. Not that there *is* an elevator in their building.

Michael is staring at her, holding back a grin.

What?

"You're turning into a Parisian chatterbox, Sarah. Back home I don't think you'd normally string this many words together in a day."

She's just excited that she's managed to figure out a few things that are probably a mystery to Michael. She wants to help.

"Now don't go mute on me again," he says. "You know you're here as my interpreter and personal guide to Paris." *Personal guide.* She won't be much good at that either. She was here for four days five years ago. She doesn't know anything. Michael starts picking up the two biggest suitcases. She'll let him this time. She really is tired, although she can also feel this surge of adrenaline, or joy, just because she's here. Paris.

They have to trudge up two tight, narrow flights of stairs which hairpin at each floor, then figure out how to turn the elaborate lock with the impressive key. But there's a pay-off when they get in the door. The apartment is just one big room all right, as Michael's Parisian colleague Laura, the one who found it for them, described it. But the ceiling rises to twelve feet or more and, after the heat of the sunny sidewalk and the climb, the room is beautifully cool. Two ten-foot French doors open out to minute balconies, more ledges than balconies. Room to shake a mop, Abe would say. Plus there's a double bed for them, a real double bed, not two singles tied together which, in Sarah's experience, inevitably, slowly, separate in the middle of the night if the occupants try to get close enough to spoon…or anything else.

And the whole place, with its kitchen nook and modern bathroom, looks spotless, not the grime Sarah was expecting. She finds some sort of a mysterious French cleaning product perched beside the sink. Does *détersif* mean cleanser or detergent? Whatever it means is suspended in translation, which feels, at the moment, as if she has to wrench herself from one way of understanding the world to another. And this is her job, now, translation, guidance; the only job she has.

Michael has stretched himself out on the bed, yawning at the same time he's grinning, and he's going on about what lucky ducks they are, getting to live here, even if the Marais isn't exactly the fanciest part of Paris. *The Jewish quarter.* It's been more or less a ghetto since the 1300's, Jews living here off and on, depending on how tolerant the regime in charge was. Sarah stands in the windows' sunlight looking out on the two half-timbered medieval buildings that Laura promised in one of her letters. They're among the oldest in Paris. The roof-lines are pointed, triangular, like a child's drawing of a house. They're special because there aren't many left. In the second half of the 19th century the city was 'modernized' and most of the old buildings de-molished. Sarah tries to picture the narrow medieval streets. The city she sees now printed over what the city used to be, translating itself.

Right below their balcony ledge is a sculpted head protruding from the wall. Michael is beside her now. "Have you met Georges? Zhat's *Georges* with an *s*," he says in a bad fake French accent. He pulls her back into the room, into a kiss. "Feel good being back here?"

Yes. Yes she does. However useful or useless she is.

"Even if you're stuck spending every night with some ignoramus who doesn't know the Left Bank from the Right?" His hands under her shirt.

"Uh-huh," she says.

He's starting to run his tongue along her earlobe.

"I should shower, Michael. I feel so grubby."

More kisses. "We could shower together. It's a nice big tub."

"Sounds dangerous."

He starts unbuttoning her shirt. "You're a dangerous woman." He's kissing her collarbone, her shoulders. "We need to get these jeans off."

"Michael, I'm stinky."

He sniffs at her neck, licks her shoulder. "You smell good to me." She's kicked off her sandals. The jeans are gone. He pulls the comforter back, gently pushes her onto the bed. His mouth on her throat. He turns her over, kisses the back of her neck. She's heard somewhere that geishas never powder the napes of their necks because it's the most erotic part of the body. The geishas are probably right. Michael's mouth is on her nape, his fingers are counting the nobs of her spine. *Glorious.*

❧

She wakes to the sound of someone fiddling with the lock. A bit of sun is coming through the white-painted wooden shutters. The door opens and Michael comes in, his hair still damp, a white paper bag in his hands. "Good morning, Merry Sunshine. Did you just wake up?"

She did. Slept in a big double bed with Michael in Paris with no dreams, no waking or half-waking.

"I got us fresh croissants. And strawberry jam. *And* crème fraîche."

"What's crème fraîche?"

"Laura introduced me to it when I was here last time. Fancy stuff. It's like sour cream, but not as sour. You're supposed to put it in sauces or on tartes, but you are *not* supposed to put it on croissants. Laura is an expert on everything Parisian – even though she's from Saskatoon by way of Tobago – because she's been living here three whole years. She's perfected her *savoir faire* and her *comme il faut*, not to mention her *je ne sais quoi*, and so according to Laura, crème fraîche on your croissant is *not* the thing to do but," he bends over to kiss her, "we're going to do it anyway, aren't we?"

Now who's the Parisian chatterbox?

"So I recommend you put the strawberry jam on top of the crème fraîche."

To be fancy. "What time is it?"

He's getting plain white plates from the cupboard. "I got us ground espresso coffee too. We can't have plain old Canadian coffee while we're in Paris. I remembered seeing one of those little French octagonal or hexagonal or whatever coffee pot things." A brief clinking and clanking among the cupboards. "Here it is. Ten. It's actually got ten sides. I got milk too." He's setting everything out on the counter. "You slept sixteen hours. It's 8:00 in the morning. I got up less than an hour ago myself. I was sure I'd wake you, but you were dead to the world."

Michael is filling the bottom of the coffee contraption with water, tamping down the coffee into the middle part. As he lights the stove with a wooden match, the gas catches with a quick whoosh. "This really is the Jewish neighbourhood, Sarah. There was a shop selling bagels right beside the French bakery. And this guy walked by me as I was leaving the bakery and I could have sworn he looked just like your dad."

Abe. What's her dad doing now? And Pat? Rose? "I thought we would have a phone."

He sits down on the bed. "A phone. Right. I noticed that as soon as we got in. I didn't check when we rented the place because I just figured there'd be one. But I asked at the *pâtisserie* – the girl spoke some English, it was great – and she said that there are booths where we can make long-distance calls at the post office right in the City Hall. It's not five minutes from here. What's the French word again for City Hall?"

"*Hôtel de Ville.*" The phrase just popped into her head – the jet-lag fog must be lifting.

"Or we can use pay phones, but then we have to have coins, or tokens. I can't remember which. But I'll find out."

A grinding and screech outside their window. Michael goes to it, opens the shutters and sun brightens the room. There's a huge tourist bus right outside. They hear the babble of voices, sounds that seem to be German or Dutch. "They're gawking at those old half-timbered buildings." The smell of coffee starts to soak through the room.

After breakfast, they head downstairs, through the lobby with its fug of cabbage stew seeping from under the concierge's door, and out into the sunlight, the day already warm.

"Where are we going?" she asks. Michael has taken her hand, is walking purposefully down the street.

"Just follow me," he says, giving her hand a light squeeze.

"I don't want to follow you. I want to know where I'm going." Which way are they supposed to go? Sarah feels in her pocket, but she's left the penny in the apartment.

"City Hall is just a little ways up here." They'll have to wait till after 3:00 to make the call or they'll wake her parents up, but Sarah wants to check the place out, make sure the girl at the *pâtisserie* had it right about being able to make a long-distance call.

A few doors on they pass a tiny shop barely the size of a closet that's crammed floor to ceiling with roughly-cut logs. They must still have working fireplaces here, though Sarah can't imagine anyone wanting a fire in this weather. A bearded old man in shirt sleeves looks up and then through them, goes back to sorting through the logs. Business must be tough.

A little ways up there's a small *supermarché*, the grocery carts stacked in the entry miniatures of the ones at home. *Entrée libre* a sign says – it means free entry or admission but that can't be right, they're not going to charge people to go into a supermarket. Maybe it means *self-serve*, something like that. Another puzzle that it's Sarah's job to figure out.

They pass *pâtisseries*, hardware stores, fabric stores, their windows crammed with goods. Fruit and vegetable shops with elaborate displays: intricate pyramidal mountains of cherries, carefully heaped, orderly piles of white asparagus-like stacks of logs. Sarah's mouth waters. Can she be hungry again already? There's an awning that says *boulanger, boulangerie* – it means *baker, bakery* but why both? And what's the difference between a *boulangerie* and a *pâtisserie?* One means *bakery* and the other means *pastry shop*. But they sell bread at the pastry shops, and pastries at the bakeries, so what's the difference? Maybe there's some arcane French rule about what you call yourself here: only someone with sixteen years of training in puff pastry assembly gets to call themselves a *pâtissier*…Sarah knows the term for puff pastry: *pâte feuilletée*. All those flaky layers that make up a croissant. She does want another croissant. And here's another puzzle for her: those odd, red lozenge-shaped signs that say *tabac*, she does know that it means that the shop is licensed to sell tobacco, but they sell stamps and newspapers as much as cigarettes. So what's that about? All these fine distinctions, refinements, specialization within specialization. She has to sort them out, get things right.

Sarah looks around. She's been so busy taking everything in, trying to parse every word, that she's lost track of where they're going. No penny to help her decide, just Michael certain he knows. "Michael, are you sure we're heading in the right direction for the City Hall?"

"Hang on, hang on," he says, looking up and down the street. "Uh-oh. I forgot to bring the map. And I have this feeling that if we've gone this far without seeing it, we might be headed in the wrong direction."

Follow me. Without knowing where they're going.

"Don't worry, it can't be more than five minutes away." He squeezes her hand again. "It's okay, we'll check it out, make sure you get your call through."

❧

She's waited most of the day so she can make the call without waking her parents, then waited again until one of the old-fashioned booths in the post office has become available. Sarah closes the door, lets the privacy of the polished wooden walls close around her, and listens to the hum and buzz as the line connects and then rings. She's got her penny tight in her fist.

"Hello?" It's her mother's voice, clear and close, as if she weren't an ocean and half a continent away.

"Mom? Mom, it's Sarah. I'm in Paris."

"Abe, it's Sarah. She's calling from Paris."

Sarah can hear the rumble of her father's voice in the background.

"Am I calling you too early?"

"No, of course not. We're polishing off our French toast, Abe says it's in your honour." Pat sounds a little giddy, she's suppressing a giggle. Things must be okay. "You're in Paris! I can't quite believe it! How are you?"

"Wonderful. It's so beautiful here." Michael makes a kissy face at her through the glass. "Michael sends his love."

"Tell him thanks. But this must be an expensive call, it's the middle of the day there."

"I just wanted to know how Rose is."

"She's all right for now, Sarah. There's no point worrying. She really is taking her meds. David is making sure she gets outside as much as she can. They even went for a bike ride to Assiniboine Park yesterday. Well, I don't think they got all the way there, but it's a start."

A start. But Rose has so far to go before she gets anywhere. Before she's saved, safe.

"So don't worry, Honey, okay? You just enjoy your trip."

"I will, Mom. Listen, give her my love, will you?"

"Of course. Of course, Sarah. Did you see Gail before you left?"

Gail. Pat's maternal radar must sense that something's awry between Sarah and Gail. Gail left a message on the answering machine the day before Sarah left for Paris: *Have a good trip. Send me a postcard.* She tried to call back but Gail wasn't in, so they still haven't spoken. She left Toronto without seeing her sister. "Didn't get a chance, Mom."

"Well, you can call her next time. She'll pass on the news to us."

"Sure."

"You have fun, okay? Just have a good time."

"Okay. Give Dad my love." The line clicks and goes silent.

Michael's waiting outside the booth. Sarah lets herself be pulled into his hug. Rose is all right. For now. One sister just starting to get better and the other angry with her. It makes her feel off balance, as if she can't keep a steady course without a sister on each side for ballast. Sarah the border collie, who needs to keep everyone together. Gail the bulldog, who won't ever let anything go. Or maybe it's Sarah who's the bulldog, the one who can never let the thread go too far or too loose without feeling herself slip.

PLACE DES VOSGES

SHE HAS TO FIND HER WAY without a map. From her last time in Paris, which was her first time in Paris, she remembers how the square held itself, made itself a world. Michael has had to check in at the office, which is all the way in La Défense, close to the construction site where his client's skyscraper is being built. So she's on her own. But she knows where she needs to go her first morning solo in Paris. She follows rue François Miron past the little shops she and Michael were examining yesterday, the *pâtisseries*, tabac, butcher shops. There's a lonesome-looking man in bright green coveralls at the curb stroking his broom ineffectually against a trickle of water in the gutter, going through the motions. What good is a tired plastic broom against all that muck?

At a pharmacy on the corner she stops to ask for directions and her hesitant French seems to work. The woman behind the counter listens carefully, *oui, Mademoiselle, Place des Vosges est très proche.* Pulls an envelope out of a drawer by the cash register and draws Sarah a little map. *Au revoir, Mademoiselle.* A little ways up, rue François Miron turns itself into rue Saint-Antoine. Sarah checks the clerk's map, walks another short block and there it is, right where the sketched map said it would be, rue de Birague.

It's a narrow street that seems as if it were made just for her, ending in a fairy-tale castle façade whose roof is punctured by dormer windows. If there are *chambres de bonne* way up in those top storeys, there must be precious little light available through the tiny windows for the maids inside. Do people in Paris still have servants, not just cleaning ladies, but live-in servants? In this expensive neighbourhood bordering Place des Vosges, maybe they do.

Maybe that's how she could stay here, even after Michael leaves – find herself a job as a maid to some rich family. *Bonne* comes from *"bonne à tout faire,"* good at everything. An all-purpose servant. Isn't that what she wants, to be good, at something?

What's good is this cool dark held in the archway opening through the castle-like façade. She moves into the solemn darkness of the arcade, the same red brick trimmed in pale yellow stone as the façade, each arched section repeating itself. Beyond it there's the brilliant splash of green of the square itself. She steps from the shadowy quiet of the arcade into the bright quiet of the square.

She's here. Place des Vosges. The heart of the heart of Paris. So much light. The square is big, much bigger than she remembered it. It's early Saturday morning, so in the strict geometry of the *place* with its circles and squares, its precision gardening, there's almost no one. The square *is* a perfect square, a model of symmetry, the same arcade running along all four sides, paths in perfect diagonals across the inner square. Lines drawn to let people in, not just keep them out. A space that can belong, at least temporarily, to anyone passing through: cleaning ladies, maids, the men in their bright green uniforms sweeping the streets with their sad brooms. The young woman she saw from the taxi with the scar across her cheek. This elegant middle-aged woman crossing the square briskly with her shoulder purse and straw shopping basket.

There are four identical fountains, one in each quadrant and their sound makes a pattern within the pattern of the garden's design. Invisible birds in the thick trees raise a ruckus now and then. Visible pigeons coo, transecting the segmented areas of the garden, creating their own geometry of flight. Sarah hears a fuffle of wings right overhead. The lampposts are topped by ornate curlicues in wrought iron and an irreverent pigeon is fluffing its feathers and settling sedately on one of them. Intricate pigeon footprints stipple the fine sand of the path beside her.

Across from her an old man is asleep on a bench, asleep or passed out, a crust of something congealed around his mouth, his trousers stained at the crotch and ravelled at the cuffs. There's a gardener right beside him, carefully ignoring him, tidying the sand paths with a venerable-looking rake and broom, erasing the traces of the pigeons' passage. The gardener is wearing blue coveralls; does that mean he's a city employee? What do gardeners earn in Paris? What if Sarah had her own pair of blue overalls, if it were her wielding the rake and broom? Gardening is what she does, what she did. Her job.

The job she doesn't have any more. She has no job and she wouldn't be able to find a job here, wouldn't be the heroine of the fairy-tale castle, eating crusts in her *chambre de bonne*, her garret. When she goes back to Toronto, to her real life, it will be her raking sand or dirt or leaves. Once she finds herself a job, another loser job. But she doesn't have to think about that now. She just got here. She feels for the penny in her pocket but finds nothing; the second time she's forgotten it at the apartment. Nothing to turn in her fingers. Nothing to decide for her. Nothing to decide, for now.

The old man asleep on the bench across from her stirs, his mouth working at some sentence. He licks his dry lips, eyes still fiercely closed. Sarah stretches, feeling the skin toasting on her forearms, the back of her neck. Nape of her neck, which Michael has such fondness for. And whose fondness she has such fondness for. Two nights with him now, two nights that she's slept right through. She stretches again. Her hands startle her: they look clean, unused. The nails are almost grown in. The hands of the old man are dark with dirt. He yawns and she yawns back. Maybe she still is a bit jet-lagged.

A breeze plays along the edges of the clipped trees above the bench. These poor trees, subject to the French compulsion for tidiness, artificiality. Some kind of linden, she thinks. *Tilia* of some sort. She'll have to check in the pocket tree-guide she brought along with her. In Europe they call lindens lime trees. How long since they were trimmed? She can see slight irregularities, the tree pushing against the limits the gardener wanted to impose. What the tree wants bumping up against what the gardener wants.

Then she catches sight of something in the shade of the arcade, shields her eyes to see what it is beyond the wrought-iron spears of the fence. Little family groups, bunches of threes, fours, fives, walking solemnly along the arcade op-posite her bench. There's something both tranquil and determined about their pace, something about their promenade that's familiar. A melody in Hebrew runs through her head: *Lekhah dodi likrat kallah, p'nei Shabbat nekabelah.*

Let's come, beloved, to greet the bride, and welcome the face of Sabbath. Something like that. She remembers her father humming the see-saw tune: it's about the happiest song she can think of. She remembers how good she felt, how holy, those times they went to synagogue for Friday night services, Sarah with her beloved sisters and beloved father going to welcome the bride of Sabbath. That rightness, righteousness. There was a straight simple thick line dividing the right thing and the wrong. The good and the bad.

Maybe that's what Gail wants from her political orthodoxy, a sense of ho-liness: what's good on this side, what's bad on the other. Whose side are you on? The party line. Maybe it makes Gail feel safe. Maybe she let herself get angry with Sarah because it was safe; she didn't dare be angry with Rose. *I hate her.* If Gail can't let herself hate Rose, she'll turn and try hating Sarah.

That's not fair; she doesn't really hate Sarah. She's just angry.

Sarah moves towards the fence for a closer look at the tight little knots of family. The people in their Saturday finery eye her briefly, with an alert at-tention, then seem to recognize something in her face, relax. *What is a Jew?* Is her Jewishness in her face, is she recognizable to them? And if so, is that good? She can see words in Hebrew script beside the door. There's a syn-agogue tucked into the building. Here. In Place des Vosges. Saturday morning Shabbat services. These families have a place where they know they have to be at a time that requires them. She watches the groups converging, congre-gating, going in. What would happen if she tried to go in – would they let her? She can go into any church in Paris, but a synagogue? And if they did let her in, she's not sure she'd feel at home. The *shammes* here would be shush-ing the ladies in French, not English. *Lekhah dodi likrat kallah, p'nei Shabbat nekabelah.* What would the tune sound like if she heard it here? She stands at the edge of the grass, watching.

Here in the heart of the heart of Paris, a synagogue. Paris can contain a synagogue and still be Paris. Some part of Sarah doesn't want Paris to be adulterated with anything that isn't Paris. It's as if the two categories are contradictory: where there are berets there shall be no kippahs. But for these people, their synagogue in Place des Vosges is as much theirs as the Talmud Torah synagogue on Matheson Avenue in Winnipeg was hers.

Can she say anything to Michael about all this when she gets home? She doesn't know how far she got last time when she tried to explain the whole *Jewess* thing. She can try. Maybe there's a new Michael, the Paris Michael, the Michael she can allow herself to sleep beside. So far. The Michael she's sharing an apartment with. Until now what Michael wanted kept bumping up against what she wanted, against what he wanted her to be. And now maybe she can be more than one thing, maybe she wants something more.

Laila

I don't know what you want me to be, Khalil. I don't know what I am, what I'm doing here in Paris with you – no friends, no job, that room. It took so much work to get here, the long road that began with its tangles of paper-work, scrabble to find money for the fares. The day you finally packed your bag, your mother came into the room, tears but no sound, a blue dish towel twisting in her hands, the flag of that blue. Her one son going, almost gone. When I told my own mother I'd decided to go with you, she cried too, but she told me to go. Paris. A place she's never seen. Any place away, distance from what happened. What am I to you, Khalil? You never said, *come with me*. Never said *love*. Didn't say anything to me. But when I told you that everything was arranged, that I was coming too, above the black-and-white checked keffiyeh tied against your neck, the stubble of your beard, your mouth pulled itself tighter. *Then you're coming, Laila*, you said. *Good. Good.* That one word, repeated.

There hasn't been much good here. No family, no work or no decent work, a room just bigger than our bed. This room that takes too much of our money, but who else would rent to us, a couple of dirty Arabs, not even married? This room I can't get clean. No hot water. A smeared toilet we share with five, sometimes six other people, no seat, clogged half the time with other people's shit. I don't know why we left.

I do know why I left. Why I went with you. Because it was you who took pity, you who bound the cut on my left cheek when you found me. It was you who took me to the clinic to have it stitched. They gave me drugs for shock. It was you who took me back to my parents' house, who brought your mother's cooking, *shish taouk*, lamb kofte, to our house when my mother wouldn't cook, wouldn't leave her room. That was kindness, or at least pity, even if it wasn't love.

And it was you who took me into your bed, what I was. A woman that another man had spoiled.

You're the one who saved me.

So I followed you, I left. I left, I followed you. You said *good*, though there hasn't been much good in this city that doesn't want us.

But today is a good day, today we claim our square foot of this city. We move through the streets and I feel I'm leaving a wake behind me, a trace of my being here that will keep. A change in the surface of things that people will hardly notice, they'll just feel that something has gone by, they've gone by something. Me. I want some bit of my life to touch others' lives, what I want bumping up against what they want, breaking the border between us. Breaking the border of where they think they're living. Where they live in this city, I don't exist. Or if I do, I'm a weed in a crack in the sidewalk, a moment's puzzle, that scar on my left cheek, what the other boy did to me. But I don't want to be nothing. I'll be a seam in the fabric of their day, like the seam left in the water by a boat's passage. A seam or a scar.

Near the bridge over the Seine, Pont Marie, a woman's voice says, *Come here. Viens ici.* A mother so clear with her daughter. *Come here.* Words in French I know. Come here. My mother would say that to me in our own language, calling me. She knew me, she knew where we were: home. But right now I can't say I know where *here* is. What if there is no *here?* I don't know what Paris is. I don't know what it can be for someone with nothing, who is nothing.

It's night now, no one is here to see us. The city for this moment is ours. I watch you reach under the green metal railings of the fence with the spray can, stretching hard to put our words in their place. You'll put the words in their place the way these people want to put us in our place. There it is, your dark scribble on the stone framing three sides of the Métro entrance. A scribble, indecipherable, like they think we are.

MÉTRO

SARAH HASN'T TAKEN MORE THAN TWO STEPS out of their apartment building when she feels lost, has to check her *Plan de Paris*, the stubby little blue booklet with detailed maps she's tucked into her purse. She needs to make sure she's got her bearings. No one can know this city without a map. Sure enough, there on the building at the corner is the little blue plaque with the street name that Michael told her about, the arrondissement number snug in the arc at the top. From Saint-Paul station, she can take the one line all the way to Concorde and then walk to the Madeleine. There's a stop right at the Madeleine, but changing lines at the bigger stations usually means cross-ing through a labyrinth of turns and stairways to reach the correct platform down grim passages with low-arched ceilings. *Abandon all hope.* The first time she was here, with Reuben, she was really scared of the Métro. She'd never been on a subway before. She still is scared of it, a bit, and this is her first ride this visit. She has the penny in her palm, rubs her fingers across the surface. Canadian penny with its maple leaf, its queen, here with her in Paris. Would a French centime bring her the same luck, different luck?

Her mission is an excursion to Fauchon, *the* haute cuisine boutique in Paris, just across from the Madeleine. Sarah is looking for gifts, and Laura has promised, via Michael, that despite the intimidating fanciness, there are bargains to be found there. Sarah wants, needs, to buy gifts, for Rose, for Gail, for her parents, however slim her savings. Because gifts are a kind of bargain with the evil eye, *kinahora*. Gifts will magically ransom them, keep them from harm.

She hasn't gone far when she's waylaid by a buttery, sugary, caramel smell that makes her realize she's hungry, despite the croissant with crème fraîche and strawberry jam she had for breakfast – her hummingbird metabolism kicking into gear. The smell is coming from a tiny crêpe stand tucked into the crook of one of the buildings, barely enough room behind the griddle for the young man who's working it. What'll she have, *oeuf et fromage* or *jambon et fromage?* The penny says *oeuf et fromage.* Her mouth waters. She likes watching the young man perform for the customers. Each crêpe begins with three graceful swipes of batter with the squeegee over the circle of the griddle. Then the man takes a narrow spatula from its holster below the griddle, taps the crêpe to determine its consistency and – at what seems to be the exact moment it's perfectly golden brown – flips it over. For the *oeuf-fromage* Sarah orders, he cracks the egg with the edge of the spatula, then quickly scrambles it on top of the crêpe with the spatula blade. He drops the right amount of grated cheese on with a scoop, spreads it, again with the blade, across what is now a semicircle of crêpe. Next he takes out a paper envelope from the waiting package of envelopes with a flourish, and with a quick graceful heft, deposits the crêpe, now a rough triangle, inside. There's one final flourish as the finished crêpe gets a quick layer of aluminum foil and thin paper napkin. *Et voilà!* Her first crêpe.

As she eats her crêpe, Sarah watches the next orders being prepared, enjoying the banter between the customers and the guy cooking. One customer is an elegant middle-aged woman who reminds Sarah a bit of Mrs. M. The man prepares the woman a lovely, fat *jambon et fromage.* But then the woman seems to be having trouble paying, even though her French sounds good, despite the English accent Sarah can easily detect. But the crêpe was five francs, no? And she had given him a 20 franc note, yes? She needs her change, then. Sarah watches as the young man disdainfully hands the woman five francs. But the crêpe was, as she said just now, only five francs, the woman insists, and so then she is still owed another ten francs from her 20, no? patiently but stubbornly refusing to be short-changed. His face gone blank, the man hands her the final ten francs. Despite her politeness, her held-back annoyance, there's something dejected about the woman's posture as she turns away, solemnly nibbling at her crêpe.

Where rue François Miron is about to spill into rue Saint-Antoine, Sarah can see the red rectangle with its 'Métro' marker just up ahead. Finishing off her crêpe, she walks first past an old-fashioned kiddie carousel, rather forlorn looking, draped in plastic, *sans* kids of any sort, then past one of those classic green newspaper kiosks with a fancy scalloped edge to its roof line and a little green dome, its stands cluttered with postcards and cheap souvenirs. Beside the Métro entrance a few trees are trapped in little metal cages, lindens, she looked them up, they're definitely lindens, like the ones in Place des Vosges. Around each tree is a miserable-looking square of exposed soil that's defended by a steel grate. A few weeds pop through the grate, opportunists, beggars collecting spare droplets of water provided for the legitimate plants that the city approves of.

Sarah starts down the grubby concrete steps of the entrance where she captures a suddenly familiar whiff of the dank, unbreathable air. She remembers this smell. Something overhead catches her eye. A dark scribble on the stone – is it limestone? – that frames three sides of the entrance, just below the green metal railings of the fence that encloses the stairs. The words stop her. The light of the day caught in them. Words in French she can't understand. She can't go past the second step, lets the annoyed crowds push by her. Three words. *Mort aux juifs*. Then the English comes to her: *Death to the Jews*. She finds herself gripping the metal handrail, staring at the white tiles on the wall, the bright silver frame at the bottom. That flash of silver, what's it for? Maybe it's a gate that shuts when the Métro closes after the last train, keeping what's not wanted out. She looks at the words again, looks around. No one else looks up. Maybe she's got it wrong. *Mort aux juifs*. Can it spell anything else? No. No, she's sure that's what it means. Every muscle in her body pulls itself tight. Someone bumps into her, a man in a dark coat goes by, his face sad. She lets go of the railing. She has something she has to do, somewhere she's supposed to go. She takes the stairs down into the stale, caustic air of the Métro.

When Sarah gets home, Michael is back from the office in La Défense, remarkably unwrinkled, given his long day. He's neatly cutting a demi-baguette into thin, slanted slices. It'll be 8:00 before they sit down to eat, but his colleague Laura has made it clear that proper Parisians never ever eat dinner before 8:00, so they're okay. Whatever this person Laura says, Sarah is starving, and she doesn't bother waiting to dig into the pâté and *cornichons* he's already set out, Laura be damned.

They've glanced at the *Herald-Tribune* Sarah picked up at the kiosk, its front-page photo of an Israeli demonstration against the invasion of Lebanon, 50,000 protesters in Tel Aviv, the largest since the war began. Now Michael is filling Sarah in on his project, the snags they're running into, some difficult personalities interfering with the negotiations. There's definitely a different character type in French law offices, not to mention the developers they have to deal with, Canadian and French. And then there are the architects.

Sarah watches as Michael pours them each another half-glass of wine. He's already *in* his life here: he has something to do, somewhere he's supposed to go, someone he's supposed to be. Meanwhile she had trouble making it through the doorway of Fauchon, those glass counters of impossibly perfect tiny fruits and vegetables, all exotic, all exquisite. Fantastically expensive bottles of wine, extravagant pâtés and cheeses. A sales clerk escorted her through the store and plucked items off the shelves for her to view – no touching the merchandise. Then he sent Sarah off to pay the cashier, whereupon Sarah was allowed to retrieve the purchases he had wrapped. Sarah presents her loot to Michael: three perfect little wooden trays with the words *Caves Fauchon* in a banner around a drawing of the Madeleine's façade. One for them, and one each for Gail and Rose. Buying Gail a present is another bargain, a promise to herself that the fight will fade, they'll go back to being sisters.

Michael hefts one of the trays. "Nice. Great stuff. Did you have any trouble getting there on the Métro?"

The Métro. She takes a last slice of baguette, spreads more pâté. "Michael."

He looks up.

"There was something there…"

"Something where?"

"At Saint-Paul station, where I went into the subway. There was some graffiti. It said *mort aux juifs.*"

He pauses, frowning. "What does that mean?"

"Death to the Jews."

He's taking another bite of the baguette spread thickly with pâté. He swallows, wipes his mouth with a napkin. He's starting to go red. "That's revolting." He reminds her of Abe when he's angry. "How can, how could anyone write something like that? Who could write that? Where did you say it was?"

"Our Métro station, Saint-Paul. Just above the stairway."

"Right here?" He clenches, unclenches his fists. Pulls her against him. "I'm sorry. I hate this. They'll take it down. I bet it'll be gone tomorrow." He pulls her tighter. "And if it isn't, I'll get my own can of spray paint and cover it over. No jury would convict me. But the city will look after it."

Probably. If this were Toronto, how long would the words stay up? Would there be outraged letters to the *Globe & Mail* the very next day, statements by the Anti-Defamation League of the B'Nai Brith? Or maybe no one would even notice it, it would be removed that quickly.

Or maybe no one would bother to object. It's just words. How much can a few words scrawled on stone mean, what harm can they do? She doesn't know what to make of it, doesn't know whether it means something or nothing.

"Hey, I've got an idea. Let's go visit the Pretzel," Michael says, going to the stove. "I'll get started on the sole. Hope you haven't filled up on hors d'oeuvres."

Sarah loves to watch Michael cook, the practised movements of his hands as he chops an onion, minces garlic. He put himself through law school working as a cook. "What's the Pretzel?" she asks. He's flouring the sole now as the butter begins to foam and brown in the saucepan. Cooking in their kitchen, the kitchen they share, for now.

"The historic centre of the Marais. Just around the corner from here. There're supposed to be all sorts of Jewish shops, bakeries, falafel joints, a real deli-type restaurant."

He wants to make it up to her, offer this consolation as compensation for the graffiti. Find her a place where she belongs: Winnipeg's North End stuck in the middle of Paris. Sarah tries to picture how the dusty little shops, crammed delis, would fit into a Parisian street, the smell of cinnamon buns infiltrating the croissant smell, the smell of galoshes and wet wool …

"We should check it out, get some home cooking," Michael says.

Home cooking. Something in her cringes. She looks at the remains of the baguette and pâté on the table, the little dish of cornichons and Dijon mustard beside them. Michael's assembling a salad that's made only of some new kind of lettuce called mâche, a delicate thing made of tiny leaves like paws. No vulgar tomatoes or cucumbers for this salad.

And then she thinks of her Baba B.'s home cooking: thick soups with clumps of fat clinging to the chunks of pale beef, wan carrots and limp celery strands. Home-made gefilte fish patties sprinkled with gag-worthy bits of bone. She doesn't want to contaminate her new life here with her narrow life back there.

"I didn't come to Paris to eat bad Jewish food."

He laughs. "Let's just go take a look, maybe get some bagels."

"Do you think they really know how to make bagels in Paris?"

"Sarah, you can't complain that you don't want to eat Jewish food, and then grumble about how the Jewish food here can't possibly be good enough." He laughs again.

But she doesn't want to see only the Paris that can be seen through a Jewish filter. She wants the real Paris, all of it. Because if being Jewish defines her, if it's everything that she is, then it's all that she is. And she wants to be more than one thing. This is the place where she can be more.

"Seriously, Sarah, let's visit this Pretzel place. It's only a five minute walk from here."

"It can't be called the Pretzel. That doesn't sound right. We can ask Laura."

He turns from the stove, waves the spatula at her. "Yes. Indeed. We will ask Laura, from whom all answers flow. You're going to like Laura."

If Laura turns out to be a know-it-all, Sarah's not sure she will like her.

She goes to the window. She's had three days living with Michael in the same apartment. Three nights beside him. Three nights without waking, without waking nightmares. She touches the glass. Looking out the window is like looking in a mirror, a long window in the building across the street echoing their window. Yesterday evening she watched a woman stand at some sort of counter, working intently at something just out of Sarah's line of sight. It must have taken Sarah five minutes of watching the ritual of the woman's careful gestures before she realized she was washing dishes. The simplest thing. Tonight Sarah can see the silhouette of a man behind a gauzy curtain. As she watches, he stoops down, and she can see then that he's lifting something, someone – it's a toddler he's raising to his chest. The child clings to him, head pressed hard against the man's shirt, and they're both still for a moment. The man moves away from the window.

∽

She knows something is wrong, can feel something wrong in the room. Some-one, something on the other side of the door of this room, which is but is not her room. She doesn't know where she is, someplace far away. Someone or thing at the door coming to take them. She's awake but isn't awake. Her eyes open, but she can't move: something at the door, something pressing on her chest so that she can't breathe. Something in the room with her that she almost sees, and it wants her. They want her. She can't move, can't do anything to save herself. Where is she? She can hear a car mutter along the street beside the room, why is the car so close to their room. Somehow she knows it's Michael beside her in bed and now she's awake enough to remember. Paris. She's in Paris with Michael beside her. What's wrong, then? Is it Michael, is it wrong that he's there beside her? She feels the pulse in her wrists, her heartbeat rapid in her chest. The door doesn't save her, something right here in the room with her. She has to do something. Her eyes are open but she can't move. Streetlight leaks through the tall shuttered windows, she can see the outline of the wardrobe, the whiteness of their little kitchen. She can hear footsteps on the street, a few quiet words in French. She's in Paris. The footsteps pause, then retreat. Her eyes are open. She's lying on her side, Michael's back against hers. She has to turn to see it, she has to move.

With a jerk she sits up. She's done it. She feels the pace of her pulse, her heartbeat. She can move. The nothing, the something, in the room is gone but she can't be here. She can feel the fear receding but she can't be here. As quietly as she can, she gets out of the bed, puts on her jeans, a t-shirt. Palms the penny, slips the key into her pocket. That leak of light from the street showing her the door. Down and down the two flights of stairs, round the hairpin turns. Out the front door. What is this place? *Follow me.* There's no one to follow, but penny says left, so she turns towards the Hôtel de Ville, away from the Métro entrance and the ugly words that are or aren't still there. It's night, no one on the street, no one here to see her. The city for this moment hers, but she has nowhere to go. She doesn't know what time it is. She can feel the river off to her left, a few blocks down, smell it. She could walk there, cross the Seine on the Pont Louis Phillipe. The air is mild and the city is almost silent, the odd car or van at a distance. Maybe there will be people in the bakeries, beginning their work on the morning's bread. She has nowhere to go, but the city is hers. The sidewalk widens, rises into steps that open into a narrow pedestrian street. *Rue des Barres* the little street sign says. Towards the far end of the street she sees someone, a thin old woman walking a little dog, some sort of little spaniel whose floppy ears seem to have tints of grey against its white fur, a colour Sarah hasn't seen in a dog. The woman is too far away to be much more than a silhouette, but Sarah can hear her crooning to the dog. The woman is very thin, seems frail, but the dog offers her something, its feathery white tail wagging in a fever, its front paws paddling eagerly at her knees. A gift. The woman sinks to her knees and at first Sarah's afraid she's had a fall, but then she sees she's picking the little dog up, bending her face to its face, which it licks again and again, its body writhing in such joy the woman can barely keep it in her arms.

CLOSERIE DES LILAS

"I BOUGHT YOU SOMETHING." Michael is grinning, something small hidden in his hand. No *p'tit paquet cadeau* this time, but he does have another present for her. They're getting all dressed up to go out for dinner. They've been in Paris a week and Michael is eager for Sarah to meet Laura, who's eager to meet her, so they're getting together at some fancy restaurant. Sarah hopes she's fancy enough for Laura, who seems like a very fancy person.

"Just a sec," he says, "hang on." He turns away from her, but he's clearly fiddling with something fussy. "Okay, I've got it now." He steps in front of her, a slim chain of some sort, silver, winking between his fingers. "Here."

He's so tall he's all she sees. She feels the arc as his hands reach over her head, a gift, but when the little nubs of the links rub against the back of her neck there's a weight to it. She puts her hand to her throat. Small, but it's heavy against her neck.

Michael leads her to the bathroom mirror, hand in the small of her back. "See? D'you like it?" A delicate silver Star of David sits below the hollow of her throat. It's a pretty design, each side slightly torqued so that the two triangles seem woven into each other. She's never worn a Star of David, never wanted that badge: *This is me, this is who I am, Jew. Jewess.* The word swollen to swallow her up, as if she's only *Jew.* Who she is annihilated by what she is. She wants to be more than one thing.

"I saw this at a little jewellery shop on rue de Rivoli and I thought you'd like it. Chain looks a little long, though, d'you want me to have a few links taken out?" He wants to help. He wants to save her.

Sarah touches the star where it's resting against her throat. "Thanks,

Michael. It's lovely. Don't worry about the chain, it's fine. Should I wear it tonight?"

He kisses her on the mouth, a long sweet kiss. "Sure. Do you really like it?" Yes. No. "Of course."

He kisses her again, checks his watch, tells her they should get going.

She knows Michael means well. *Mort aux juifs* and here's her declaration, Michael's declaration to her, showing her he knows what side she's on and, more than that, that he's on her side.

The graffiti is still there. Every time she goes down into the station, she has to walk under the words, feel their weight. *Mort aux juifs.* Masculine plural used to include male and female. If it were *morte aux juives*, it would be specific, death to Jewesses. And *juif, juive* means Jewish, also, gendered adjectives as well as nouns. She's looked it up. *Manger en juif* means to eat by oneself without sharing. *Le petit juif* is what they call the funny bone in French, though she doesn't know why, isn't sure she wants to know. *Mort aux juifs.* No one pays any mind.

Somebody wrote those words; the city didn't just produce them by itself. And what made them want to, what is it about life in this city that made them write those words? What would the old man drunk on the bench in Place des Vosges think about the graffiti, the man raking the sand, the concierge in their building? Would the word Jew, *juif*, be enough, would it tell them everything they needed to know? Would they agree, or would they just be tired of seeing the subway walls, chairs, public telephones all smeared over with words no one wants to read?

When they went down into the subway this morning Michael coloured when he saw the graffiti, his neck going rigid. He muttered something about a midnight raid with a bucket of whitewash. Maybe he'll do it. Maybe she wants him to do it. Someone to do something. Maybe it's easier for Michael to be angry because he doesn't have to mix in any shame – *this is everything you are and it is nothing* – with his anger. Lucky Michael. They were visiting the Carnavalet Museum. Michael was tired, he's been working long hours despite, or perhaps because of, the French penchant for two-hour lunch breaks. He stretched himself out on one of the chilly benches in the museum, his head on her lap, hands across his chest, and, in an instant, he was asleep. On the hard bench. On her lap. An act of faith, to fall asleep like that, exposed, in a public space. To trust the world that much. A guard came up to her, *Mademoiselle, sleeping in the museum is not permitted.* Sarah gently shook Michael's arm. He woke relaxed; not startled, not afraid.

What would it be like to be unafraid like Michael? Michael, who's standing there, waiting for them to get going to their dinner, their restaurant, still grinning. He does mean well, and he doesn't know that this badge, his gift, weighs on her.

✑

The restaurant is at the corner of Boulevard Montparnasse and Boulevard Saint-Michel, streets Sarah knows she should know, but doesn't exactly, though the names smell, like so many others in the city, of romance, of the Eiffel Tower and the Seine. She's wearing the skirt Michael gave her in Toronto and a new white cotton knit boat-neck sweater. *All dolled up*, her dad would say. When they were on the Métro a slightly older, worn-looking woman was staring at her, at Michael. The woman, with her heavy shopping bags and weary skirt, her crumpled mouth, seemed maybe envious of her. And Sarah was, after all, all dolled up. Michael too. He was wearing the new shirt they bought him at Alain Figaret, an intimidatingly Parisian shop, formal and perfect with its organized rows of stiff shirts in their blond wooden shelves. It was Laura who told them to get the shirt at Alain Figaret, Laura who picked the restaurant they're going to. She seems eager to ensure that their introduction to Paris goes smoothly. Introduction or indoctrination. Michael is clearly pleased with having an express route to becoming a real Parisian. He has another quote from Laura: while the French won't ever let you become French – especially someone like Laura, a girl from Saskatoon by way of Tobago – anyone can become Parisian.

127

They've come up from the underworld of the Métro and are back on the streets of Paris. And it's a beautiful evening, a light breeze lifting the smell of exhaust, the smell of dog shit and human pee that never seem to go away completely. But they're not sure they are where they want to be. "We got off at Port Royale so we *have* to be near the corner of Montparnasse and Saint-Michel," Michael says, deep in his *Plan*. "I know it's supposed to be the 6th arrondissement, and this *is* the 6th, but I can't even find the corner."

Sarah points – it's at the very bottom of the page, the intersection jutting out beyond the tidy little border of the grid. They really must look like idiot tourists, standing at this complicated intersection, peering alternatively into the booklet and then up, trying to locate a street sign on a building façade. "Okay, we're right here. Now we have to spot the Closerie des Lilas." Michael looks up, scans for a moment, then points. "There it is, kitty-corner across the street. Tucked away behind those hedges."

The restaurant is squeezed in implausibly where the two famous streets meet at a sharp angle. Closerie des Lilas. *Lilas* means lilac; somehow Sarah knows that. Knows it and suddenly can smell the lilacs outside the window of her bedroom on Rupertsland, their scent almost dizzying. Rose has checked under Sarah's bed for a wolf, tucked her in, and they're both breathing the smell of lilacs. She knows the word *lilas*, from the inside out, but what can *closerie* mean? She'll have to look it up, though the paperback French-English dictionary she brought to Paris isn't much good. After, when she looks it up in the big fat Harrap's she has at home, it's still not there, still a small impenetrable mystery.

Michael takes her hand, steers her across the busy street. Laura has asked them to meet her at the brasserie side, which is less expensive than the restaurant side with its white tablecloths. The brasserie has the feel of a greenhouse, a glass-roofed, glassed-in extension to the main building. It sprawls itself out onto the sidewalk, a space between spaces that's guarded by thick hedges in sturdy green wooden boxes – a garden and a building, a private and a public space.

And now Sarah and Michael are standing in the lighted entrance, in between being there and not being there, waiting to be seated, looking into the brilliant rooms. The maître d' smiles at them both, gestures to a table in the corner beside the fish tanks where a woman who must be Laura is waving at them. The tables are all squished together, but people smile as they squeeze by.

Laura stands up and leans over the table to kiss first Sarah and then Michael on each cheek. Hair a stylish halo held back from her forehead, makeup that doesn't announce itself. It's the smile that makes her beautiful, a smile that pulls each pretty feature into a whole that's much more than pretty. She's wearing a slim fitted red scoop-neck dress with three-quarter-length sleeves. She's slim herself, but not as small as Sarah; there are curves where Sarah has planes. And she's soignée, every element put together. So this is the inimitable, the irresistible Laura.

The waiter deftly pulls out the table so Sarah can slide in beside Laura, then smoothly slides it back in. Laura hands them a large menu, smiles again. "We finally meet. I was getting tired of listening to Michael yammer on about you. *Bring her to Paris already,* I told him. Good thing he obeyed." The smile briefly vanishes behind the menu, then reappears. "So *are* you enjoying your time here? Michael says it's mostly holiday, but I think he said you're interested in landscape gardening. My friend François – the guy who owns your apartment – his boyfriend Charles teaches landscape architecture. I can ask him to get you a list of gardens to visit. Maybe he can take you on a bit of a tour."

So Laura's been told that Sarah's interested in landscape gardening. This is Michael conniving. Sarah still hasn't said anything to him about her taking courses at Ryerson, about starting her own landscaping company, Mrs. M.'s ideas. But clearly he has his own ideas.

The waiter comes up, smiles first at Laura, then Sarah, raises a delicate eyebrow of appreciation for Michael.

Sarah figures the waiter's smile is more for Laura than it is for her.

However hard Sarah's tried to gussy herself up, she can't begin to compete with Laura and her highly polished *savoir faire*, her *comme il faut* and *je ne sais quoi*.

"Would you like a kir? Should we have kir royals? We should celebrate." Laura's smiling at Sarah, then Michael.

It's the smile. Sarah probably should be envious of this beautiful woman, jealous of the way Michael has come to rely on her advice, her prescriptions and proscriptions. But the welcome of that smile – it's for Sarah as much as Michael.

"*Kir?*" Michael asks. How could he not smile back?

"Kir, Monsieur," the waiter explains in English, "is a cocktail, a mix of white wine with crème de cassis, blackcurrant liqueur. If you make it with champagne, it's a *kir royal*."

"*Trois kir royals,*" Michael tells the waiter, looking pleased with himself.

"Some places will serve you any old sparkling wine when you order kir royal," Laura says. "At the Closerie we're safe, though." She winks at Sarah, who has to resist winking back.

"So it has to be real champagne, not sparkling wine?" Michael asks.

"Yup. There are all sorts of good sparkling whites but only wine grown in Champagne can be called champagne. It's the idea of *terroir*."

"*Terroir?*" Sarah asks, sure that Laura will have the answer.

"I don't think there is an English translation," Laura says. "It means soil, or region, but when you're talking about wine, it means everything that adds to the taste – the type of soil, the climate, even the particular slope of the land, how it catches the sun. So even if you take the stalks from the champagne grapes and plant them someplace else, they won't taste the same."

Sarah takes a sip of her water. *Terroir.* What do those poor fig trees in Toronto think of their lives, so far from the *terroir* that made them? Do the figs taste at all the same as figs that are grown where they belong?

"Sarah, do you like fish?" Laura's frowning over the menu. "They have *loup de mer*; it's one of their specialties. They make it with fennel. Or maybe *coquilles Saint-Jacques?"*

Loup de mer or *coquilles Saint-Jacques*; how do you choose? Sarah fingers the penny.

"Lucky penny?" Laura asks, putting her hand lightly on Sarah's.

"Bad habit more than anything else." Sarah hands her the penny. "I like having it on me."

Laura flips the penny with her thumb; it takes a little hop towards Michael's water glass.

"I picked it up back when I was studying at U of M, and I've kept it on me ever since. Actually, it's lucky because a friend gave it to me as a good luck charm." She tucks the penny back into her skirt pocket. "Drives Michael nuts."

Michael grins.

"It came from an ex-?" Laura asks.

"No. An older woman who was taking a class with me. Helen. I really liked her."

"Does it bring you luck?"

"I don't know." It helps her decide. Helps her choose when she doesn't know how to.

"Did you notice these?" Laura asks, pointing to the little brass plaque attached to their table. "I love 'em. The restaurant engraves these plaques with the names of celebrities who were regulars. Hemingway is supposed to have written *The Sun Also Rises* at one of these tables."

"Do you know who the guy on this plaque is – *Max Jacob?"* Michael asks.

Laura bites her lip, then shakes her head. She screws up her face, determined, then reaches over, gently taps the arm of the man at the next table. His tie is slightly askew, his eyes merry. *"Oui, Mademoiselle?"*

Laura asks in rapid French whether the gentleman knows who Max Jacob is. "A politician of the right," he replies promptly in English. His friend across the table grabs his arm. *"Non! C'est un journaliste de gauche!"* A journalist of the left. The men briefly glare at each other and then crumple into laughter.

"Well, Mademoiselle," the first man says, "he's either a politician of the right or a journalist of the left... or vice versa. Or possibly both. Or neither."

Now everyone's tucked into a tight fit of laughter at their squished tables. The waiter brings a second round of kir royals, sets it on the table.

"You know," Sarah says, "*Max Jacob* sounds like he could be one of the regulars at the Salisbury House on Main and Matheson, or any other greasy spoon in the North End of Winnipeg. Do you have Sals in Saskatoon, Laura?"

"I think it's just a Manitoba institution, sadly. I'm sure we don't know what we're missing."

"I'm trying to figure out which names would be engraved on plaques at the tables there, and what the reason for their fame would have been," Sarah says. "Maybe: Beryl Greenstein, who drank a record sixteen chipped mugs of bitter black coffee in a single afternoon... Benny Plotkin, who never ate a Sals French fry without first dunking it in exactly one dollop of ketchup..."

"And the list goes on. Okay, Sarah, are you ready for another kir?" Laura asks, raising her glass. "And please tell me that you like this place."

Sarah loves it, the waiters with their fitted white shirts and long white aprons, a uniform, but a dignified one, like a doctor or scientist's white coat. The sign that they're professionals. And she's taken with Laura too, how much Laura wants Sarah to like these offerings.

Laura smiles again and then the smile wavers. "Sarah, Michael mentioned that your sister in Winnipeg was sick. How's she doing?"

"She's stable, we think," Sarah answers.

"We've spoken with Sarah's parents a couple of times," Michael says, "and it sounds like Rose is holding her own. She's had some ups and downs, but they're still adjusting her dosage. It takes time."

Laura takes Sarah's hand, gives it a squeeze. "When she's all better, we've got to bring her here, right?" Laura nods to Sarah, the light pressure of her hand on Sarah's. Sarah squeezes back. "Let's drink to Rose."

To Rose. To Rose when she's better, when they all come to Paris together. They wind their way through dinner, two kir royals each and then the entrées, accompanied by a bottle of wine, and then mains, accompanied by most of a second bottle. After the cheese course, Sarah excuses herself. Despite her flat-soled sandals, she finds she has to hold tight to the banister of the spiral staircase that takes her downstairs to the washroom. When she comes back up and gets to the top of the stairs, the room gives itself a brief twirl. She smiles at the linen-covered tables, no longer sure where she was sitting. The waiter smiles at her, gently nods in the right direction.

Yes, yes. That's where she's sitting. Is it possible? That she's sitting here, in this fancy place? That she's getting to be friends with a woman like Laura, who belongs, who knows everything? When Sarah was in Paris with Reuben, she might have looked through the window or open door of a restaurant like this to catch a glimpse of the lucky ones inside. She wouldn't ever have dreamt she would be sitting at one of the tables, laughing and eating and drinking. Lucky duck that she is now.

But what about all the not lucky ones, the unlucky ducks, who are still outside, what about them, the woman with her shopping bags, the drunk on the bench? And what about Rose? Lucky her, unlucky Rose.

Sarah has always had to know what it is that she *can't* have. Because what she can't have is so much more than what she can. And up to now, she tried to school herself so that what she couldn't have, she didn't want to want. But she wants this. And has it.

She shakes her head to clear it, sees Michael waving her to their table.

Michael. It's thanks to Michael that she's on the inside, that she's in this beautiful place where she doesn't belong.

As soon as Sarah is back at the table, Laura announces that they must have dessert too, because the French will be offended if they don't have dessert. Michael must have a *crème brûlée*, and Sarah must have a *tarte aux fraises* because strawberries are still in season, but only barely. They're eating their dessert and Laura is smiling and Michael is smiling and Sarah smiles too, because there's nothing to do but smile. That's how good the *tarte aux fraises* is, and the *crème brûlée*, which she tastes from Michael's plate after he's smashed the pretty crust on it. That's how good the restaurant is, that's how much she's drunk. But even though Michael has gallantly paid the bill and they're leaving the Closerie, Laura tells them the evening must not end. She's pulling on Sarah's arm, she has to take them to rue de Fleurus, that's where Gertrude Stein and Alice B. Toklas lived, did they know that? It's somewhere off the Luxembourg Gardens. Laura was there once, with the guy who owns their apartment, François, and François was almost in tears, that's how much he loves Gertrude Stein, do they love Gertrude Stein? Laura can't say she loves Gertrude Stein, way too obscure a writer, though she does like *The Autobiography of Alice B. Toklas*, they should read it, it's the one readable book Gertrude Stein wrote, do they know Gertrude Stein was Jewish? Of course everyone knows she was Jewish, it's one of those obvious Jewish names. Gertrude Stein was down in the south of France during the war, that's how she got by.

As they walk out into the warm night, Sarah is wondering how Gertrude Stein could possibly get by if she was Jewish, even in the south of France, how did she get by? Now Laura is explaining that she can't find rue de Fleurus, it has completely vanished, but she is going to take Michael to see something, he's going to love this. There's a sweet little shop, she's sure it's on rue de Vaugirard, and he has to see it because he has to buy himself a suit there, he will not be allowed to leave Paris without buying a suit at this shop. If she could only find the damn shop. She's almost sure it's on rue de Vaugirard.

Sarah thinks they've probably closed all the metal shutters on all the stores by now, which would make it hard to even find the store, much less window-shop effectively, but Laura is in the lead and Sarah's game.

It's a beautiful night. And here they are, out in the Paris night, and in front of them instead of the buildings she expects, there are cobblestones and rows of trees cut into rectangles which Laura explains is the Luxembourg Gardens. Another garden for her to study. Because apparently she's studying gardens. Laura's explaining that not only has rue de Fleurus disappeared, but rue de Vaugirard, which she knows runs around the Luxembourg Gardens somewhere, also seems to be elusive and they seem to keep going round and round the perimeter of the garden, which is locked at this time of night, locked inside the black wrought-iron fence with its bars like spears, gold-tipped, and Laura's taken off her high heels and is walking barefoot, which doesn't seem like a very good idea, what with all the dog shit, and they can't find it, rue de Vaugirard, and no one's around to ask. Michael's *Plan* doesn't seem to be helping at all, they have to turn it around and around and suddenly Sarah's feeling a bit dizzy. So she sits down. She's going to sit on this little stone step in front of a lovely old set of wooden double doors till she feels better. And until Laura's finished giving her very good advice. About pickpockets, it's important for Sarah to know about pickpockets and cut-purses because Laura wants this to be a very good visit to Paris and wouldn't it be miserable if she had her purse stolen?

"You hold your purse like this," Laura says, her purse strap across her chest, her hand firmly gripping the close on its zipper, her beautiful face un-smiling this time. "See? That way nobody can grab it. Even if they cut the strap. I had a friend, they grabbed it off her shoulder and took off on a mo-torcycle, the whole damn purse, not just the wallet."

"I'd chase them," Sarah says.

"No," Laura says. "You shouldn't do that."

"I would."

"She's fast," Michael tells Laura. "She's very fast. She'd catch 'em."

"Uh-uh." Laura's shaking her head. "Not a good idea. Dangerous. Oh my gosh," Laura says, looking at the clock in the pharmacy window across from them and sounding like she's from Saskatoon, which she is. "Look at the time. We missed the last Métro."

The last Métro. Isn't there a film with that name that came out not long ago, something with that beautiful French actress, that blondey-blonde, the blondest of blondes, Frenchest of Frenchies, Catherine Deneuve? Something about Jews in Paris during the war that Sarah was supposed to go see but didn't? Jews in Paris. Jews in Paris. Death to the Jews in Paris.

Something cramps in Sarah's chest. The last Métro. They've missed the last Métro! Laura told them all about it, don't miss the last Métro, she'd warned them, and now it's Laura's fault they've missed it and what will they do? Sarah's very far from home and she's trying to be someone else and they've gone and missed the last Métro. Sarah closes her eyes, for a moment sees her sisters' sad faces as the last train in Paris pulls away. Rose and Gail, both of them gone.

She opens her eyes. Michael has sat down beside her, and then Laura pushes her over a little bit and sits on her other side. "It's too far to walk. For either of us. Any of us. None of us. We can't walk," Laura says, setting her shoes in Sarah's lap.

"We better find ourselves a couple of taxis," Michael says. Laura's apartment is in the opposite direction from theirs.

"Taxis are rash," Laura tells them. "Girls from Saskatoon don't just go around taking taxis every which way."

"We know," Michael says, "but in this case, I think you need to take a taxi. We'll walk you to the stand. If Sarah can get up."

"I can get up." She can always get up!

"Okay, there, upsy-daisy." And he holds out his hand and things tilt a bit again but then they right themselves.

The three of them are quiet as they walk Laura to the stand, where a taxi is languidly waiting, the rumpled driver looking up in an irritated fashion from his newspaper when Michael raps on the window. Laura gives them each a smoochy kiss on the cheek before she gets in, smoochy and only one cheek each, she must have forgotten some of her French manners, and she's giggling, waving a large elaborate wave as she closes the door, then opens it again to get her shoes, which Sarah for some reason has been holding.

Now it's just the two of them again. Nobody else at all on the street. Paris so quiet at this time of night. "I'm sure another taxi will be along soon," Michael says.

"I don't want a taxi. I want to walk. I want us to walk."

"I think it's a ways."

"Not that far. Forty minutes, maybe less. We'll sober up."

"Bad idea. I don't want to sober up."

"C'mon, Michael. It'll be fun."

Michael takes her hand and soon they've found Boulevard Saint-Michel. Straight as an arrow pretty much all the way to the Seine, that's what Michael says their *Plan de Paris* says. She looks up. Above the stores and banks and cafés are apartments, most of them dark, a few with the flickering blue light of a television coming through the window. The city's so quiet, just the faint sound of a radio through another window. Hardly any traffic. They walk down the middle of the street till a taxi honks softly at them, then scramble, giggling, holding hands, for the sidewalk. Now and then they hear a baby crying, or the hushed sound of a TV. Light filtering through the shutters of a window, a smell of toast, someone making toast at 1:30 in the morning.

The city only theirs.

Laila

I don't like the faces on the buildings in this city, above the windows and doorways, their blank eyes. When I say this, Khalil, you laugh at me. You tell me that buildings don't have faces, but they do. I'm the only one who notices, you say, I'm the only one crazy enough to mind. We're at a café, you want an espresso, it costs less if we stand at the bar. As you count out your coins, counting each centime, I tell you I don't want anything. The buildings have faces, not me. You're looking at a newspaper on the stool beside you, *Le Monde*, which means *The World*. You're reading in French about the world, the blood, the guns, how many are dying. A new alphabet here, a new way to read. I want to read this city the old way, right to left, the French would call it backwards, but to us it's the only way it makes sense.

Though there are three words that are mine, even in this foreign language, foreign alphabet. *Mort aux juifs.* That's what we have to say. What we said.

You sip your espresso, read the newspaper on its stool. I don't say anything. I want to tell you about the city I've seen underneath the city, the hatches in the sidewalk that open under people's feet. But I don't. I want to tell you about how the workers go down there, lower themselves into the mouth of that other city to keep the city above working, its electricity, phone lines, water, sewage. I don't tell you because you're not in the mood to listen.

If you'd listen, Khalil, my friend, I'd tell you how every morning Paris is washed clean of its sins. If you looked down some morning when you were walking, you would see the sewer floodgates open and water rinse through the gutters. The openings are called *bouches de lavage*, mouths for washing. I'm learning these words. And stuffed against those mouths are pitiful pieces of rolled carpet, filthy, water-logged. They're useful in some way, I don't know how.

The water gives itself to the gutters and a battalion of men come by with their imitation witches' brooms made of plastic twigs, and they stroke at what they find, debris. This army brushes at what the city doesn't want, what has been spent, lost, discarded. They sweep it away so it doesn't offend the ones on top, the ones the city belongs to.

You're finished your espresso and I've finished the nothing I have and we leave, turn the corner onto a bigger street, the museum there in all its finery, the Louvre. Louvre, I know its name. I know all about it. A jail for beautiful things. In the gutter here across from the museum I see a crumple of pale feathers, a silvery glint playing off them only now and then, light caught. Something crushed, its body splayed so that at first I don't know what it is and then I do: *pigeon*. Another item for my collection. I have a collection in my head, Khalil, a catalogue; I'm keeping track. Gutter treasures. The pigeon, and the bundled corpses of carpet at every sewer mouth. What else? Candy wrappers, beer cans, empty cigarette packages. And things that are worth something, a five centime coin, a cigarette butt.

Every morning Paris is washed clean, all that good water wasted because the city still stinks. I'd know this place with my eyes closed: diesel exhaust and dog shit, human piss. Garbage gone putrid. Though I have to remind myself there are other smells too: through the vent from a hotel laundry the scent of cotton sheets, fresh smell I remember of washing on the line, sheets pinned against the sky. My mother's hands with the wooden clothes pegs, pinning our clean sheets against the sky. And there's the flowery smell of detergent from buckets of water the concierges throw onto the sidewalks in front of their buildings, making a show of cleaning. When my mother cleans it's not a show, our house is clean, our house holds us safe.

I know what they're up to, the concierges. Making a show of clean. Because it's not just them and it's not just the army of men with twig brooms who clean the city, it's me. I've made myself useful. I have work now, washing Paris. That's what I'm doing here, I know that now: washing myself clean with work, wasting myself.

It's because of my mother that I finished high school. And she wanted more for me. She would set aside the dress or cushion she was working on, she'd look up and tell me she would do it, find a way for me to go to college too. My father too, that's what my father wanted for me. For both of his children. The blue of his cigarette smoke curling against the white walls in our living room. Curling behind the newspaper he read, the newspaper that would tell him everything. He'd watch TV too, try to catch the news, watch in the shop window, or at his cousin's, as if knowing the news did anything for him, for us. He would have sent me to college. If he could have.

10,000 dead. That's what the French newspaper you needed to read told you, Khalil. 10,000 wasted, or less, or more. The newspaper says *a reliable accounting isn't possible because of the chaos of war, the devastation of neighbourhoods and refugee camps, the haste with which bodies were buried in mass graves, the absence of impartial agencies gathering statistics. There may be extreme exaggeration on both sides.*

And if only 1,000 died?

One is too many.

JEU DE PAUME

Jeu de Paume, Jeu de Paume. Sarah can still hear Michael sing-songing the words. She's almost there, at the Jeu de Paume, an art gallery at the foot of the Tuileries Garden, where she'll meet up with Laura. Visiting art galleries is what you do when you go to a city like Paris, but Sarah hadn't even heard of the Jeu de Paume until Laura suggested the visit. Laura wants some time with just the two of them, and so does Sarah; time to get to know each other. The bars Sarah passes are hectic with their lunch-time traffic, corner cafés where each table is an island of conversation, each couple wound into their own tight intimacy. The back of a thin young woman watching a man finish his newspaper, his espresso – why isn't she having anything? At their breakfast this morning, another breakfast together, over his café au lait, his cigarette, Michael was declaring that the French had ever so kindly designed those three syllables, *Jeu de Paume,* specifically for the comfort and enjoyment of English speakers. The easiest words in the French language for an English speaker to pronounce. The word *Tuileries,* on the other hand, had been invented just as deliberately to make the English sound ridiculous. So he claimed. *Twee-leh-ree.* It isn't easy, remembering that the *l* is an *l,* not a *y,* getting the *r* sound right, silencing the *s* at the end.

Another breakfast with Michael. Another night she's been able to sleep beside him.

She's past the Louvre, almost at the end of the unpronounceable Tuileries. Before she hits the chaotic traffic at Place de La Concorde, she has to cross from the shade of the arcades on the north side of rue de Rivoli, with their mix of designer boutiques and kitschy souvenir joints choked with gewgaws, to the heat and light of the south side. Maybe it's the stink and racket of the traffic, or the bleak stone wall guarding the museum, but there's something barren about this corner. Sarah hurries up the stone steps behind the Métro entrance. The museum is a long rectangular box with four large dour columns at the entrance. Laura says it used to be a handball court: word for word, *jeu de paume* means *game of palm*. As Sarah heads for the doors, a clutch of scruffy kids comes up, talking away in fragments of French and some other language she doesn't recognize. *S'il vous plaît, Mademoiselle*, if it pleases you, Miss. It doesn't please her at all, in fact she's good and irritated as they crowd around her, coming close but not actually touching her. One is holding a frayed piece of cardboard. He's taller than Sarah, though he looks to be only about 12 or 13, his face dull with dirt, lean. He comes right up to her, *Mademoiselle, Mademoiselle,* shoves the cardboard against her arm, the one holding her purse. She pushes past him and he flinches, stumbles back, drops the cardboard, then stoops to pick it up. Sarah pulls her purse closer, goes into the museum. Little jerks. Such a stupid, inept attempt at picking her pocket. She checks for her wallet, then touches the penny in her pocket. Still there. What would they have done with a dull Canadian penny? She looks back and sees they've moved on to another target, a well-dressed American couple who are also pushing by them as if they were some kind of debris. She was pretty brusque herself; she doesn't like kids ganging up on her like that, especially the tall boy.

A few minutes later, Laura hurries into the quiet lobby, scanning for Sarah, the smile rising to Laura's face when she spots her. "There you are. Hey, did you make it okay through the gauntlet at the door? I usually try to give people something if they're panhandling, but that pack of kids is intimidating. Did you check your wallet?" Sarah nods. "Will you let me treat you to the tickets? This once?" She sees Sarah hesitate. "Hey, this is a foreign country. Yer money's no good here."

"Thanks, Laura."

Laura comes back from the ticket counter frowning.

"Were the tickets more expensive than you thought?"

"No, no. The cashier was rude."

"Rude? Why?"

"Why?" Laura laughs. "Sarah, you're a clever girl. I think you can figure it out."

"I'm sorry…"

"Actually it doesn't happen as much here as it does at home. Here, if I'm soignée enough, I'll often as not get a free pass, despite my *complexion*." She looks up. "Don't worry. Let's not waste our time. I only have an hour and a half for lunch."

"Did you eat already?"

"Um, well, I usually skip lunch once or twice a week. Helps me keep an eye on my figure."

Sarah would pass out if she missed a meal. She made herself a fat cheese sandwich, baguette and brie slathered with butter, and ate it on the way here.

Are the kids she pushed through hungry, is that why they were swarming her? Or is it all an act? That tall boy was skinny, his cheekbones sharp, like a fox's. And that flinch that moved across his face when she pushed past him.

"You skinny little thing, I guess you can eat whatever you want." Laura pretends to glare at Sarah. "It's hard to like you, Kid." She takes a floor plan from the ticket desk. "Despite the rude ticket-taker, this is my favourite museum, all Impressionists."

"My mom used to have a book of reproductions: Degas, Cézanne, Monet," Sarah tells her, thumbing through the postcards by the ticket desk. "I remember stretching out on the living room floor when I was a little kid, poring over them." The eternal winter sunlight painting a patch of brightness on the yellow carpet. "There were all those still lifes and ballerinas and jockeys, of course, but it was the nudes that I wanted to look at most." All women, of course, and women painted by men. Gail would no doubt speechify about the male gaze, how it objectifies women, but the women in those paintings seemed somehow to own themselves. They were just ordinary women, a little plump or a little thin, unselfconsciously clipping their toenails or combing their hair, their faces almost always obscured. A painting of a heavy woman, the broad landscape of her back, the soft arcs of the folds of belly below the equal arc of breast, serenely scratching her back, at ease. "I remember my sister Rose explaining that if it was art, it was all right for ladies to be naked." What will she do if she doesn't have Rose to spell out the world for her? She does, she will have Rose, always. Every day out of hospital is a promise that Rose will be all right, no matter how long it takes.

Laura touches Sarah's arm. "You're still worried about her, aren't you?"

"I can't stop. Not that it does any good."

They move into the first gallery. Sarah stations herself in front of a Renoir, takes her time watching the crowd. People don't seem to stop for long. They'll pause at a painting, say, *Degas*, or *Renoir*, and then nod, satisfied, and move on. They have the right word, they know the name, so they've tamed what they're seeing, know what they're looking at – art. It was Rose who taught Sarah the one thing she knew about art: you stand close and then far. When you stand close, you see bits and pieces. When you stand far, you can see the whole thing.

In the next room there's a painting by Monet of the front of the cathedral at Rouen, bits of white and blue and yellow and even some red making up the stone façade. Were there pickpockets, panhandlers in front of the cathedral? Beggars, that's a more honest noun. Beggars in front of the Jeu de Paume, maybe beggars in front of the cathedral at Rouen. Did Monet see them but choose not to paint them? There are no people in the picture, none she can see, but is she looking hard enough? This painting pulls her in, makes her want to look at it as long as she can, until she sees past the names of things. Sarah sets her hand against her throat, testing for Michael's necklace, that it's still there, still invisible below the collar of her shirt. Then on instinct back to her pocket, checking for the penny. Sometimes it's hard not to look away. Making herself look in Prof. Koenig's class, trying to will starved, saved figures back into their own lives. Looking for a way to save herself.

She holds her gaze until the dab of white she's looking at in the Rouen cathedral isn't a dab of paint any more. It's not a bit of stone either. It's the light of the day caught; the moment it was seen. The painting goes into her, colours and the patterns they make moving through her body. The world made of light, not just things and the words for them. Someone taps her on the shoulder and she startles. It's Laura. "Earth to Sarah."

Sarah looks out the window of the gallery, startled to find the city there, Paris, because the painting has taken her someplace else.

This is what she's been doing with her days in Paris, days with nothing to do but what she wants to do – looking at things until they seep right into her. Until she's more.

"C'mon," Laura says, "onwards and upwards. Let's have a look at the next gallery before I lose you to another Monet."

The first thing Sarah sees when they move on to the next room is a Cézanne her parents have in the living room of the house on Rupertsland, a framed reproduction of a still life of apples and oranges. But this is the real thing.

Laura comes up behind her. "You like Cézanne?"

"My mother has that exact painting in her living room." There's a tipsy, slightly crooked look to the cloth and dish and bowl that the fruit is displayed on, as if the painter has almost but not quite figured out the rules of perspective. Something childish about it, less than dutifully perfect.

"*Nature morte,*" Laura says, "that's what they call still lifes in French. *Dead nature.* Such a weird expression – should landscapes be called *live nature,* then?"

Landscape or still life, you don't usually see living people in either. No beggars and no bosses. But maybe in the still lifes you do see the imprint of ownership, because those objects – the oranges or plates or rabbits – did belong to someone. As did the rooms that held them.

"Oh, I've been meaning to tell you – François told me that during the war the Nazis used the Jeu de Paume as a storage facility for art they'd stolen from Jewish families. Other families too, I guess. He says there was a curator here who secretly kept exact detailed lists of the works that had been taken, and of the original owners, so that the art could be given back after the war. If you like, I'll look up her name for you."

"Sure, thanks." An exact count. *Mene, mene.* So all through the Occupation, the curator kept believing not only that the war would end, but that the Nazis would lose, and the owners come back, alive. Live nature. As if that hope would save them.

Laila

It's quiet here. You're tired. You've laid your head on my lap and, quick as that, you're asleep. We found this place together. It was hidden so people like us wouldn't find it, but we did. You have business nearby, you have to go soon, but for now we can rest in the quiet shade. Except for a sideways glance now and then, nobody bothers with us. A gardener in blue coveralls sweeps the sand path, wiping away the traces of pigeon footprints. He doesn't look at us. He's busy with his work. His business.

I don't know what your business is. Though I do: part of your business is finding more work. For you, for me too. And you're selling things, I know that, a duffle bag with bottles of water, plastic toys, plastic souvenirs. What other business I don't know. But for now you're peaceful, your eyes closed, hands for once at rest.

And I can sit and watch this square, which is a square, symmetrical, laid out in strict geometry. Divided in four by paths cut as exact diagonals: in each section, an identical fountain. Here on our bench there's shade, shade also held under the arcades that wall in the square, their red brick trimmed with pale yellow stone. But there on the paths, on the four fountains, only sunlight. A bright quiet. Peace. A pigeon fluffs its feathers on the curlicued lamppost beside the lawn.

I close my eyes, listen to the sound of the water. Open them. Each fountain has an urn at the top, then a basin; a stand, another basin; another stand, and at the bottom a shallow pond. The second basin so big you could take a bath in it. You'd like that, a bath. Me too, I'd like a long bath in hot water, and then a sleep in my own bed at home, the sound of my mother humming as she kneads dough.

In this fountain water spills off the top urn and then the top basin, a little wind catching so it falls crooked there. But at the second basin, the water moves through narrow pipes spouting through the mouths of lions. Paris lions. My father told me that he saw the Lions' Gate in the walls of the Old City in Jerusalem once. The Lion of Judah, the Lion of Jerusalem. The lions carved into stone there centuries older than these. The ones here are worn so that each lion's head has been changed to wear a slightly different look. Bored with us, maybe, or maybe curious. Patient. The water keeps spilling itself.

Over years the water scours the metal of the pipe too, shaping it so it flows differently from each lion's mouth. Lion of Paris. Lion of Jerusalem.

Tell me why we're here, Khalil.

I want a country and you've given me this square.

LUXEMBOURG

SARAH'S BACK AT THE LUXEMBOURG GARDENS, sober this time, solo, and in daylight. She can remember it only hazily from her first glorious dizzy expedition with Laura and Michael. Yesterday, as she and Laura were leaving the Jeu de Paume, Laura ran into her landscape-architect friend Charles, and quickly talked him into giving Sarah a tour of the Luxembourg Gardens. Sarah really is *interested in landscape gardening*, but she couldn't help feeling like a problem child being handed off from one caregiver to another.

Which she probably is. The family black sheep. The woman who can't even spend the night with her boyfriend.

Until now. Until these Paris days, Paris nights, when she can.

Charles is supposed to meet her in front of the Grand Bassin, which is a funny shape, an uneven octagon, two sides longer than the others. Sarah's taken a seat on one of the little metal chairs sprinkled around the edge of the pond where the immaculate French children are sailing their wee boats on the placid water. Just the lightest breeze today, so the little multi-coloured sails are a bit lax. The stone lip around the pond takes an elegant slow curve to its rippled edge, but that curve seems a bit dicey for the toddlers leaning towards the water with its tempting ducks and wooden boats. The mothers are nonetheless nonchalant, smoking, flipping through magazines.

Sarah moves her chair into the partial shade of a linden. She's learned that linden is *tilleul* in French. As soon as she saw the illustration on a box of *tisane de tilleul*, Sarah knew what they were – no mistaking the distinctive heart-shaped leaves and their tiny frilled yellow flowers cupped by narrow yellowy-green bracts. That play between the vivid green of the regular leaves and the pale glow of the bracts, as if they had a special way of holding the light, which perhaps they do... The sun is playing off them now, a green ripple in the bit of breeze.

Tilleul is another word in French that Michael claims he struggles with. *Tea-yul*: she can see how he's buffaloed at the proximity of those *l*'s and vowels. Laura has persuaded them that they have to try *tisane de tilleul* instead of regular tea. *Tisanes* are infusions, and this one is made from the dried flowers of the linden. Another Parisian must, Laura claims, the kind of beverage preferred by women who are BCBG – *bon chic, bon genre. Tisane de tilleul,* visits to art galleries, all elements in Laura's gentle but insistent campaign to infuse Sarah herself with *savoir faire,* to transform Sarah into a new category of being. Ugly duckling into swan. Wooden puppet into real girl. Statue into living woman. She's a project. And learning more about landscape gardening is part of the transformation.

Sarah would be resentful of the instruction, but Laura's proposals always come with a tang of ironic appreciation that this isn't how either of them were raised, it's not how things go at home. There's nothing condescending about Laura. She would be the first to admit that she has also metamorphosized herself, turned the girl from Saskatoon by way of Tobago into an honest-to-goodness BCBG *parisienne*. Laura hasn't made any bones about how hard she's had to work to make that sea change. She says she can hear her parents tsking – *sucking teeth,* she says, taking on their accent – in disapproval of her *airs and graces*. As if the change were a betrayal. And maybe it is. Though Laura knows they're proud too, that she's *made something of herself.*

And she has. Laura has made herself a career at a fancy legal firm in Paris. Sarah's the one who doesn't even have a job.

She looks out, away from her thoughts. The trees here at the Luxembourg, the lime trees in Place des Vosges, that big basswood in Mrs. M.'s front garden, those poor captive saplings caged near the Saint-Paul Métro stop, they're all lindens, all genus *Tilia,* all in the *Tiliaceae* family. What's in a name indeed. You know something by naming it, but common names depend on where you happen to be. She looked up *Tilia* taxonomy in her pocket tree guide. Though they're not a citrus at all, linden are called lime trees in Europe because the Middle English word *lind* got twisted into *lime*. *Lind* from the Latin word for flexible, pliant, yielding. So the words *lithe* and *lenient* are from the same root; *liana*, those clingy woody vines, too. Because they're so compliant, linden are great trees for cities: they can tolerate all soils, various degrees of sun exposure, they can tough out air pollution, survive a fair bit of drought. Adaptable, pliant.

If you were a linden tree, what kind of linden tree would you be? Mrs. M.'s basswood back in Toronto is *Tilia americana*, one of the larger varieties, fast-growing but not as long-lived as other species in the family. Bigleaf lindens, *Tilia platyphyllos*, grow more slowly, but according to Sarah's book, they can last over a thousand years. *Tilia cordata*, littleleaf linden, also have that ability to endure. *Littleleaf linden*: Michael would probably get a kick out of that name too, all that bouncy alliteration. A linden by any name would smell as sweet – all the *Tilia* cultivars have beautifully fragrant flowers.

A bit of wind again in the leaves. It's so quiet here. Peaceful. The city is speckled with these pools of quiet, and Parisians seem as drawn to them as she is. Refuge from the stink of the Métro, the noise of stalled traffic, horns honking, construction. No graffiti here, no litter or panhandlers. There is a middle-aged man in a rather jaunty fedora slumped in a chair in the shade who may be sleeping it off. Sarah can just barely hear the murmur of human voices at a distance. Sounds here are birdsong, the scratch of a rake against the gravel and dirt path. Someone is always looking after things – here, and at Place des Vosges. Public gardens for the public good. Public spaces that ·create public goodness. The clock on the palace façade has chimed the quarter hour and now the hour, discreet notice. A pigeon approaches, inspects the dirt around her sandals for crumbs. No luck.

And then Charles is beside her, briefcase in hand, a natty bow-tie, ever so slightly askew, on his trim, striped shirt. He extends his hand. No cheek-kissing for Charles. He's English. "Hope I haven't kept you waiting. You've had to rent a chair."

"Oops. No, I just sat myself down. I didn't realize I was supposed to pay." She's done it again.

"Well, you've gotten away with it. I hope you and Michael are enjoying the apartment. François lived there on his own for a couple of years before we moved in together, so it should be quite habitable." Charles digs into his briefcase, shuffles a few papers, hands her a creamy thick envelope. A list of gardens to visit. Because she's *interested in landscape gardening*. And she is. She wants to open up the envelope right away. She's begun to see how the gardens she's browsed in work on people and how the people work on them. Begun to see what happens when what the gardens want bumps against what the designers want, and then what happens when they both bump against what the people who use them want. Her thumb strokes the paper and when she looks up, Charles is smiling at her.

"I've jotted down some notes on each garden, just a few quick facts or points of interest, but it could easily keep you busy your whole stay. Though you may want to take some side trips too. Versailles, of course. And maybe Giverny, you know Giverny? Monet's garden is there, the water-lilies garden. Both the house and the gardens have been restored. They opened to the public just a year or two ago. I haven't gotten there yet myself, but I hear it's quite something."

Monet's garden. If she went there, she could see at least something of what Monet saw, that world made of light.

Charles is walking briskly away from the pond, down the wide gravel path of the central allée, its trees as sternly disciplined as the children she's been watching. She hasn't been in Europe in winter, but she has seen illustrations of pollarded trees with their top branches lopped off, pruned so brutally that they look like elongated stumps. It's hard to believe the trees could ever recover after having had so much taken from them. They've been pollarding in Europe for centuries, and it's supposed to promote growth, but it's difficult to picture how something can be so stunted and still live, much less thrive.

To the side, a group of intense men who look to be in their sixties are playing a game of *boules*. Sarah listens to the quiet click of the balls. It reminds her of the sedate elderly gents and ladies in their whites on the exact green of the lawn-bowling centre just off Bathurst beside the Wychwood Library. There's a gorgeous huge catalpa tree on the north side of the library that's probably covered in pale orchid-like blooms right now, its scent haunting the sidewalks. For a moment she misses home.

"I hear ice-curling is as popular in Canada as it is in Scotland." Charles is grinning as they watch the boules players.

"My dad likes to curl," Sarah tells him. Big Abe on the ice in his giant Cowichan sweater with the moose parading across it, the one his mother knit him; Abe watching the lazy turns of his granite stones and calling *sweep, sweep* at his teammates louder than anyone else at the rink.

"We've never had the chance to visit Canada. You and Michael are in Toronto, right? I hear High Park is interesting, I suppose you've been. And the city itself, I understand there's an impressive canopy of trees, an urban forest."

"I used to work as a waitress at a rooftop bar in Toronto, 17 stories up. I remember looking south beyond the patio and seeing treetops all the way down to the lake."

"My mum worked as a waitress but she had to retire. Thirty-five years on her feet and her legs are spoiled. Is that where you're working now?"

"I work for a garden centre." Worked. She isn't working now.

"Right. I think Laura mentioned something of the sort. How is that suiting you?"

She looks at Charles. "I lost the job just before we left. Got fired, in fact." She looks at him again, but Charles' face is steady. "That's why I'm here with Michael. I'm at loose ends."

"Did you like it, then?"

"I liked the work. I like getting my hands dirty." She holds both hands in front of her. "We've been here two weeks, and I've actually got fingernails again."

He laughs, a genial sort of snort she wasn't expecting. "Is that a plus or a minus?"

"Hard to say."

"Well, I don't get my own hands dirty often enough. My mum had a backyard vegetable garden in Liverpool. That woman could grow a cabbage in a teapot."

Liverpool has to be farther north than Winnipeg; they'd have even longer hours of summer sunlight.

"Let's just follow the allée here, and I'll start my spiel. After Good King Henry was assassinated in 1610, Marie de Medicis, his second wife, was so down in the mouth that the only thing for it was to move out of the royal residence at the Louvre. So she had the Luxembourg Palace and the Gardens designed after her childhood home in Florence – the Pitti Palace and its Boboli Garden."

The Pity Palace, perhaps. So strange that the model of a French garden was built by a homesick Italian princess.

"The gardens have grown and shrunk over time, especially when Haussmann was busy reorganizing the streets, but a lot of the original design is still intact, and it is a model of the garden *à la française*. The French are that keen on formality, symmetry." Charles purses his lips in imitation of the *moue*, that pouty discerning French face, and Sarah can't keep from smiling. *Charles fait la moue.* "I'm not as partial to the French garden as I should be, living here," he says. "There are times when it feels too much like an act of will, working against nature rather than with it. I'm more fond of the English style."

Maybe it's that the English style allows more of what the garden wants, not just the designer.

A toddler goes racing past them. The mother looks up from her magazine, gets up from her wooden bench and somewhat reluctantly pursues him.

"D'you like the double-sided benches?" Charles asks. "I think of them as Janus benches."

"Two-faced benches. I think I saw them in Place des Vosges."

They've reached the wrought-iron fence that borders the park. Sarah puts her hands around the bars. "We were so drunk the last time I was here. I have a foggy memory of wandering round and round here after we finished dinner, following Laura on some wild goose chase. We couldn't get in, it was all locked up."

"I'm glad you're seeing things more in focus this go-round. Sarah, did you know we have beehives in the Luxembourg? There's been an apiary and bee-keeping school here since 1856. The apiary is just up the walk, at the corner of the garden. There's a plan afoot to repopulate Paris with beehives. And not just in parks; there's talk about using the roofs of some of the big department stores, hotels, even the Opera House. And they've already got good evidence that bees are happy here, productive, too. Gobsmacking, isn't it, urban bees?"

They come up on a cluster of square wooden hives behind a pale wooden fence, the sun so brilliant that the hives' tented roofs seem white in its light. A little city of hives. The hives are perched on metal platforms of some sort. Their wooden walls have been polished to a beeswaxy sheen by age and weather. And those pitched roofs on them – like straw rice-paddy hats or pagodas topped by knobs that probably are handles for lifting the roofs off to access the honey. There's a larger structure to the left, a gazebo that seems to have come directly from a fairy tale except that it's housing a cluttered bunch of equipment, mostly more wooden boxes for hives. She tries the handle of the gate. It's locked. Another locked gate.

"Yes," Charles says, "I meant to get us the key ahead of time. We can just go into the little building over there, and I'll fetch it so we can get a closer look."

There are painted stencils of bees at the tops of the gate posts. The bee outlines look as though a very clever child has drawn them, flat and slightly crude and perfect, and Sarah suddenly needs them, needs to have them stencilled as a border along the walls of her room back home, they're so much the shape of what she wants.

But she doesn't have a room.

She wants one. Her own room.

They walk a few steps to an odd-shaped little building, a pavilion of some sort with mosaics running cheerily across the top of the façade. Palms in tubs flank the door, which is open. It's musty and a bit dreary inside, a contrast to the exterior. Behind a battered table, there's a man about their age. He rises, and he and Charles do the quick male double-kiss. So Charles *can* be French with the French... Then he and the man at the table start to chatter in such rapid French Sarah can't follow. The key, *la clé*, she gets that much. The man is shrugging, being emphatic, but no, but yes, Charles isn't sure, and now Charles is agreeing.

"I'm sorry, Sarah," Charles says as they leave the little pavilion. "You didn't follow?"

"It was too fast."

"André says we shouldn't go into the enclosure itself. It's unwise, *ce n'est pas sage*, as André says, because the hives have already been accessed today and the bees are more agitated than usual. And we haven't any protective gear."

She wants in. She isn't worried about the bees; in all her work at the Centre, she's been stung only once. She wants in because she wants to be on the other side of the locked gate that Charles could have gotten the key for. Every lock in Paris has its key, but only for those with a right to them. Not for the clochards, the tramps with no place to live but the streets. Not for the panhandlers and not for the drunks and not for the downtrodden women with their sagging shopping bags. But Charles has the kind of life here where he has the keys to things. And because of the kind of life Michael has, Sarah knows Laura, who knows Charles, who can get into places where others are kept out.

She wants in, but she won't get in, not this time.

They walk back into the sunlight. Little signs are placed in the grass: *Ne pas marcher sur la pelouse. Danger abeilles.* Do not walk on the lawn. Danger bees. Sarah and Charles circle on the path at a respectful distance. She watches the flecks of sunlight that are the bees as they swerve and flicker above the hives. Light is a wave and a particle and so are the bees. The arcs of their flight paths seem intense, more determined than anxious. The breeze has picked up a bit, and the leaves of the chestnuts shiver and pause. Charles is also watching silently as the bees perform their intricate arabesques of approach and departure, drawing corkscrews in the air above the hive.

"When they get inside the hive, they do some sort of dance to let the other bees know where the flowers are. It's called the 'dance language' of bees," Charles says.

Dance language. What would Rose say about that? Is that how Rose feels when she's dancing, that she's speaking in some way, that the body itself can be articulate? "My sister's a dancer."

"Lovely. Can she make a living at it?"

"Yes and no. It's hard."

"Of course."

"Are the bees actually talking to each other when they dance?"

"There's controversy about exactly how they communicate. As they leave the hive, those bees that are new to foraging will start off flying in that spiral we're watching. They aren't yet using scent for direction, just whatever they learned from the returning bees' dance –"

"I'd like that."

"What?" Charles asks.

"To speak with my body."

He laughs again, the same boisterous roar. "I'm pretty sure you do, at the appropriate moment."

She smiles. "That wasn't what I was thinking about."

"I understand that research has convincingly shown that men are almost always thinking about that."

She's caught again by the spiral dance. The bees seem so businesslike. She wishes she knew with as much certainty what her day's, her life's work, was.

They *must* know what they're doing, to get done what they get done: the hives, the wax, the honey. That has to amount to knowledge.

"Well, then, how about you?" Charles asks.

"Me?" What does she know with her body? What does it tell her to do?

"What are you keen on doing? This interest in gardens, where does it come in? You won't get your hands dirty researching."

"I don't know, Charles. Like I said, I'm kind of at a loss these days." Loser at a loss.

Charles studies her. "About time you find yourself, then, right?"

She smiles. "One of the people whose garden I've worked on thinks I should start my own landscaping business when I get back home."

"And what do you think?"

"I'm not sure I'm up to it."

"Why on earth not?"

She looks at her hands. "I'm afraid." Afraid of failing. Afraid of trying.

"Of course you're afraid. I think the real question is, would your hands get dirty enough running a landscaping business? We've established that you need to get your hands dirty. Let's say you weren't afraid, or you got over that hump. Would landscaping suit you?"

Would it suit her?

"I don't know."

Charles smiles again, checks his watch. He has to run, but he wants them to meet up again, wants to walk her through the Palais-Royal.

They shake hands, he's gone back into English mode. Is it subconscious, this switch from cheek-peck to handshake? It must be. She watches for a moment as he walks quickly off through the shaded paths and back towards the pond.

She'll walk home.

On the central lawn, people are stretched out on the grass, behind a sign that reads: *Pelouse autorisée.* Sitting on the lawn permitted. This is a space where everyone is allowed. No locks, no keys. It belongs to everyone, a public terroir. Maybe that's what makes Parisians so distinctive. Not the language, but the soil, maybe they pick up the scent and spice of the earth that's around them. When they can, when it's not covered with concrete or stone, or locked behind a grille. And not just the scent of the earth, the slant of light too, the winds that work their way among the buildings.

How much of Toronto has she soaked up? Is Winnipeg still in her, after so many summers, winters, away?

And can a Jew ever have their own terroir, or is every bit of land provisional? Every land but Israel, where she can't imagine living. Not now.

Laila

Three nights a week Agnès waits for me at the shining entrance to the office building, its glass doors, bright lobby. I work here, clean offices, three nights a week. I don't have a key but at 8:00 I meet Agnès at the entrance and she lets me in. She takes me into the ladies' bathroom, we change into our uniforms, baggy grey dresses. I don't know why we need uniforms, nobody is here to see us. She doesn't bother much with me, Agnès, but she tells me what to do: where to clean, how to clean, where the bosses' offices are, how they like things done. And when she saw how the bleach hurt my hands, she gave me rubber gloves, paid for them herself. Even with the gloves my hands are red and clean now, from scouring, from the cleansers and detergents. Their skin tight and pink like the scar across my cheek, they look like they don't belong to me. When Agnès asked me about the scar, I didn't say anything, shrugged.

Because I have a job, I have 15 francs of my own in my jeans pocket. Fifteen francs. Agnès pays me cash. At the Marché d'Aligre market the piles of food set out in the stalls are bright, gleaming. It's a long walk to the Marché d'Aligre from my room, but the prices are good here. I can buy anything: lettuce, grapes, cheese. Eggplant, lemons, garlic, mint. I could cook a meal, if I had a kitchen. I could make food I remember. I touch the bills in my pocket, the money I worked for, the dull feel of the paper.

In the square in front of the market building is a table with cardboard boxes full of clothes, everything the same price, 10 francs. The women go through them, mauling the fabric, hunting for bargains. I want something for me. I want something pretty to wear in this ugly place, a fitted white blouse with a square collar, a striped t-shirt, boat-necked, French. Across from me a tired-looking woman, her plastic shopping bags at her feet, stops sorting through the clothes to stare. My hand goes to the scar on my cheek. But it's not the scar she's looking it, it's me, *dirty little Arab*.

My hands are clean.

I don't want her look. I don't want to want what she wants, I don't want anything in these boxes. I don't want to want anything.

I leave the market with nothing, no lemons or mint, the money still in my pocket. I'll walk the crooked streets to meet you. You said it shouldn't be more than a half-hour walk from the Marché d'Aligre to the Cité Métro station, if I'm not lazy. I'm supposed to look for you there, I'll find you working, Khalil, I'll find you foraging for cigarette butts so you can roll yourself a smoke from the leftover tobacco. *Your* fingers are dirty, your hands.

I'm walking the crooked streets, watching these people and their pretty paper shopping bags. Shopping bags full of things they've bought, things they wanted and didn't walk away from. Pretty things, pretty nothings because nothing is itself here. Clothes can't be clothes, food can't be food. Even the simplest thing isn't what it is. My mother would set grapes in a wooden bowl on the tablecloth she'd embroidered, set cheese on a white plate, fresh bread beside it. Everything my mother served tasted real.

Coming up the side of the cathedral, I can't escape the gauntlet of music I don't want to hear, each tune a slap: a duet on the sidewalk, violin and bass, the case open for coins. Then singing from inside the cathedral, so many voices, a choir. Then a round woman singing opera, her voice scratching at the sky. And finally the bells themselves, their song riding over the other voices, the music.

As I cross the square, I feel a touch on my shoulder. I turn and jump to see my own spoiled face. The man who touched me bows, a real mouth smiles. No, he's not like me, there's nothing wrong with his face. It's an ugly, twisted mask he's wearing over his eyes and nose. He doesn't say anything, tips his beret, waits a moment, is it money he wants? I can feel the light pressure of the bills in my pocket – they're mine, not his.

He bows to me again, goes off to a woman who's snapping a picture.

He poses just beside and behind her, he's snapping a picture too. She turns and sees him and she startles as well, but now she's bent over laughing, a heavy woman, German maybe. I can see now that the man is a mime, in his beret and tight trousers and striped sailor t-shirt, a t-shirt like the one I wanted to buy. He's one of the entertainers in the cathedral square.

The tour buses vomit out their swarms. More tourists in the famous square. They raise their cameras and take what they want to take home with them: themselves. *Here's me in front of Notre-Dame. Me in front of the Eiffel Tower.* They want to be *next to* something they recognize, they want themselves to *be* the picture. They come here looking through the filter of themselves, looking only for themselves.

Someone snaps a shutter and, by mistake, I'm in the frame. They don't know I'm caught in their picture. The light of the day captured but also me, and a dozen, maybe twenty, other strangers, here, in front of Notre-Dame Cathedral, by mistake. And then, someone takes a picture of that photographer, by mistake, and takes his face home. Our lives bumping into one another, a brief collision, a moment's mistake. The call – *I was here, I was here* – thinner and thinner in each repetition as the echoes of their images fade. None of them will see me, but I'm here.

The clochards and the pickpockets, they see me. And the drunks. The clochards and panhandlers and pickpockets see me but they don't bother with me, they don't think I have anything for them. The drunks, the men, they make that sloppy chirping sound with their mouths, lips puckering, calling me like an animal, a pet. They think they can have me cheap, they think they can have me for the taking, already spoiled. And the women drunks, with their own spoiled faces, what do they see when they look at me, that brief collision? A warped reflection, like the mime with his ugly impersonations, something they recognize.

I don't recognize myself now, I don't know where to look. What do you see when you look at me, Khalil, a spoiled face, spoiled woman? The one you took home, out of kindness or pity or honour, or a moment's mistake? I don't recognize you. I don't know what business it is that keeps you busy. I don't know where to look. I see the pictures on television, soldiers and their guns, how the city is hurt, its wounded buildings, walls gouged with bullets, the corpses of burned-out cars. I don't understand why they don't give us the faces of civilians, why we aren't shown their wounds. All we're given is a child's hand dangling from her father's hold, a man's arm loose from a stretcher, blanket over his face, a leg hanging. A woman in a pink dress, balancing a bundle on her head, her face turned from the camera. I want to see their faces. I want to give them their names.

✿
CALL

SATURDAY SUN IS SLANTING IN ON THE TABLE, giving even the crumbs on its surface their own long shadows. Sarah brushes the table clear, then picks up the penny, turns and turns its chill, light weight in her hand. A quick flip into her palm, then she switches the penny into the other palm, opens: *yes*.

"Michael?" The penny closed in her fist. He's walked into the room, freshly showered, towelling off his back. Sun haloing the damp blond curls on his head. He'll want a trim soon. "I wanted to talk with you. I've been thinking about my plans – for when we get back to Toronto." He reaches for his shirt, nods.

"I have some ideas. Actually, not me so much. It was Mrs. Margolis who put me on to them. She thought –" Sarah worries the penny between her fingers, "she was talking about me taking some courses in landscape gardening. At Ryerson. Maybe even getting a certificate."

Michael sits down, buttoning up the shirt. "Ryerson."

"And once I'd taken the courses, she was saying – my designs are good, she was saying – she thought…I could start my own business. She figured I could make a go of it." What Mrs. M. thought, she keeps talking about what Mrs. M. thought. What does *she* think? What will Michael think?

Michael takes the penny from her, skates it back and forth in front of him along the table. She can see him measuring his words. "Really. A landscape business. You'd be good at that."

"You think so?"

"I know so. And if it was your own business, you'd still be able to work a shovel whenever you felt like it," Michael says. "But you'd have larger

164

projects, ones that really grabbed you."

"That's what Mrs. M. said."

He nods again. "You know how rare Mrs. M. is. Most of the time at the Centre, you'd be digging a pond for some god-awful plastic statue of a boy peeing or something. If you had your own business, you could develop a more sophisticated clientele, people like Mrs. M. You're still in touch with her, right?"

Sarah nods. She'd dropped by Mrs. M.'s before she left for Paris, sipped the requisite glasses of iced tea.

"She might even be able to get you some customers, word of mouth. Her garden would be a showcase for you. You think she'd be okay with that?"

"I think so."

"This is really something," Michael says. "This is good."

"Up till now," Sarah says, "I'd never thought that far beyond my job, making the rent. You know." She takes the penny back from him. "But being here, seeing all these gardens, it's got me thinking about what a garden is for."

He nods again.

"I like the idea of designing spaces, backyards, gardens, anything. Then at least the work I do won't just wash away after a season. I could start with the Ryerson courses, see how they go. See if I like or not, if I can do it."

"You can do it."

Michael so sure. But school never was hard for her, except that one course. "I need honest work –"

"You've never done anything but honest work!"

"– but I like the idea of making some sort of mark too." Leaving some sort of a wake behind her, something to show she was here. Doing something that not only does no harm, but does some good.

He looks up at her, eyes cautious. Through the caution she can see how happy he is, the happy tension running through him. A solution. The solution to the problem of Sarah. The possibility of her half-life turning whole. "Sounds good, Sarah. Really good. Start with the classes. I can front you the money for school. If you'll let me." He slips his hand under her t-shirt, and she takes hold of it, presses it against her ribcage. "You should do this. You know you should."

෴

Later that morning, Sarah and Michael and Laura are lingering over brunch at Laura's apartment. She lives on a tiny street, rue Agar, in the 16th, the fanciest of all fancy arrondissements in Paris, where *parfumeries* surely outnumber grocery stores. Laura has made them *pissaladière*, a flatbread with onion, olive and anchovy topping, and then a green salad which she's served, French style, as a separate course *after* the main course. The pièce de résistance is dessert, a tarte Tatin, apple upside-down pie, which Laura has also made herself – she was just putting it in the oven when they came in. They're squeezed around the table on her little rooftop patio, Laura and Michael delicately sharing a cigarette. He's trying to quit. Sarah's standing on tiptoe, looking across the river where she can just see the top of the Eiffel Tower.

The view is part of the reason Laura rented the place. She confesses that she loves the romance of it, even if real Parisians don't like the Eiffel Tower – or didn't when it was first built. It was the entrance arch to the 1889 World's Fair and when it first went up, it stuck out like a tacky, vulgar, sore thumb. So says Laura's friend Marie-Claire, who was born here. After almost a century, though, the Parisians are finally adjusting... Sacré Coeur too, the big white church at the top of Montmartre with the three elongated domes; even though construction on it started more than a century ago, lots of Parisians still think it's hideous, a white elephant with those bloated, awkward domes.

Sarah isn't sure what Sacré Coeur looks like, she hasn't been to Montmartre yet, but she can't imagine Paris without the Eiffel Tower. Paris *is* the Eiffel Tower.

But then, up until 1889, Paris was Paris without any Eiffel Tower.

The view makes the apartment worth the eight-storey climb, Laura says. It used to be several *chambres de bonne*, but walls were taken down to link

166

them. Now it's a string of small but lovely rooms that she's furnished sparingly with refurbished flea-market finds.

The building was designed by an art nouveau architect, Hector Guimard. Guimard designed all the finishings, every aspect of the building, the fireplace with its swooping lines, even the doorknobs. The doorknob a wobbly white oval that fit snugly into Sarah's palm. Guimard is famous for designing the green entrances to the Métro. He's back in fashion now, Laura says, but when the Métro station entrances first were built, people hated them. They called his designs *le style nouille*, noodle architecture, to make fun of all the droopy green flourishes.

So, the Eiffel Tower, Sacré Coeur, the Métro stations – nobody liked them at first. Everything that was new offended. And now Parisians can't do without them: icons, emblems of the city. This city that Sarah is living in for now, an accumulation of pushes and pulls, change and resistance to change.

Guimard also designed a synagogue in the Marais, Laura says, the arcs of its narrow façade meant to represent an open book for the People of the Book. It's on rue Pavée, right near their apartment. But in 1941, on the evening of Yom Kippur, it was among a bunch of synagogues dynamited by French anti-Semitic collaborators. French collaborators, not the Nazis. Guimard and his wife, who was an American Jew, had moved to New York before the war because of the anti-Semitism in France. So at least they weren't in Paris in any danger when the synagogue was dynamited. After the war, the building was restored. Sarah and Michael can still go see it, if they want to.

Mort aux juifs.

Michael and Sarah haven't said anything to Laura about the graffiti, which hasn't been removed. They know she'd worry about the stay being spoiled for them, though she's been candid enough about the racist slights she's experienced here herself. Not as bad as home, though, she says. It's worse at home.

"Is it an act, do you think?" Michael asks. "All the formality here, the politesse?"

"Well, it works for me. Let's face it: I'd rather have insincere courtesy than honest rudeness. And these French women," Laura says. "They are perfection. They knot the sleeves of their sweaters at their necks just so. They make their chignons just messy enough to be sexy. Not to mention the *moue*. The *moue!* I've been working all out on mine for three full years now and I don't come anywhere close to these French women.

"I got the chance to observe a real pro in action at lunch the other day." Laura sets down her fork, a wicked grin on her face. "She was sitting at a table across from mine, and I was positioned so I could watch the whole performance. She was wearing this blouse that was impossibly white, with a collar that was impeccably crisp. It starts with her giving this totally serious, unsmiling summons to the waiter, her eyebrows arched just a bit. There's already a hint of disappointment in that eyebrow. I mean, more than disappointment, maybe even *sorrow* – She's about to discuss the menu and clearly there's so much opportunity for the waiter to let her down. Standards might not be met. Which would be a calamity.

"But there's also in this very same arch of the eyebrow the opportunity for the opposite to occur. There's the faintest chance that a smile might play at the edges of her mouth." Laura shakes her head in mock world-weariness at this point. "Because if the world plays its cards just right, if the food, the service, the conversation, are exactly as they should be, the waiter, and the world, might be rewarded with a smile. The smile *has* to be held back at first, so that if, in the end, it is in fact offered, it will mean something. The intimacy of a smile shall be granted if and only if all expectations and standards are met."

These little back-and-forths, so intricate they seem choreographed.

Now Laura is practising an extreme version of the *moue* on Michael, who's completely cracking up. Rose could master the *moue*, if she wanted to, which she wouldn't. But Gail, Sarah can't begin to imagine Gail making that flirty little French face.

She's sent Gail a couple of postcards, got one very funny one in return but she still feels unsettled. Michael keeps telling her just to call, act as if nothing was wrong. Give Gail an opening to apologize. Fat chance. Maybe

Sarah should apologize to Gail, though she doesn't know what she'd be apologizing about – punching herself in the face? She still hasn't mentioned that little slapstick anecdote to Michael.

Gail no doubt would have a full and complete analysis of the position of petit-bourgeois women in French society. If Gail were here, the talk would probably be more battle than banter. But if Rose were here, sitting at this table, admiring the view, she would find a way to say her piece without running around in circles or letting herself get shoved into some corner. At least the old Rose would. Sarah has had a postcard from her. One postcard. She thinks she's doing a bit better.

"So how does feminism fit in, then?" Sarah can't help asking.

"Feminism?" Laura takes a big bite out of her salad, puts down her fork. Chews with satisfaction. Then she shakes her head. "It's really sad – it's *really* sad – but if you ask the average French woman whether she'd rather be pretty or smart, the answer will always be *pretty*.

"C'mon, you're on dish duty, Mr. Scott," Laura says. "Grab some plates. We'll wait a bit before we dig into the tarte Tatin. Meanwhile, Sarah, why don't you make that call now?"

For days now Sarah has been wanting to know how Rose is, to hear Pat's voice. Wanting to tell her mother about the bees in the Luxembourg Gardens, the Cézanne at the Jeu de Paume. She weaves past the narrow kitchen to the little parlour, seats herself on one of the re-upholstered chairs beside the phone, which is on a refinished side table. She has to dial twice before she gets through, maybe she did something wrong, didn't wait for the signal after the country code – she's used to the operator at the Hôtel de Ville – but then the call connects. The phone rings and rings until she's about ready to give up, but then the line clicks and she hears her mother's *hello?*

"Mom? It's me, Sarah."

"Are you in Paris?" Pat's voice sounds fuzzy.

"Yes." Where else would she be? "I was just calling to hear how Rose is doing."

"She, she seems not too bad." Pat sounds like she's waffling about what to say.

"Are you okay?"

"Me? Well, I haven't been sleeping all that well. It's early here."

Damn. Sarah got the time difference wrong: Winnipeg is an hour earlier than Toronto so it's six in the morning, not seven, and even though Pat is an early riser, Sarah's either woken her or she's just barely up. "I'm sorry, Mom."

"Oh it's all right. I would have gotten up soon anyways."

Anyways. That's where Sarah gets it from. Michael mentioned it the other day: you don't say *anyways*, you say *anyway*. It's like *irregardless*, her dad always used to tweak her about that one and trained her out of it, but she never even thought about *anyways*. These slips make her feel *less than*.

"Sarah? You there?"

"Sorry, Mom. I just wanted to call to check in with you. We're over at our friend Laura's, and she's got a phone, so I thought I'd try catching you."

"I'm glad you did."

"You sound worried, though."

"Me? I guess so…" Again that hesitation.

"What's wrong?"

"Rose has had a few bad days. When I dropped by Wednesday with some Hutterite chickens for her freezer, she seemed withdrawn. I spoke to David yesterday and he's been worried. They're taking her back to the doctor to see if she needs her medication adjusted. David said they might try a different antidepressant."

"Do you think she's taking her medication?"

"David says she is. I mean, she would. Now. After all that. We have to expect setbacks, if that's what it is. It takes time."

"How about you? Are you okay?"

"Me? I don't know. It's just… I don't know. I just can't seem to get my balance back."

Pat, the eternally unflappable, always in charge. Their mom. Someone who worries about them. Someone they never have to worry about.

"Sarah, you know, the funniest thing happened yesterday. I was walking up to get the bus at McGregor, the car's in the garage for a check-up, and this older lady was walking towards me. She was well-dressed, tidy. Maybe in her early seventies. She smiled at me, and then as we passed each other, she said, 'You must be picking up your children from school.' It *was* four o'clock. But me picking up my children? 'My children are all grown,' I told her. And that was that. I have a feeling she wasn't quite in her right mind. I certainly don't look like someone young enough to have kids in elementary school. But, it kind of threw me off and I thought, they *are* grown. But how, how are they grown? I really don't know, couldn't say."

"Mom, don't worry."

"Don't worry?" Pat's voice rises. Sarah can hear her take a breath. "How can you tell me not to worry? Rose tried to kill herself!"

"Mom –"

"How can I not worry?"

Laura and Michael are still chatting out on the patio. Sarah holds the phone tight against her ear. "Are you crying, Mom? You sound like you're crying."

"I don't get it. I don't get it. Why did she do it? Why would she? What's wrong with her? And what's wrong with me?"

"There's nothing wrong with you, Mom –"

"– and what's wrong with you? What are you doing there in Paris? Why can't you settle into your own life? And what's wrong with Gail? Why is she so awful?"

Sarah doesn't know why she's in Paris, why Rose tried to kill herself, why Gail is so awful. She doesn't know anything. "Mom –" She can hear Pat take another deep breath, sigh. "Shall I call you back? Do you want to talk later, when you're more awake?"

"No. No, it's okay. Don't hang up." Another sigh. "I'm sorry, Sarah. I don't know what's gotten into me. I'm half-asleep still. I had a bad night."

"You can call me back in a bit. I can give you the number."

"No. No. Just give me a sec to take a sip of my coffee, clear my head." Sarah can hear her swallowing. The line is crackly and Pat's voice comes through staccato. "I don't want you to be upset. I don't want to spoil your trip."

"Should I come back? I can change my ticket."

"Of course not. There's no reason for you to come back. It'll be okay. I just have these moments when I doubt everything."

"I know. I get it."

"Oh, here's your dad up now. He wants to say hello." The line's clearer now.

Abe's rumbly voice comes on, how's the weather, how's Michael, have they been to the top of the Eiffel Tower, did they see the fireworks on Bastille Day, is she thinking about what she'll do when she gets back? The barrage of parental concern is a relief, it's what she's used to from her parents.

"I'll write you, Dad. It's been great here. We're at a friend's house and we can see the Eiffel Tower from her patio. It's amazing."

"Well, that's terrific. Don't you worry about anything here."

"I won't. It's so good to hear your voice."

"You too, Sweetheart. Take care, won't you?"

"I will. Give Rose and David my love, Gail too, if you speak to her."

"Will do. Bye-bye."

Sarah stays on the line after he hangs up, the dial-tone buzzing in her hand.

FRENCH LESSONS

GIVE IT A TRY, LAURA SAID. She has a friend, Marie-Claire – the woman who still disapproves of the Eiffel Tower – who gives French lessons. Sarah might like to add a bit more polish to her accent and Marie-Claire is a real parisienne. She gives tourists lessons all the time, she's very well educated. And Laura admitted she had an ulterior motive: Marie-Claire was having a bit of a hard time, and could use some extra income, things were a bit tight for her. Michael immediately jumped in, another damsel in distress, sure, why not, he'd be happy to cover the modest fee. Sarah was pretty sure this was another element in Laura's campaign to improve her, but she didn't really mind. It'd be great to come home speaking better French. So she dutifully walked out to the payphone on rue Saint-Antoine and called the number. Marie-Claire answered in correct English, then switched to a slow, clear French Sarah had no trouble following, even on the phone. They'd meet Wednesday at Marie-Claire's apartment.

Sarah is resisting the Métro these days. She tells herself that she just wants more exercise, it has nothing to do with the *mort aux juifs* graffiti by her stop – which is there, and stays there, and never goes away, however much Michael mutters against it. And she does need more exercise today, because she has to shake off the bad dream she had about Rose last night, something stupidly obvious, the two of them near a cliff and Rose not careful enough, Rose dancing at the edge. That willowy body in an Isadora Duncan costume of some sort, gauzy white, paying too much attention to music that only Rose could hear, paying no attention to the cliff. Corny and obvious and terrifying. The worst part about it was that Sarah was furious with Rose, she'd shouted at her, *I've been trying my whole life to live and you want to die.*

She's still rattled by the call to Winnipeg though she has to believe that things will get better, that some day Rose will be herself again, her sunny, serene self. But she needs to walk. She takes the route to Marie-Claire's that goes along the Seine, where the water seems to calm her thoughts, then crosses at Pont Royal to follow rue du Bac almost to Boulevard Saint-Germain. She likes the feeling that she's walking Paris into her bones. It's hot, probably hot in Winnipeg too, though in their phone call back at Laura's apartment, they didn't talk about the weather. There's not much in the way of shade on this route, but there is a bit of a breeze off the river.

She gets to Marie-Claire's apartment building early, so she distracts herself by window-shopping the pâtisseries and pharmacies. Why are there so many pharmacies in Paris? It probably takes a lot of beauty products to keep all these French women soignée. She can hear Laura wisecracking about the cost of Parisian beauty. Laura's looks always seem effortless, but there has to be some work involved in all that sophisticated understatement. Rose is so beautiful but she doesn't ever seem to have to go to any fuss about it. She doesn't even seem to wear make-up, maybe a little lipstick when she goes out someplace special.

And now Marie-Claire is here, on the sidewalk, apologizing in French for being late (*we will speak only in French, all right?*) though she isn't late at all. She is indeed soignée, very kempt, if that's a word. A bit older than Sarah, very blonde too, just slightly heavy, and looking somewhat schoolmarmish in a tweedy skirt that touches her knees and a single strand of pearls under the collar of her pale green blouse. They walk across the courtyard, the clip clop of Marie-Claire's heels echoing. "We wear these shoes so the men will know that we're coming, to attract their attention, no?"

Sarah doesn't own a pair of heels.

It takes a moment for Marie-Claire to open the door, the lock is clearly tricky. It's quite dim inside, but she doesn't switch on any lights and the windows are heavily curtained. Despite the gloom, Sarah can see that the apartment goes on and on. It must be ten, fifteen times the size of their little place on François Miron. They have to step around heaps of papers stacked almost waist high on the scuffed parquet floors. Similar heaps are scattered over the dusty antique desks, at least three ornate desks in the one room they cross. She's never seen an apartment this size in Paris, never imagined such an apartment could exist here.

"I must apologize for the condition of the apartment. It's one of my father's properties, and he sometimes works here still, so I am not to disturb anything." Marie-Claire shrugs, that classic Gallic shrug. How to explain inexplicable French parents, especially to a somewhat rough-around-the-edges Canadian?

One of her father's properties? How is it that Marie-Claire is so short on funds, then, if she's living in one of her father's properties? Sarah can't imagine Marie-Claire ever having a minimum-wage job shovelling compost or digging weeds. Maybe 'short on funds' means something else in Paris – being able to afford only one bottle of champagne a week, real champagne of course, not that ersatz Spanish stuff... Is this apartment Marie-Claire's terroir? Has she soaked the dust and faded respectability and gilded exhaustion into her bones?

They sit at a slightly brighter corner of one of the rooms, on sofas across from each other, and Marie-Claire offers a chocolate from a box that is open on the elaborate coffee table. Sarah can't help but feel that the chocolates themselves must be dusty, and she can't bring herself to accept one, though she's hungry as always. The lesson begins with Sarah's imperfect r's, and then continues on to polishing her vowels, which aren't quite what they're supposed to be, though they're not bad at all, not at all. Sarah does want her vowels polished, she wants to be better at what she knows she's already pretty good at, but still something in her is reminded of her worst days at Hebrew school, the shame of being wrong, shrinking because she's gotten something wrong which must be corrected, something wrong by which God Himself will be offended.

At the end of the lesson, speaking in English as a reward, Marie-Claire tells Sarah that she's done very well, she's already made excellent progress.

When Sarah sets up another lesson for next week – she feels obliged to do two lessons at least – Marie-Claire smiles, tells Sarah that she is so very pleased that Laura introduced them. Might they follow up on Laura's suggestion that the three girls meet up for drinks this Friday, say 6:00, and perhaps then Michael, and Marie-Claire's beau, Henri, will join them afterwards, for dinner? That would be so pleasant. She would love to have further conversation, in French of course, Laura speaks so beautifully, and Sarah will have a chance to demonstrate how well she's already doing.

⁊

Laura teases Sarah until she agrees to have their Friday drinks with Marie-Claire at the bar at the Ritz in Place Vendôme. The people-watching is stupendous, well worth the price of admission of one stupidly expensive drink. Laura promises that they won't need to buy more than one drink. *Pretty pretty please?* Sarah can't say no. It's very hard to say no to Laura, who says yes to so much.

The Ritz. Sarah can't really believe it's a real place; it seems like another fairy tale from her mom's black-and-white late-night TV movies. *Puttin' on the Ritz.* Fred Astaire tap dancing in a top hat and tails. She can hear Pat humming along with the silly, sparkly tune, Rose joining in with her fine soprano, adding a few tap-dance steps to match Astaire.

Sarah walks into the quiet of the glittering lobby and is immediately, politely, accosted by a groomed officiary. Can he help her? When Sarah starts to explain, her French stumbling, that she's meeting some friends at the bar, before she can complete the sentence the man smiles, replying in English that the bar is just to her left. She nods, smiles back, taking the requisite left and then stands, immediately hesitant, at the entrance, wondering when the next interrogation will begin, when she'll next be identified as an imposter. What on earth is she doing at the Ritz? She can't help fidgetting as she waits for someone to come up, probably to inform her that she's improperly dressed and must leave immediately. Is she standing in the right place? Has she done something wrong yet again? Why isn't Laura here to rescue her? Sarah turns and sees an elegant man just ahead of her poised at the periphery of the bar itself. The maître d'? She touches his arm and, in shaky French, explains again that she's joining two friends.

A look of shock registers just for a moment on the man's face, and then is supplanted by a broad smile that he quickly covers with a more subdued polite one. "I am terribly sorry, Mademoiselle," he says in lightly accented English. "I'm afraid I don't work here." The broad smile breaks out again, then is again immediately suppressed. The maître d' hurries up, as though his social antennae have detected the faux pas as it is occurring, and he hustles Sarah to an oval table close to the bar where Laura is sitting, a welcoming grin on her face. Sarah's shoulders begin to shake and when the maître d' leaves, she has to hide her face in her hands, ripples of laughter running through her. It takes a while before she finally gets over the fit and can lean in to Laura to explain what happened.

"The guy is probably president of some corporation – or maybe a count," Laura says, keeping her own voice low. They haven't dared look around to see where he's seated. "I'm bloody sure it's the first time in his life he's been mistaken for a waiter. And by a girl from the North End of Winnipeg –" Laura can't finish the sentence, she's laughing too hard, neither of them can stop themselves, though they do manage to keep the volume down.

"I put it on sometimes," Laura says when they've recovered.

"What?"

"That hauteur, that eyebrow-cocked look, so you get good service. I remember the first time I tried it here in Paris, setting my shoulders back, looking faintly irritated. The waiter couldn't hustle over to me fast enough, *oui, Mademoiselle,* what could he do for me, where would I like to sit? I just took on that self and it worked. Instead of the *golly-gee, don't trouble yourself with me, I'm from Saskatoon* self. I just hope I can shuck this bit off when I need to, when I go home."

"Will you go home?"

"I always think I will. Not necessarily home to Saskatoon, but Canada, yes. But not soon. Not till I've conquered Paris." Laura raises her glass. She's joking, but she's not. Sarah wants Laura to win, to learn everything she wants to learn, take on whatever self she'd like to take on. It doesn't mean she has to erase Tobago and Saskatoon.

By the time Marie-Claire joins them, twenty minutes late, Sarah has made Laura promise, *cross your heart and hope to die*, not to tell Marie-Claire about her blunder, though Sarah's dying to tell Michael all the gory details.

The drinks have been served, and Laura and Marie-Claire are chatting away in rapid French. Sarah is back to feeling out of place and under-dressed amid the red velvet and polished wood panelling, the sleek hush and murmur of the place. Marie-Claire is decked out in a slightly fussy but impeccable outfit, and Laura is her usual understated fashionable self. Sarah has on the new *frock* – she can't think of it as anything but a *frock* – that Laura helped her buy. They'd gone shopping together, and Laura spotted a dress in creamy cotton with a pattern of poppies scattered over it, the waist nipped in for a full skirt. "Here you go. Gorgeous. This dress actually gives you some curves, who'd a thunk it?" Laura told her when Sarah tried it on.

They're carefully sipping their kir and Sarah is gobbling the dishes of olives and nuts set on their little table. She's starving, as usual. The waiter has already come by once to quickly refill the nut dish, smiling widely and kindly at her, and she can't remember if he's the one who witnessed her gaffe at the entrance. Surely the *bon chic bon genre* clientele endlessly obliterate the memory of the endlessly lesser beings these waiters come across… She hasn't been paying attention to the conversation and she needs to, because Marie-Claire is saying something in French about *les juifs*.

Mort aux juifs.

Of course that's not what Marie-Claire has said.

"Sarah, dear, have you done the complete tour?" Marie-Claire asks in French. "Of the Marais? It's very colourful, very charming, if a bit insalubrious."

Sarah shakes her head.

"I know Michael's been bugging you about seeing the Pletzl," Laura says. "I do think you might like it."

Sarah hasn't yet been to the Pletzl, the correct term Laura gave them for Michael's 'Pretzel.' The first synagogue in Paris was built in the Pletzl; a famous yeshiva was based there way back in the twelfth century.

Marie-Claire nods. "The square's actual name is Place Saint-Paul, but since the late nineteenth century, when it became a centre of Jewish immigration, people have been calling it the Pletzl. Diminutive of *place* or *square*. From the German of course."

"There are these neat little shops packed with menorahs and mezuzahs, souvenirs from Israel, that kind of stuff," Laura says. "And there's that famous deli. The restaurant owner – Rosenberg's, I think it's called – his family were Holocaust survivors." Laura takes a nut from the dish. Pauses. "I don't know if you've already looked this up, Sarah, but I've read that over half the Jewish population of the Marais was deported and died in concentration camps during the war." Laura polishes off her kir, takes a look over at Marie-Claire.

Marie-Claire sighs. "What you don't mention is that three-quarters of the Jewish population in France survived the Occupation. That is the other side of the statistics. But is it necessary, so many years later, to dwell on the experiences of the war?"

Sarah can understand perfectly every word that Marie-Claire says, her enunciated, polished French honed by the years she's given lessons to visiting Anglophones. Sarah looks over to Laura, who is grimacing into her empty glass, who seems uncomfortable in her seat.

Marie-Claire nibbles at one of the olives, places the bald pit in its special receptacle. "I know it was very sad, Sarah." She touches Sarah's arm, a light stroke. "And of course *you're* not one of those types." She's using the informal *tu*; she explained to Sarah that since the language classes are being given on a casual basis, there's no need to maintain teacher-pupil etiquette and use the formal *vous*. Their primary relationship is social, so the *tu* is just fine, completely appropriate. Sarah felt vaguely honoured as well as miffed. "It is just that there are others, certain people who feel they must go on about the war, how they suffered. The other night I was having dinner with a friend at Dominique's, a truly lovely Russian restaurant. The cuisine was delightful, but sadly, the dinner was ruined by the clientele. The place was just full of those people, very noisy, very rude, people elbowing past our table. They were so loud I could hardly think, much less enjoy my meal." Marie-Claire stops to cover her ears as a demonstration. "Where are people's manners? It makes one very uncomfortable. Sarah, really, don't you find that these types – the hostility and aggression – it's unpleasant, no? No wonder we have such a hard time getting used to this continual intrusion into civil society."

"What did you say? Civil society? I don't understand," Sarah asks.

"I'm sorry, Sarah. Yes, *civil society*. I'll try to speak more slowly."

"No, no, you don't need to translate, that's not what I meant. I'm astonished," *étonné*, the word *étonné* comes to Sarah, "I can't, I don't understand how you can be so harsh..." She needs the French for harsh – *sévère*, "so harsh speaking of people you know nothing about."

"But really, Sarah," Marie-Claire is smiling still, "I have so many dear friends who are Jews. And of course there's *chère* Laura, who is so very special..."

Laura is drumming her fingers on the table. "Marie-Claire, *really*..." She looks ready to pounce.

Marie-Claire sighs, shrugs. "I suppose they must feel they were badly treated. But really, there is no excuse for their behaviour now. They have developed a certain style of complaining, very elaborate. They are aggrieved, in a permanent fashion, and perhaps this is where the rudeness comes from."

Grossièreté, this is the word Marie-Claire is using, the French filtering into Sarah's brain. Grossness, rudeness, the crude consistency of these loud Jewish voices, unpleasant Jewish thoughts.

"Especially," Marie-Claire continues, "when you think how well you people have done since the war, your successes everywhere – banking, the press, entertainment – well, you see, it is very hard to be tolerant of this continuous grumbling on top of the rudeness."

"But," Sarah is searching for the words in French, "but the Jews *were* treated badly in France, from what I've read. As Laura says. The deportations –"

"Sarah, it was the Nazis, not us, who deported the Jews. The Gestapo. You exaggerate. You always exaggerate, *Cherie*." She's switched from *tu* to *vous*: *Vous exagérez toujours*. The plural, not the formal. *All you people exaggerate*. She strokes Sarah's arm again. Sarah involuntarily flexes, her bicep twitching. "You're such a strong little thing," Marie-Claire laughs. "And what about the Resistance fighters who sacrificed their lives to save all those Jews?"

Laura, who has kept opening and then closing her mouth, at last has the chance to say something in French that Sarah can't quite follow. "Pardon?" Sarah asks in English. "What was that, the raffle of the *velodive?*"

Laura answers in brisk English. "I was talking to Marie-Claire about *la rafle du Vél' d'Hiv*. *Vél' d'Hiv* is short for Vélodrome d'Hiver, the Winter Velodrome. It was a stadium for bicycle races. Not far from the Eiffel Tower."

"Yes, yes," Marie-Claire says. "They took it down in the late 1950s, I think."

"There was a raffle there?" Sarah asks. Were they raffling off bicycles? What does this have to do with French anti-Semitism during the war?

"*Rafle* means *round-up* or *raid*, something like that," Laura explains, her mouth working. "This is in fact an established event during the war; no one, Marie-Claire, no one questions that it happened. Though you don't hear much about it in so-called *polite circles*." She looks at Marie-Claire. "Jewish civilians were arrested en masse. During the Occupation. 1942, I'm pretty sure."

"I don't believe they were French," Marie-Claire says. "They were foreign nationals."

"My understanding is that many long-term residents who were Jewish weren't in fact allowed to become citizens. People were kept in the Vélodrome under barbaric conditions," Laura says. "I've heard only bits and pieces because it's been very nicely hushed up. I need to learn the full story." Laura's still drumming her fingers on the table.

"Is that so? I really don't know anything at all about that incident, whatever it was," Marie-Claire says in French, gently pressing on Laura's hand so the drumming stops. "Once again, people do tend to exaggerate, you know?" She smiles lightly at a passing waiter.

"How do you spell that?" Sarah asks in English. She's done with French.

"Spell what?" Marie-Claire asks.

"*La rafle du Vél' d'Hiv.* I'll look it up."

Marie-Claire takes a pen out of her purse, carefully prints the words on a paper napkin, ever the instructor, hands it to Sarah with a gentle flourish. "Soon my little student will be teaching the history of Paris to me."

Sarah fingers the napkin, reads Marie-Claire's elegant hand: *la rafle du Vél' d'Hiv. Vélodrome d'Hiver.*

Mort aux juifs. The *grossièreté* of the mannerless *juifs*, their intrusion into civil society.

She doesn't want to be here. "I have to go," she says.

"But we were going to order another kir," Marie-Claire says.

"I'm sorry," Sarah says, picking up her purse. Why is she apologizing? Gail wouldn't apologize. Michael wouldn't apologize. Every other sentence she says is an apology. *Non, rien de rien. Non, je ne regrette rien.*

Marie-Claire stands, pecks her on each cheek. Sarah doesn't return the pecks.

"I haven't upset you?" Marie-Claire asks.

Sarah can feel her cheeks hot. She hardly ever blushes.

"You are very sensitive," Marie-Claire says, touching Sarah's shoulder. "Perhaps we can talk about this again?"

Sarah shakes her head, walks away. She can feel someone following her.

"Sarah?" It's Laura. She catches up with Sarah, reaches for her elbow. "It's crap, Sarah. I'm so sorry. I didn't think she'd go off like that, though she has bloody done it before, just not about Jews. I'll talk with her."

"It's okay, Laura. I just don't want to see her again. I'll send her a note. I don't need lessons from her."

"Of course not. I understand. I'm sorry…"

It's not Laura's fault. Marie-Claire is the one who owns these opinions. *Those types who are so very hostile and aggressive. Those people. Those people who exaggerate things. Those people who were not treated badly.* Marie-Claire, who owns her proud heritage, her endless apartment full of rubbish. The history of Paris.

Sarah walks out into Place Vendôme. A couple get out of their chauffeur-driven black Mercedes, head up the red carpet into the hotel. Behind them, a man in uniform is brushing invisible bits of trash into an elaborate mono-grammed dustpan. The Ritz. How does *he* feel about the Ritz, how much is he earning working at the Ritz? She doesn't even know what minimum wage is here in Paris. And what on earth is she doing at the Ritz, what is she doing in Paris? What does she want from this city?

Right now what she wants is to walk away. Walk it off. This is what her tough body can do for her, take her places she wants to go, let her leave places where she doesn't want to be. Place Vendôme. She doesn't want to be here. This ornate, artificial glitter. She walks quickly down the short block to rue Saint Honoré, then down rue Royale to the Métro station, heads down the stairs. Concorde is big and she's not paying attention, forgets which Métro line she's looking for. The floors down here are made of some hideous grey-black material – is it cement? – a colour that seems as if it were itself just the product of decades of grime. The walls are plastered with ugly shit-brown ceramic frames for the movie ads, the shampoo, department store ads, as if the idiotic ads were works of art.

She's down on a platform, starts to sit on one of the harsh, inhospitable plastic seats that discourage, no, make it impossible for anyone to stretch out and sleep on them. As if anyone would want to sleep in the Métro. Unless they had no other place to sleep. Enormous steel beams support the ceiling, the machinery of the Métro made clear. How far down has she gone? She loses all sense of direction, depth, when she's in the Métro. As she hears the train approaching she suddenly realizes that she's at the wrong platform, waiting for the wrong train. She gets off her awkward chair, heads down a tunnel, up a set of stairs but she's not heading for the right line, and she can't see any signage at all to tell her where to go. That doesn't make sense, why can't she find any signs? She has the feeling she's going the wrong way down one-way hallways, but that can't be right, the corridors aren't one-way.

She goes down another flight of stairs, the station feeling empty except for herself, comes around another corner and sees a young man her age pressed up against the wall, she doesn't understand why. He looks quickly left and right, doesn't seem to see her. He's loosened his filthy trousers, his filthy duffle bag is at his feet and as she approaches, she understands that he's pissing against the wall. He doesn't turn around, doesn't look at her, but she can feel the shame radiating out from him, or is it her. She has to get home.

Laila

The streets are wide and almost empty. No crowds, no tourists. Not here. Just sun on the broad pavement. Quiet. Streets that are big and beautiful and clean. I'm done cleaning. Not at the office building now, Agnès got tired of me, I was late one time, she said she didn't have any more work, not for me. Now it's Mme Dupont I work for, here in this quiet part of Paris. Mme Dupont's apartment is clean in the clean sunlight that comes through the clean windows. Because of me. My hands running a dust-rag over the polished wood, my hands wiping the counters down, drying them off so there are no streaks. Scrubbing down the sinks in both bathrooms, changing the towels, straightening them so they hang just so; the tap, the faucets polished so they shine. I do good work. Mme Dupont wants me back next week. *Merci Madame.* Mme Dupont hasn't asked me what happened to my face, just told me I do good work. *Merci Madame.* But no pay in my pocket today, no white envelope. I have to come back for it next week. She says. She forgot to go to the bank. Last week it was M. Dupont who tucked the folded bills into my back jeans pocket with his nasty clean fingers. *There you go*, in my ear, in French, his fingers resting on my money, my pocket. No M. Dupont today. Will he be there next week? Maybe next week it will be Mme Dupont again. Mme Dupont will give me my francs, two days' pay. My pay, in a fresh white envelope.

No pay, no money for the bus or the Métro. The street is so wide. No pay, so I'm walking across the empty city to get back to our room. You haven't given me any of my francs back, Khalil, you need them to pay for the room. You say. No money so I have to walk. I'm so light. Wings a blur, that dizzy hum. If I try a little harder, I'll float above the sidewalk. My head a balloon tied to my body by a string, the string thinned, ready to break. I ate yesterday, lunch, soup and bread. When I came into the big apartment this morning, Mme Dupont was drinking coffee, finishing a *pain au chocolat*. The smell of coffee in the room, the smell of butter, chocolate. I had to wipe my mouth. In her kitchen I washed everything, wiped down every shelf in her refrigerator. Moved the food from shelf to shelf to clean but didn't taste. Just the smell.

I'm following the wide street, walking back to our room. Maybe an hour to get there, maybe more, and my head a balloon. You won't be there. You're working. You say. At your business. I'll have to wait for you on the sidewalk, my head swollen. I don't have a key. All this light, for me. I pass a café where people are drinking their coffee in small white cups and eating pretty bits of food. I pass a grocer's where chickens are turning on a spit and I have to smell the smell of crisp brown skin. I pass a crêpe stand where I'm waylaid by a buttery, sugary, caramel smell. I stall and then move on, pass a bakery and it's here that the smell of bread just baked comes into my mouth. The smell, but no bread. I don't have the key.

The smell of bread in my mouth makes me dizzy. I have to sit for a minute on the curb of the sidewalk here. My head so light, it's going to fly away. People sidestep me. A dirty little Arab, skinny little Arab they don't want to touch. Even though my clothes smell of sweat, even though I know I smell of sweat from carrying the bucket and mop up the back stairs, I know that inside I'm clean. My hands are clean. The smell of soap on my hands from washing Madame's delicate things. She doesn't want them put in the washing machine, it has so many bright dials. She trusts me. With her delicate things. I like touching them, burgundy and lace, chocolate peau de soie. I like touching them. Nobody going by on this bright street wants to touch me.

I close my eyes, sitting on the curb, hold my head so it doesn't float away. That dizzy hum. And then a man leans over me, what does he want, I open my eyes, an older man, he's asking me something in French, his voice soft, am I sick, I think that's what he's asking me. I shake my head. He smells like cigarettes. He smells like my father. Creases around his eyes. His face is sad. Am I all right, he's asking, and his hand is at my elbow, he's helping me to a bench in the shade, sit here, I think he's saying, and he's gone and then he comes back with a bottle of water. It's hot outside, he says in French. I must be tired, he says in French. Am I all right? I nod. He starts to go, then stops, very quietly reaches into his pocket and quietly puts some bills in my hand, francs. My hand, not my pocket. I want to say no, but he's already gone, he doesn't want to be thanked, doesn't want anything from me. I must be tired, he said.

I drink all the water. Nobody is looking at me here in the shade where it's cooler. I close my eyes again, open them. There's a little grocery store across the street, a cooler with soft drinks on the sidewalk in front of it, fruit set out on a stand, grapes, melons, bananas. I go into the store, open my hand, show them the bills. My other hand resting on the counter, holding me up. *May I have some bread*, I ask in French, and the man looks up from his paper, which tells him Beirut is on fire. He looks up at me. A young man. His face also is sad. He puts his hands on the counter too, as if his hands were thinking. Then he turns away, his face sad, his back my brother's back, blue cotton of his shirt, blue sky above my house. He takes a loaf of bread in a plastic bag, a chocolate bar, a bag of peanuts. *Assalamu alaikum.* Peace be with you, he says, in Arabic. Peace be with you. Softly he folds my fingers into a fist. The money is still in my hand.

HISTORY

THE DREAM COMES BACK. The night after drinks at the Ritz with Laura and Marie-Claire. Again she's awake but not awake, eyes open but not able to move. Glass breaking, boots coming up the stairs, people shouting, pounding on the door, shouting orders. Outside the room the sound of motors and trucks, the awful barking of dogs. Why is she remembering something that didn't happen to her? The thing pressing on her chest. Somehow she knows Michael is breathing beside her. The dream won't stop. Finally she must have called out, because he rolls over beside her, wraps his arm around her, almost asleep, muttering, *you okay?* No. But his arm around her moves her out from the nightmare. *Michael*, she says, and he stirs, pulls her towards him. *Michael*, she doesn't say, *save me from the dream.*

The next morning, the dream a hum at the back of her mind, she's heading down to the public library in the Centre Pompidou at Place Beaubourg, ten minutes' walk from their apartment, to study history. *Histoire.* The history, the story, of Paris. What is the story of Paris? It may be that for her, Paris is a puzzle, or a test. *La rafle du Vél' d'Hiv.* The Holocaust history course taught Sarah so much but it didn't teach her this story and now she needs to know.

In the story of Paris, the Centre Pompidou, like the Eiffel Tower and Sacré Coeur, like the Eastern European Jews who took refuge here, is another unwelcome recent arrival, a newfangled building opened five years ago to general public displeasure. Covered in gaudy tubes, with a weird exoskeleton of mechanical parts like a squid or octopus with its guts on the outside, the

188

building certainly makes Sarah grumpy. The stepped plastic tube that holds the escalator looks like something that belongs on a hamster cage. Such a show-off of a building, a building that looks forwards, never back, that has no regrets. Maybe it belongs to a brave new world, a world in which *la rafle du Vél' d'Hiv* never happened. Or happened and can be ignored.

Sarah's been meaning to come to the public library here ever since Charles gave her the list of gardens; she wants to look things up, learn about the history of the parks he's suggested she visit, see some scale drawings, some old engravings that show the various stages of development. She's more and more interested in public spaces, what can happen in them. What can happen in public spaces – what was it that happened in the Vélodrome d'Hiver? That's why she's here, this is the story she needs to learn about today, not the Palais-Royal, not the Bois de Boulogne or the Tuileries.

It's clear what *can't* happen in the public space of this enormous square in front of the Centre Pompidou – it isn't made for sitting. No benches, nowhere at all to be comfortable, though people Sarah's age or young families are picnicking on the cobblestones, or perching on the concrete stumps of columns that help control traffic. Laura says the slang word for the stumps is *bîtes*, which is also slang for penis, something like *putz* or *schmuck*. Is the square meant only as a space to move through? It must be perfect for big demonstrations or for shepherding giant tour groups, but what if you're tired, what if you need to rest?

What does get to happen here? There are the usual little kids feeding the usual pigeons, and the usual pamphleteers, some of them touting shops, some political causes. No doubt the usual pickpockets. Sarah pulls her purse closer, Laura's slightly tipsy words of wisdom still in her head. Despite the few lonely-looking lindens, that amenable tree – littleleaf, by the look of them – at the western edge of the square, this is not a park, certainly not a garden. The space feels harsh, controlled, despite the fun the picnickers are clearly having, especially on a day like today, all sunshine.

There are buskers here as well, musicians playing jazz, a guy dressed up as a mime, wearing a beret and striped sailor t-shirt, tight trousers. He's got a mask over the top half of his face, an exaggerated clown face of some sort, that's vaguely frightening in its distortion. And he's very clever, walking up to people who are self-absorbed, mimicking them for the brief moment before they notice him, and startle, or shriek, and then mostly laugh, others laughing at their bemusement or fear. There's something about him Sarah doesn't like, the way he pushes into other people's spaces. So clever. She doesn't want him to come up to her, so she hustles into the building. The inside is the inverse of the square outside, a lidded, rather than a lidless, giant box. It feels slightly less unfriendly than the square, but there's still no place to sit: you must never be tired at the Centre Pompidou. She lets herself be taken up the short escalator ride to the library and she's soon absorbed in the quiet, the public privacy of its reading rooms.

It takes a while, but eventually she finds a few references. The librarian helps her find more articles, points out other possibilities. Sarah starts reading painstakingly through the French sources. It's hard to find much, just as Laura predicted, though Sarah does learn that the round-up at the Vélodrome d'Hiver, which happened on July 16 and 17, 1942, was part of one of the largest operations against Jews by the Vichy government, and it was mostly hushed up. Marie-Claire was wrong: the Gestapo weren't directly involved. The operation was led by the French police and by officials who were working with the Parti Populaire Français, a French fascist organization, to round up thousands of Jewish civilians, mostly women and children, many of them living in the neighbourhood around the Pletzl. The neighbourhood she now wants to visit, to be able to imagine how this story unwound. Because something real happened there. People, civilians were taken away, held in the Vélodrome and then deported to Auschwitz. The sources note the Vichy government's 'enthusiasm.'

To ensure compliance, the government officials recommended that only foreign nationals be included in the round-up. So Marie-Claire was right about that. But Laura was also right: many of the 'foreign nationals' had in fact lived in France for decades, but hadn't been able to become citizens. The decision was made to round up children as well, to avoid 'unpleasant scenes' when they were separated from their parents. There were Parisians who applauded as their neighbours were herded into busses. There were concierges who looted empty Jewish apartments. *Collaboration.* It's the same in French and English. A word the French don't like. Would Marie-Claire have been one of the ones applauding as *those people* were taken away? There were Parisians who did help: church leaders, journalists, even some of the police officers involved in the round-up. Prof. Koenig would want Sarah to determine the numbers, objective evidence, and she finds them: 4,115 children, 2,916 women, 1,129 men. They were held for up to seven days, they were given next to no food, no water, next to no access to the restrooms. She finds no record of an apology, no claim of responsibility by the French government after the war. *Rien de rien.*

What she does find is a photograph of a family: the father in his dark suit and tie, his face under the fedora obscured in shadow, a yellow star stitched to his jacket pocket; two little girls who remind Sarah of photos of her mother when she was a girl, one in a neat plaid skirt cut fashionably on the bias, her hairband tidy. It's hard to see in the print, but it looks like the mother is bent over beside the bleacher, probably reaching for some food she packed. Yes, it's the mother, there's a patch of light caught on the back of her hair, one hand. The dark cloth of her coat. One strand of light. Their little brother is in his suit jacket with his yellow star stitched to the left breast pocket, bedrolls on the bench beside them, one, two, three, four, five, one each. A wooden horse on the bench as well, just within reach. He looks to be about five or six. It's probably his favourite toy, the one he decided to take with him.

Who took the picture? And how did it get into the book? There's nothing in the caption that gives the names of the family. She wishes she knew their names. That would help. It wouldn't help them but it would help her.

She closes her books, puts them on a trolley to be shelved.

When she comes out of the Centre Pompidou she notices for the first time the graceful, welcoming slope of the plaza. This space built so many years after those thousands of people, women, children, men, were taken away to the Vél' d'Hiv so they could be forgotten. Such a big space, where only certain things can happen, where no one can rest. Another Paris.

Laila

I'm not going anywhere. I'm going nowhere, one step at a time, down the grubby concrete steps, to breathe the unbreathable air. A dirt-coloured floor, a floor that could be made of dirt. The Métro platform empty except for me, empty with me, alone with its dirt, its ugly plastic seats. Mme Dupont's money is in my pocket, two days' work. I came into her apartment and his face was on the television, the Prime Minister of Israel, Begin. A photo of him, a man with the mouth of a frog, the eyes of a frog. And a map of Israel and Lebanon – no Palestine, for them there is no Palestine – with cut-out soldiers, Israeli soldiers, cardboard heroes. Then footage of the battle, first the sound of missiles, a sound like the rush of wind around the wadi by my house. And then machine-gun fire, *dit-dit-dat, dit-dit-dat-dat, rat-a-tat-tat*, a cartoon noise. Mme Dupont got up, turned the television off. She had things to do. She wants me to come back next week again. I do a good job, she says, I'm a good girl. Because I'm a good girl and do a good job, she has a friend, Mme LeBlanc, who wants me to work for her too, tomorrow. Mme LeBlanc, an older lady who needs help, who might need me to work for her every week. More work is what I need, Mme Dupont says.

I need you, Khalil. You're gone, I don't know where. I don't have a key to the room. I ask M. Laval, the man who rents us the room, to let me in, he says why don't I have my own key, why didn't you leave me a key, where did you go? He can't let me in if you haven't given me the key, it's you he's renting the room to, you're the one who pays the rent. I give you money for the rent, I tell him, I give you almost all my money. Why don't I have a key then, he asks me. He shuts the door in my face, shouts at me to go away, leave him alone, who do I think I am, disturbing him like this, while he's eating his dinner? The smell of beef stew coming through the door, the sound of his voice.

Only you can let me in. I don't count.

I count Mme Dupont's money in my pocket, enough for food but not for a place to sleep. Where can I sleep? I think about the pillars covered with posters for movies on the kiosks with their onion-dome turrets. I could take some of my francs and pay for a ticket, sleep in the movie theatre, sleep somewhere clean. But if I slept there, who would find me, what would they do when they found me?

When we first came to Paris you told me that there were places in the Métro to hide, blind spots, dead spots. You told me that was where you took your business. That was where you took your duffle bag, sorted through what was left to sell, no one could see what you had, take what you had. Blind spots, dead spots, that's where you'd catch a quick nap, take a piss, no one could see. Though sometimes someone would catch you, by mistake. But there were places, you said. Maybe today there's a place for me, a place to sleep.

I don't know where you are.

Everything you do is by mistake.

I sit on one of the ugly chairs but there's no place to lie down, no place in Paris where I can sleep. I have to go to work tomorrow for Mme LeBlanc, the white lady, but there's no place for me to sleep. I want to do good, I want to do a good job, earn my keep. But how can I work if I don't get any sleep? Thick steel beams above my head, the machinery of the Métro on display. I have to find a blind spot, a dead spot, down a tunnel, up a set of stairs, but there aren't any signs to tell me where to go because I'm going nowhere, going the wrong way down one-way halls.

And then I find my little nowhere, a hidden corner down an empty hallway and I must fall asleep for a while because I have the dream again, the one I dream too often. You aren't there. I go for water, I have the plastic jugs with me. My brother's friend comes up as I'm going home beside the wadi, the jugs are heavy with water. He says hello, polite, my brother's friend, and he walks beside me, can he carry the water jugs, can he help? Yes, I say, thank you. The jugs are heavy. He wants to help. When we've walked to a place that is empty, a place where no one else is, he changes. Pulling my arm. *Let go*, I say, *no*, but he doesn't let go. *No*, I say, *no*. Pulling me behind an empty building. And when I start to scream, I won't let him do this to me, I'll scream and someone will come, he takes the knife out of his coat pocket. A kitchen knife, ordinary, the kind my mother uses to slice sweet circles from oranges. He holds the knife against my throat and then I'm quiet. He hits and hits me and then he's inside me and it hurts. He says words to me that I don't want to remember, they're that sharp.

And when he's done, more words and then he pulls the knife across my cheek. I can feel a wetness and I know it's the blood emptying out of me.

It isn't a dream. I dream it tonight in Paris, but it isn't a dream. It doesn't happen in Paris. It doesn't happen in my country. I've never seen my country. The Jews took it away.

It's them who cut my cheek.

They took my country, made my father leave so I had to live in the place where my brother's friend raped me and cut my cheek.

I've never met a Jew.

I met my brother's friend and he raped me and cut my cheek.

DINNER

FROM HER TABLE AT THE *traiteur chinois* Sarah watches an old woman slowly cross the street. She's hunched like a narrow question mark inside her leopard-skin coat in the warm evening, wearing a brimmed hat with a veil, labouring her frail way with her wobbly bundle-buggy. A bag-lady, they'd call her at home, as if what weighs her down identifies her. Head down, intent, she just misses being levelled by a bus heading down rue de Rivoli. Sarah sees a brief rage quickly suppressed on the driver's face. He doesn't even honk, probably doesn't want to startle the woman as she plods ahead. *Civil society.* The bus driver must somehow recognize the woman as a fellow citizen, and so worthy of his civility.

The Formica table smells of vinegar, the waiter has just wiped it down, gathering every crumb. A middle-aged man in a rumpled white shirt is standing at the cash, waiting for his take-out as the cashier piles the wire-handled cardboard cartons into a brown paper bag. It's only 6:30, but Sarah's starving as usual. Michael said he wouldn't be home till after 9:00, so she's eating alone. She's come to the *traiteur* to feed up on nostalgia as well as wonton soup – the last time she had Chinese was Gail's apartment. She'll order honey garlic ribs and beef with broccoli in black bean sauce, Gail's standard order, in her honour.

An older woman, perhaps in her mid-seventies, is seated at a table across from Sarah. When she catches Sarah glancing at her, the woman looks back with quiet disdain. Sarah looks away, but she has taken in the woman's stolid solid stout form, her cardigan, the distinguished wooden cane one hand closes austerely over. The woman's skirt goes unfashionably to mid-calf, her thick ankles end in grave, sombre shoes. Sarah can imagine her wearing the same outfit a decade ago, a decade from now, immutable, unmoveable. She seems Parisian through and through. What would it be like to really live here, to live here so long she grew old here? What would it be like to live her life in another language? Would she be a permanent foreigner, a 'foreign national' like the Jews who were rounded up in 1942, or would she be able to become a part of *civil society*, the real thing, Parisian?

And now yet another old woman has come into the *traiteur*, a desiccated, bird-like woman, who, though she's elegantly dressed in a light-weight cream blouse and narrow cream skirt, seems more than half starved, the grim corners of her mouth turned permanently downwards. She hesitates in the doorway, peering round for a seat. Something familiar about her. Then Sarah spots the dog at her feet, a little spaniel whose floppy ears are tinged grey against the white of its fur, its tail swaying eagerly. It's the woman Sarah saw in silhouette walking her dog on Rue des Barres that night she was startled out of sleep with the waking dream, the first time she had the dream in Paris. The waiter nods the woman to an empty table. She carefully picks her way to it, steadies herself on its surface as she sits herself down, the little dog at her feet, no rules against dogs in Paris restaurants. The woman must live in the neighbour-hood.

Sarah rests her chopsticks on the plate; she's already made a big dent in the beef with broccoli. Yesterday she was at the Post Office trying to reach Rose. When she couldn't get through, she found herself asking the operator to dial Gail's number. Listening to the empty rings, she tried to imagine her sister's voice, what they'd say to each other. How many weeks now since they've spoken? She doesn't even know if there's any fight left between them, whether it's just a residue, a sediment of resentment building up, making it harder and harder to pick up the thread. When the ringing finally stopped and Gail's recorded voice told her to leave a message, all she could think of was a feeble, *It's Sarah, I'll try later.*

Maybe she should call now. She takes the penny from her pocket, flips it into the air, turns it over on the table. *No.* The penny says no. But suddenly Sarah doesn't care what the penny says. She's so tired of being a stranger. She's hungry for family. She can't wait, she has to hear her sister's voice. She'll try a pay phone, keep ringing till Gail has to pick up. She polishes off the rest of the food, goes to the register to count out her francs. She's being careful; she doesn't want to have to borrow from Michael. Even with the expense of the presents, that one drink at the Ritz, her share of the food costs, her savings should hold out. She sees a public phone just across the street, its windows smeared with graffiti. If she's lucky, it will actually work and she'll be able to talk to Gail, at the very least hear how Gail thinks Rose is doing.

When Sarah picks up the greasy earphone, she's surprised to hear a dial tone. She listens to the thunk as the coins drop, flips her penny inside her pocket as she waits for the line to connect.

"Hello?" Gail picks up almost immediately.

"Gail, can you hear me? It's Sarah."

"Sarah. Wow. Are you in Paris?"

"Yeah, I'm in a phone booth not far from my apartment." A bus snorts and chuffs down the street. She closes the door against the noise, against any bit of breeze as well. "It's a bit noisy here, the traffic, can you hear me?"

"It's loud, but I can."

"Did you get my postcards?"

"Yeah. Did you get mine?"

She can hear Gail slurping coffee. "I did. Very funny. Do you know how Rose is doing?" Sarah asks. "I spoke with Mom a while back and she sounded worried." The couple of brief letters that Sarah has had from Pat since the call have been noncommittal, and she needs to hear what Gail has to say.

More coffee-drinking sounds. "Yeah, I guess you know we've been worried because she seemed down again. The docs changed her meds, and we just have to hang in there, see if it works. They think she might be perking up a bit, these last couple of days."

"Is that what Mom says?"

"Yeah. Mom *and* Dad. And I spoke with Rose yesterday."

"You did!"

"Yeah. I did. It's not hard, Sarah. I picked up the phone. You could too."

Except that she doesn't have a phone. Except for the time difference. Except that she did call. "I tried calling her from here yesterday but she wasn't home. I called you too. I left a message on your machine."

"Damn. I didn't know. I never check my machine."

"Well, I don't have a phone here anyways." *Anyways.* Why is just talking to Gail rattling her like this? "So how was she, Gail, what did she say?"

"Well, she didn't talk for long. Then David got on the phone."

"What did he say?"

"He said the doctors told them that the new meds seem better, but the dosage still probably needs tweaking. She's had some nasty side effects, appetite loss, which isn't great because she's so thin already."

Her big sister even thinner. That slip of a girl, fingernail paring. Moon crescent waning.

"That's too bad."

"Look, we just have to wait it out. Eventually they'll get it adjusted right. Look – really, she's pretty stable. The setbacks are minor. She's at home, not in the Psych ward. Just stop worrying so much and go back to eating croissants or whatever it is you're doing there."

Clicks and buzzes on the line and then an unintelligible mechanical voice says something in French.

"Gail? Gail? Hang on a minute. I have to add more coins." Her hands are shaking as she fumbles in her pocket, drops the coins into the slot.

"You there?" Gail asks. The line is clear now.

"Yeah, but I don't know how many minutes I still have in my pocket. Just fill me in a bit more."

"There's no reason to get into a flap, Sarah. At least her colour's better. Mom says her colour's much better. Before we know it she'll be looking like her old beautiful self."

Another garbled interruption by the French voice.

"I think that means I have ten seconds left or something."

"Well, okay. When are you coming home?"

The line goes dead.

Sarah thinks about fishing around in her purse for more coins, but she's not sure it would do any good, another two minutes of hasty conversation with Gail. At least they spoke to each other at last. At least Gail thinks Rose is pretty much stable. *A minor setback. Minor side effects.* She'll get better. She has to get better.

Sarah's sweating in the airless booth, it's stifling, a little hothouse, but she waits a bit before hanging up, feels the weight of the handset, the weight of Gail's voice. *Go back to eating croissants or whatever it is you're doing there.* She'll walk back to the apartment, to do whatever it is she's doing here. She's gone on her own to the Palais-Royal, one of the urban gardens from Charles' list. The square is right across from the Louvre, about a twenty-minute walk from the apartment. It reminds her of Place des Vosges – another refuge in the city, another garden walled by perfect façades. She's going to write up some notes, do some decent diagrams from the sketches she made there. She has so many questions for Charles when they meet next. Whatever it is she's doing here, when she sees Charles, she wants to talk with him not just about the design of the Palais-Royal, but about going to school when she gets back to Toronto, what he thinks about it, whether it makes any sense to him. And she's starting to think about what it would be like to take on public projects, maybe work for the City. She wants to talk with Charles about that too.

When she makes it up the stairs, the apartment is cool. She's opened the door to the smell of apricots. She left a little bowlful out on the table, they didn't seem quite ripe. And now the scent is intense, essence of apricots, a smell she can almost taste. Real apricot, not the apricots they have in North America, imitations, impressions of apricots. Here in Paris food gets to be food.

And when Sarah gets back to Canada, will Rose be Rose, not some pale imitation of herself? And what will Gail be – her usual impossible self? And what will Sarah be, what will she decide at last to be?

⁓

Later that week Michael comes home earlier than usual, brings a broiled chicken from the street vendor, the room filling up with the smell of crisp brown skin. A whole chicken and roasted potatoes too. A Michael form of apology for the spat they'd had the day before. Michael had been super nervous about the dinner they'd been invited to at a famous Danish restaurant on the Champs-Élysées. They met with a group of partners from the Toronto office who'd flown in for the week, some of the local Paris lawyers too. Sarah had been specifically invited, though she wasn't quite sure why. The food was a nice change, no heavy buttery sauces, and, as Michael had promised, there was very little shop talk. Sarah was way more talkative than usual, chatting about the design of the Palais-Royal, the differences in layout as well as use between it and Place des Vosges. She'd been pretty sure she held up her end.

But in the taxi home, it turned out Michael was ticked off with her. According to him, she'd flubbed things at every point. He really needed her to brush up on her French manners. There was a whole list of offenses: when they got to the table, she just plunked herself down without waiting to be told where she was to sit; then, when the cocktails were served, she started sucking hers back before they'd had a chance to make the toast; she started eating before they said bon appétit; she used the wrong fork for the main.

Michael had told her all about these kinds of rules when they were on the subway to the restaurant, but she hadn't paid much attention. And it was all new to her. They don't eat like this at home. She doesn't know French manners. She knows Winnipeg manners: Feed people the second they walk in the door. Have at least three times as much food as anyone could possibly eat. Food first, alcohol next, if at all. Nobody in her family drinks. Keep offering more to eat no matter how many times people say no until they just give up and accept more helpings. Send everyone home with leftovers.

Winnipeg manners. There's nothing wrong with Winnipeg manners, even if this isn't Winnipeg.

She hadn't ever been to that kind of fancy schmancy dinner before. And as far as she was concerned, everybody seemed to be having a perfectly good time. Michael was the only one keeping score. When Sarah pointed this out, he seemed to settle down a bit, and she figures the broiled chicken for dinner tonight is a peace offering. Michael takes a bite or two, spears a roasted potato, then asks Sarah what she was up to today.

What *is* she up to? *Go back to eating croissants or whatever it is you're doing there.* It's fine and dandy to want more, to want to be more. And she does feel the city filling her up, feel her ideas about gardens coming into being, coming clear. But she's not sure any of it counts. All her fine new ideas, will she even be able to spit them out on paper if she does take some courses, much less make them work in her clients' suburban gardens back home? She puts down her fork. "I was at the library at Centre Pompidou. And I met with Charles; he's giving me a reading list for when I get home."

"Glad to hear it. Listen, when you do decide to take those courses, I want you to know I'm happy to bankroll you."

"You know I can't do that, let you pay for things."

"Okay, don't get on your high horse. Make it an interest-free loan. To be repaid when your business takes off."

"I want to do this on my own."

"I get that. I just want to back you any way I can. So please, don't waste the little time we have left here worrying about what you'll do when we get home."

Michael always pushing her, hand at the small of her back, nudging, prodding. "Will you stop telling me what to do? *Quit this job. Get that job. Go to school. Come here, go there, do this, pick that.* And all the while you have your own agenda."

"What's my agenda?!"

"I don't know. Having a girlfriend who follows you everywhere you go.

Who doesn't embarrass you at company dinners." She sets her napkin down. "Did anybody say anything at the office? About last night?"

He bites his lip, smiles. "About last night? Um, not anything negative. In fact, both my bosses John *and* François made a point of telling me how charming you were, how intelligent, what a lucky dog I was, etc. etc. I was urged to propose before someone else snaps you up."

A lucky dog. With a chicken in its mouth as an apology.

"It's just, look – I don't want you to feel that you don't know what the right thing to do is in those situations. I want you to feel that you're as good as anyone else. But that was just dumb," he says.

"What was?"

"Bugging you about manners nobody else was worried about." He's grinning that irresistible Michael grin. "Was coming with me to Paris really such an awful idea?"

"There have been worse ideas." Sarah grins.

"Hey, are you still taking French classes from that friend of Laura's, Marie-Claire? I asked Laura at work but she kind of skittered around the question."

"It's a long story." Part of her wants to be pissed off at him, grin or no grin, chicken dinner or no chicken dinner. But it isn't easy, not with Michael. And when she fills him in on the fiasco at the Ritz, he goes predictably ballistic, stops eating, starts pacing the room.

"Just who in the hell is this woman? And what on earth is wrong with Laura, why would she introduce you to someone like that?"

"Laura was mortified, Michael. She looked quite ready to slice Marie-Claire into bits herself."

"Yeah, well, I don't figure Laura has much patience for bigots."

"She doesn't. She told me that Marie-Claire has made that kind of remark once or twice about Black people, but that she hadn't fully twigged on to just how bad it was."

Michael's still pacing.

"Why don't you sit down and have your dinner?"

"I am starved." He sits down, settles into the remains of his meal. "Listen, Sarah, I wanted to let you know that we might iron out the last details on the contract a bit earlier than we planned, and I'm pretty sure I can take the extra time as a bit of holiday for us. Italy maybe? The South of France?"

"Sounds great. Either." Maybe they can go to Giverny, see Monet's garden.

He takes another sip of his wine. "Hey, I've got an idea –"

Before he finishes the sentence she knows what he's going to say…

"Let's go visit the Pletzl tomorrow." He's finishing off the last of the potatoes. "Otherwise we're going to run out of time. I've got an appointment nearby. Why don't you meet me in there about 12:30, 12:45? There's this deli called Rosenberg's, we could get knishes. Or we could just get a quick falafel if I'm held up and there isn't time. There are a bunch of falafel joints right nearby."

She can't help thinking about the salade niçoise she had for lunch, perfect fresh skinny green beans and tiny new potatoes, black niçoise olives, hard boiled eggs and tuna, all artfully arranged on the serving plate.

"Sarah?"

Even though she didn't come to Paris to eat bad Jewish food, she does have plenty of reasons to visit the Pletzl, the *little place* where so many *foreign national* Jews were rounded up and then sent to extermination. The place where Jewish life intrudes on *civil society*, where a different Paris can surface. She gets up, carries her plate to the sink. She doesn't need to flip the penny. *Yes.* She'll visit, figure the place out. "Sure. Sounds good."

Laila

This is what I remember. What my mother, my father, wanted for me. My mother's hands busy with the needle, the embroidery cotton, flash of that needle. Her hands reaching for mine to take me into the yard, let me hand her the sheets, the shirts and the handkerchiefs, clean and wet, and then hand her each wooden peg as she pinned them all to the line, clean against the sky where the sun would scour them white. Or we would be in the kitchen and she would tell me to go and wash my hands, I had to wash my hands first before I helped her, because in our kitchen we keep everything clean. Then she would lift me onto a chair, let me put my hands in the bowl to help make the dough, we would carry it in a pail covered with a red striped cloth to my aunt's house, to the oven she had there, to bake. My mother taught me how to eat properly with it, to tear each piece off correctly, just the right amount, I had to know where to dip my piece of bread in the serving bowl, how much it was right to take, how to cup the bread in my hand so that nothing would spill, nothing would be lost. I was learning to read and write in school, she told me, and that was good, but I had to understand that there were also things I could only learn with my hands, know with my hands.

My father would be sitting on a chair in front of our house, the blue of his cigarette smoke curling like the letters of his script, like handwriting, against the smooth white-washed walls. I'd come to him, and he'd take me on his lap, his shirt a blue like the sky. I'd ask him to tell me a story, and he'd touch the tips of his moustache, smile. What about my brother, he'd ask me, didn't he want a story too? I'd beg him to tell me, just me. I wanted a story just for me. And he'd smile again, and the story would begin, a story just for me. About Antar and Ablah, a slave and a queen. About a fool and his son and his donkey. A poor man and his seven hungry daughters, his lemon tree and his dream. About a fox and a dragon and a frog. A sparrow and a locust. About how burning can turn you back into yourself. How some day justice might come even to the poorest woman, the poorest man, if the dreams they dreamed were proper dreams, if they listened to them and waited.

And they would tell me, my mother and father, about the place I've never seen, the hills and the valleys where our fig trees grew, the taste of the ripe figs from our yard a taste you couldn't find anywhere else. Never look for flowers on the branches of a fig tree, my mother would tell me, because on a fig tree, the flowers grow inside-out, they grow like a miracle inside the fruit. Thousands of tiny flowers that give us the seeds inside the ripe fruit, it's the seeds that give taste to figs, texture. My father would tell me about waiting, about the patience needed to grow fig trees, five or six or seven years of waiting till the trees truly bore fruit, but that waiting was worthwhile because the trees can live so long. They live and bear fruit up to a hundred years, feeding us for a hundred years, if there isn't a frost, if they aren't torn down, if they aren't bulldozed or taken. On our land we had fig trees, we had trees everywhere, figs and also apricots, almond and apple trees, carob and olive trees. Fields of wheat we had, and barley, lentils, peas and beans and chickpeas. In my grandmother's garden tomatoes and cucumber, onions, garlic, zucchini, eggplant and cauliflower, beets. Everything we needed. Everything we needed we had, there. The place I've never seen. A place they wanted me to see in stories, that they wanted me to know like a miracle inside-out, to know with my hands.

LUNCH

THE NEXT MORNING MICHAEL'S DRESSED before Sarah is up, busy packing his briefcase at the table. "See you 12:30, 12:45, then? In fact, if you can, could you go a bit early, get us a table at Rosenberg's? Laura says it can be busy."

"Is Laura coming?"

"Don't think so, she has to be at the office. So, the Pletzl is not even five minutes from here." He pulls out his *Plan*. "Just go up rue Pavée, where the synagogue Laura told us about is, and turn left on rue des Rosiers. It's on the corner of rue des Rosiers and rue Ferdinand Duval."

"Ferdinand Duval?"

"Yes. Get this: Laura was telling me that up until the Dreyfus affair, Ferdinand Duval was called rue des Juifs. And rue des Rosiers – I guess you know that means rosebush street – the name goes all the way back to the 1200s, when the street followed the walls of the city, and roses grew along the ramparts."

Roses on the ramparts. A different Paris.

"Gotta run." He gives her a long kiss and then is out the door.

She starts making her coffee, gets out her notes on the Tuileries Garden, the next on Charles' list. Clears the breakfast table, gets down to work. She's using the pretty orange Clairefontaine notebook she just bought herself here, eking out her francs. It doesn't feel like a *notebook* or a *scribbler*: somehow it's a *cahier*. Funny how in Canada she was surrounded by French words she didn't think she was paying any attention to, but that clearly seeped into her brain – those old Hilroy notebooks with the map of Canada on the cover and the words *cahier d'exercices* below *exercise book*. Some of the French she has now absorbed subliminally that way. What would Marie-Claire say about that as a method of learning French?

She doesn't care what Marie-Claire would say. She's not interested in Marie-Claire's French, Marie-Claire's France, Marie-Claire's Paris.

When she looks up, it's already 11:50, so she hustles to get changed, fusses a bit over what to wear, then pulls on the dress Laura helped her pick out, the one that gives her curves. It's summery, fancy and simple at the same time. She reaches for Michael's necklace, then sets it down. It doesn't really go with the dress. She slips the penny into her pocket, her thumb following the thin edge for a moment before she releases it. She's already decided to go – she doesn't need the penny to make up her mind for her.

But when she gets out the door with the directions in her head – up rue Pavée then left on rue des Rosiers – she feels a funny pull to the east, towards Place des Vosges, or south, to the river. She likes taking her crooked path across Île Saint-Louis and surprising Notre Dame by coming up behind its towers, seeing the flying buttresses spread their spindly spider legs towards the little neglected park at the back. She knows the city in such a disorganized way, through familiar nodes she connects by familiar paths, this corner tabac and that little café floating along the routes she's worked out in her head. So then she can be surprised to turn a corner and find a familiar building or café where she doesn't think it could possibly be. She has to remember to go back to the map, locate things where they really are, not in the personal map in her head. And right now for some reason, she's drawn to rue de Rivoli, to the Centre Pompidou, not the narrow streets just to the north that will take her to the Pletzl.

But she's decided. And she has a date with Michael. So at rue de Rivoli she takes the first small street north, checking her watch. She should be okay for time even if she does get a bit lost. She's a few buildings up the street when she notices, peripherally, a shop window that feels familiar. She turns back a few steps. Bazar Miriam. A little store whose shop windows are crammed with an odd-ball display of kippahs and menorahs and mezuzahs, inexpensive Seder plates, *yahrzeit* memorial candles. A window full of tchotchkes, her dad would say. There are Star of David and *chai* necklaces too, though none identical to hers. She touches her neck, startles for a moment because the chain isn't there. Feels in her pocket for the penny, gives it a few turns. What a jumble of merchandise in that window. If everything were written in English instead of French, the shop would be right at home in North End Winnipeg. *She'd* be right at home. She must be near the Pletzl. She hadn't noticed any Jewish shops before. She's tempted to go in, smell the musty smell of sanctity, community. She checks her watch: no time to dawdle. Maybe she'll stop by after lunch if she's still in the mood for nostalgia. Maybe there's something Rose would like, or Pat. Something for Gail, maybe.

And suddenly she's there, at the Pletzl, which isn't a square at all but a nondescript triangle. She checks the street signs and finds she's been wandering up rue Ferdinand Duval and now has found herself at the point where it meets up with rue des Rosiers. Here she is in this anonymous space, a place she's taken herself to without knowing it's where she's supposed to be. This arbitrary meeting of irregular streets, the famous Pletzl, is more an intersection than a square.

Though she wanted to come, to see this Paris, she can't help wondering why Michael made such a big deal about the place. Some crummy little falafel joints, a peculiar mosaic of yellow tiles making up the façades of Rosenberg's, as if to establish a Disneyland link with the mysterious East. An appliqué of one culture on another, but the applied culture is thin. This 'little place' doesn't feel like a place at all, it's more a non-place. It doesn't really feel like any kind of Paris, doesn't feel like anywhere.

But of course it's also the place where so many were rounded up in July, 1942, taken to the *Vél' d'Hiv*. Almost exactly 40 years ago.

She checks her watch, 12:45. Michael should be here any minute, unless his meeting has gone late. No time to explore, to try to find out more about the deportations. She should go in, get them a table, since it's pretty crowded, but instead she studies the façade of Rosenberg's. It has the feel of a child's drawing: above the arched doorway are crude little schematic flowers picked out in tile, the borders circling them black against the bright, impossibly cheerful yellow of the mosaic tile – no colouring outside the lines!

The windows are cluttered with notices and placards: *specialists in all kinds of smoked fish, caviar, salmon, sturgeon; blinis with sour cream.* Once she's inside, she finds the interior both familiar and strange. In some ways she really could be in a deli on Main Street. The black-and-white tiled floor, glass display cases, they're as much Winnipeg as Paris. The bustle and clutter of any deli she's ever been to, but behind the long counter are upside-down bottles of hard liquor you wouldn't find in any deli on Main Street.

The room is packed, there must be fifty people eating lunch, standard Winnipeg fare: gefilte fish, chopped liver, chicken soup, schmaltz herring, perogies, boiled beef with horseradish. A waiter glances at her, there are no tables free, so he gestures with his head, his hands full, towards the counter. She sits down on a red stool, puts her notebook on the stool beside her to save it for Michael. Chicken soup with matzo balls would probably be tasty or at least safe but it's too hot a day, too hot for borscht either. She could try a potato latke but nobody makes them the way Pat does, thin and light and not greasy at all.

There's an older woman seated at the table beside her, painfully thin but fashionably dressed in a white blouse and narrow navy skirt, who looks somehow familiar. She's deep in discussion with two young men, pointing an animated crooked finger at them, her sons perhaps, and both men crumple into laughter, the woman smiling in mild triumph at them. It suddenly clicks into place where Sarah saw her before – she's the bird-like woman who was walking her dog, though there's no dog in sight, the same woman she noticed the other night at the *traiteur chinois*, the woman she thought of as a Parisian 'type.' The woman is wearing a different stylish outfit, the blouse looks like silk, the skirt is beautifully tailored, and the little dog is nowhere to be seen. She is intensely gaunt, but she seems so at ease at her table, so much a part of the place. That's it. Sarah can see just the edge of the faded blue of the tattoo on her wrist, it's peeking out of the cuff of the woman's white blouse. The woman is a survivor. Half-starved, Sarah thought at the *traiteur*. More than half-starved at one point, if the tattoo that Sarah's glimpsed is what she believes it is. That look of deprivation that Sarah had pictured as self-inflicted, thinking her a victim of style, not of the Nazis. And now the two images collide. But look at the woman here. In her element. The waiter is standing at their table and all three josh with him in rapid French as they hand him back their menus. Sarah can imagine the woman swapping the same jokes in Yiddish at Oscar's Delicatessen in Winnipeg. She probably speaks Yiddish.

Sarah feels someone standing beside her. Michael.

"Hello there," he says, giving a somewhat lop-sided kiss to the cheek. "No luck getting us a table?"

"Nope. I got here twenty minutes ago, but it was already packed."

"Have you seen the menu, Sarah? What do you recommend?"

Oh dear, what can she recommend? She can't help thinking of French food: steak-frîtes. Bouillabaisse. Vichyssoise. Something with a lot of s's and vowels in its name. "I think they have knishes. I like the cheese ones, not the potato ones. You might like those. Or blintzes."

Michael's leaning towards her, smiling, trying to decide.

The light changes behind her.

She turns her head, looks back.

Michael is standing right beside her and then he's not.

Everything stops. There's some sort of shift in time, a hiccup. Something splashes into the room, glass is breaking, something has broken the window of the restaurant and there's a noise, mechanical, sharp and then there are human noises, cries, screaming, and light, a sharp light.

She has to do something. Michael isn't there, but the older woman is on the floor and Sarah knows that this is something she can do. In the shock of the moment, she twists herself so that her body is covering the woman, whose white silk blouse is a banner now, blowing in some wind Sarah doesn't understand. Sarah crouches over the woman, whose eyes are open, looking at her. *This is a person.* The woman's eyes are open and she is herself.

Two shadows, two people, they're wearing something on their heads, hoods maybe, two shadows at the doorway holding metal in their hands, something silver, shining and there's more noise, it's like a movie soundtrack or a cartoon, but loud and close, *dit-dit-dat, dit-dit-dat-dat, rat-a-tat-tat.*

And then she's not crouched any more, she's fallen, and she makes herself fall so that her body covers the woman's body. And in the sound and light and terrible brightness, in the sudden light and pain, the worst thing is that Michael, who was beside her, isn't there and the worst thought, before the merciful darkness, is that he's gone.

Michael's gone.

Her eyes must have closed because when they open, the sound is different, sirens, *wee-woo-wee-woo-wee-woo,* the special sound of a French police siren all around her. She touches her neck but the necklace is gone, it was never there. Michael's gone.

Her eyes close and she's gone too.

Her eyes open. Somebody's standing over her, a slim man in green pyjamas, no, that's not right, green scrubs, he must be a doctor, or a medic, and the bottom of the pants that are loose on his slim body are soaked, dark. He looks down at his pants, holds out his hands as if he's asking a question, then wipes his face with the back of his wrists because his hands are wet and dark too and he looks very tired and he looks down at her, tired and sad, saying something. She can't understand the words. French. She's still in Paris, some sort of Paris. She looks down at the slim man's feet and the floor is wet and dark too. Where is the woman she was hiding with her body? Where is Michael? Somebody's kneeling beside her, saying something in French, she can't understand, but she feels open, she feels as if her body isn't itself anymore, she's open and, worse, she's meat. Everything's red, over her, over the medic, and she can't look, her eyes close.

With her eyes closed, nothing hurts. Nothing hurts because she's not in her body. The pain has taken her outside her body and she knows something terrible has happened, is happening. Her eyes close and she's gone and they open and close, they can't stay open, she's back in her body and she knows the terrible thing is the pain, which she can't escape without leaving her body. The terrible thing is the pain, it's not at the door, it's come into the room. She can't move.

Her eyes open.

The light is silver. There's something shining silver above her. There's another man standing above her, not the slim green man. This man has a shiny silver helmet – Halloween, a comic-book hero. Or a Greek god, the messenger god with the helmet, wings at his heels, the one who travels to the underworld. The light of the day caught in his helmet. That's where it went, that terrible light. He has a dark coat, his face is sad. He's saying words to her in French, but she can't answer. Because she looked back. Kneeling in front of her, he's all she sees. His hands lift to reach over her head, she feels the arc as they move behind her neck, a gift, something small, light against her face. A gift with no debt attached, nothing to repay. And now some of what was tight in her loosens, she feels her chest lift. And she's being carried into the air under a blanket, tan blanket with a band of dark brown. Her mother cuddled up under it on the sofa in the house on Rupertsland. And there's a sound, herself. She's screaming. She's screaming – it must be her – because it hurts, where her body is open. Where are they taking her, these shiny men, into the air, the underworld?

She's gone.

Laila

You think this is your story, don't you, Khalil? But it's mine. I remember now it's mine.

You're happy. You were gone, and when you come back, you take the key out of your pocket and open the lock and let me back in, and you're happy. I've never seen you this happy. But it's not for me, it's not because I remembered what my parents wanted for me. It's not for me, it's for the thing you're cradling in your arms, a gift, you say. You've been given a gift. You unwrap it and put it on the bed. I watch you touch it in a way that you never touch me, never will touch me. You stroke the barrel, the stock, the safety, the trigger. They gave you this gift and they taught you to take it apart, you say, they taught you to clean it.

I want to tell you that I'm the one who cleans things, it's me who washes Paris clean. I'm the one who washes my hands in my mother's kitchen, who helps her take the sheets and pin them up against the sky where the sun scours them white.

And you show me, before I even have a chance to lie down at last, before I can sleep in my own bed, you're so happy that you show me right away, spreading a cloth carefully on the floor, how you clean it, take it apart. You set each piece tenderly in order on the cloth, a beautiful thing, you keep telling me, a beautiful thing. Beauty right here on the cramped floor of our terrible little room.

And you keep talking, you keep telling me you're in love, you can't stop talking. It's your very own. They gave it to you. You have so much to tell me. The graffiti's still there, you say, nobody has taken it down. We left our mark. And now you're planning to leave a different kind of mark, do something that everyone will see, everyone will notice. The whole world will see.

214

We will create our own victory, however the PLO fighters are suffering.

And I can be part of it. I can help you.

You laugh, maybe this is the reason you saved me, you say. And you tie the black-and-white keffiyeh around my face. No one will even know I'm a woman, you say. I'm so small, so skinny, my breasts are hardly breasts. You touch my chest, but not with reverence, not the way you touch your beloved.

10,000 dead. The Jews will pay. The Jews and all their friends will pay. Israel will pay. I can be part of it, you tell me. You'll let me be a part of it.

I know what it's like to be taken apart.

You think I'm afraid, but I'm not afraid to touch it, taken apart.

You put it together, clean.

I'm not afraid to touch it, whole.

I can hold it, you tell me.

No.

You pull the keffiyeh off my head. It was a joke, you say. There may be a woman who isn't afraid to do what you're going to do, but it isn't me. You laugh.

I'm not afraid.

I know what it's like to be taken apart. I could do it if I wanted to. But I know what a knife can do. What a bullet can do. Skin can be opened like a book, a door. What's whole can be taken to pieces. That book, that door, opens and what spills out.

Before you left, before you took away the key, I got into bed one night in the dark. I hit my leg on the bedstead in the dark, the tender meat of my shin hard against the hard wood, and it hurt so much in the darkness that my hands went to the leg and they came away wet, the whole calf, my hands wet. I turned on the light, not understanding, afraid. All I'd done was knock against the bed, and my hands were red, blood surging down the shin, the hem of my nightgown dipped into it. I told myself, don't be stupid, it's just a nick, a vein right at the surface of the bone, it's nothing.

215

Blood wetting a corner of the sheets, how would I get it clean, how would I clean my nightgown?

I was afraid the blood would empty me out.

The way my brother's friend emptied me.

Hate can do that. Your hate could do that.

I know what a bullet, a knife, can do. Skin opened like a door.

What spills out is life.

I say no. No.

RIEN DE RIEN

IT CAN'T BE RIGHT. SHE CAN HEAR SOMEONE singing through the bright nightmares, that terrible silver light. Something in Sarah loosens, she feels a weight lifted. It's Gail. But that can't be right. Her sister is far away, isn't she? When Sarah opens her eyes Gail is all she sees. Sarah feels the arc as her sister's hands move, a gift, and there's something small, light against her face. She can breathe. Her sister is giving her a gift. The penny is gone, and now she can choose. When she opens her eyes again, she can see it's not Gail, it's someone else, Laura, Laura in a green dress, touching Sarah's forehead. Then it's not Laura and it's not Gail, it's someone in uniform, a nurse. Sarah closes her eyes and when she opens them it *is* Gail, here, beside her. Gail in the room, knitting a red scarf. Gail's body an edge to her own, so she isn't open any more, won't dissolve. Gail's body holding her on the earth. She can breathe, she's been handed her life, but what is she going to do with it?

Michael. She can hear his voice, even with her eyes closed. She thought he was gone, but he's here. *Sorry sorry sorry.* That's what she hears him say, she doesn't know why. It can't be right because Michael doesn't say he's sorry. He's saying *sorry* and holding her hand. She can feel his hand on hers, even with her eyes shut. She thought he was gone into the noise and light but he's alive. And Gail. Michael and Sarah and Gail, they're all alive. But what about Rose? Where is she? Where did the penny go? Sarah's eyes seem to open and shut by themselves, but she doesn't know when they're open because everything she sees is too bright. Vivid. That's a word. There's a dull pain all around her ribs and a sharp one in her left arm, she's trying not to move it. Something stuck into the back of her right hand, too, something sharp that hurts when she moves it but not as sharp as the pain in her left arm. Michael is holding her hand, very gently, her left hand doesn't hurt if she doesn't move her arm. *Sorry sorry sorry.* Why is he sorry if they're alive?

Non, rien de rien. Non, je ne regrette rien.

She closes her eyes and that song is in her head, the Little Sparrow singing her to Paris where she has no regrets. No, it's Laura singing a quiet song Sarah remembers, *all day, all night, sifting sand.* And now there's another song, outside her head, the old lullaby, Simon and Garfunkel, the song with a bridge in it, troubled waters, and she's lain down and when she opens her eyes she thinks she sees Rose, Rose in Paris, crying and smiling at the same time. She closes her eyes and someone is singing, the soprano wobbly this time; it can't be Rose but Sarah wants Rose to be here, wants her to lay herself down alongside Sarah again the way she did all those years ago but it hurts too much. It hurts because there was something she could do. That banner, the white silk blouse, Sarah crouched over the woman. Something she did. When she closes her eyes against the hurt, she can see the penny spinning on its own, she can see the bees dancing, their intricate arabesques, corkscrews in the air. And now there's Rose dancing. Mrs. Margolis too, Mrs. M. and her hummingbirds, dancing, the hummingbirds diving in and out, playing. And then the hummingbirds are attacking each other. *Rat-a-tat-tat. Attentat.* A hummingbird dogfight, a drumming whoosh, *dit-dit-dat, dit-dit-dat-dat, rat-a-tat-tat*, two hummingbirds dive-bombing the deli because they're territorial, they're fighting over the land of Israel. Palestine. Palestinian terrorists. *Terror* from the Latin *terra*, earth, from the Latin *terrerre*, to frighten. Paris belongs to who, Paris is whose terroir?

❧

It can't be right, it can't be her mother in the room, Pat wearing her jelly-bean pink sandals and a soft white shirt. Pat touches Sarah's face and Sarah touches her blouse, she wants to touch the softness of her mother's blouse. But what's Pat doing in the room? Sarah knows she's in hospital, she was hurt in the *attentat*; the doctors, the nurses with their gifts, they keep saying that word, a word in French she keeps hearing. She doesn't know what it means, but it must be important. It can't be right that Pat's here, so she must be in Winnipeg, they must all be in Winnipeg and Rose must be sick again, that's terrible. But Pat is explaining that Rose is okay, she's doing okay, and Abe and David are staying in Winnipeg to be with Rose, but Rose is just fine. Her mother's hand is cool against her forehead. She can feel the smooth skin on her mother's hand, lovely soft skin, the bump of a ring. She's watching the ring, her mother's wedding ring, a band of small diamonds set in white gold. Beautiful. Not much light caught in them, not much light in her mother. Pat is saying that Gail is here in Paris because Sarah was hurt. In the *attentat*. Even her mother is saying *attentat*. Sarah remembers now, the green man, the shiny silver helmet, being lifted, how the light changed. The older woman her body protected. The day the light caught. The penny spinning, then gone. Sarah was caught but now what was tight has loosened. Hands lifting to give her a gift, her life handed back to her. She was taken apart, a rift, but now the gift has put her back together, she can put herself together. And Michael isn't gone, he's here and alive, looking after her. He's telling her that there was an attack on Rosenberg's deli and people were hurt, Sarah was hurt. She hurts, but when the nurses come, the pain goes quiet for a while. And Gail is here in Paris with Pat, with roses, are there roses in the room, is Rose in the room?

Sarah needs to tell them about the roses. She doesn't know if she's talking inside or outside her head. Can she talk now, are there tubes in her throat? Maybe the tubes are gone. She's talking inside or outside her head about rue, the sorry street, the street that carries her sister's name. Rue des Rosiers. Rose's sorrow, a current that almost carried her away from them all. Rue the street that carried Sarah into a small dangerous place. That rue. *You'll rue the day*, that's what Abe says. What day was it? The day of the abortion, the day of the *attentat*. *You have to wear your rue with a difference.* Someone said that. *There's rue for you, and here's some for me.* The drowned girl. Common rue, herb-of-grace. Rue and rose bushes on the lovely ramparts, along the wall. You build a wall to forget what it is you rue. You build a wall to keep your enemies out, you let the penny spin, let it choose for you. You're pulled along the ramparts by that current of rue, you turn your head and go under.

Rosaceae, she needs to tell them about *Rosaceae*. A catalogue to arrange things in categories, to keep the rue at bay. *Mene, mene.* The place for roses is in the kingdom *Plantae*, thine is the kingdom, and the rose family is the family *Rosaceae*, genus *Rosa*, *Rosids*, order *Rosales*. A medium-sized family, just like theirs, three sisters, father, mother, almost 3,000 species. In the rose family, it's not just roses, it's cherries, apples, apricots, plums of course, peaches, even almonds. You can't grow those in Winnipeg, can you, whatever the power and the glory. Glorious Rose. And Gail. Glorious Paris. And Michael. Why is Michael sorry, what does he rue? The glory of apples, too, fruit of knowledge, and pears, and quinces, she wants them to remember the Japanese quince bush in the yard of Michael's apartment on Howland. She wants to be there now. She wants to be there, not Paris, where it hurts. Quinces and raspberries, Rose's raspberries, strawberries. All in Rose's family, their family. The boundaries of the family are not disputed. Sarah has studied *Rosaceae*. For ever and ever. Amen. Cherries and pears. Hawthorn and roses. The same family holding such different things.

And now she remembers what they tried to tell her, here in the hospital in Paris. People died. In the *attentat*. She remembers the sad man who didn't know what to do with his hands, the rueful man in green scrubs, and that other man in the cartoon silver helmet. They didn't save everyone. What about the older woman in the narrow skirt, the white silk blouse, the birdlike woman, what happened to her, to her family, her sons? Sarah remembers what her own body did, twisted itself to hide the woman, save her, whoever she was. Did that woman survive, she survived once, did she survive again? Did Sarah save her, did the sad men save her, did they save Sarah? Is she saved? Now that they've handed her back her life, what's she going to do with it? The green man holding out his hands as if he were asking a question.

People died at the deli. Someone broke through the day and killed them. Cherries and pears. Hawthorn and roses.

The sad men want to know, Sarah wants to know: the people who killed, and the people who were killed, do they belong to the same family?

❧

Michael's fixing her pillow, her blanket, the tilt of the bed. Laura was here and Pat was here and Pat was so small beside Laura, who put her arms around Pat's shoulders, who took Pat's hand as they both left. They left, they needed to rest, but Michael's still here. Michael the Boy Scout, Mr. Fix-It. He's fixing her the way he always wants to, she's a problem to be solved. Sarah is X, solve for X. He has a bandage on his forehead but it's nothing, he says. *Rien de rien.* She's glad it's nothing, because now they can solve the problem, they can figure out what to do. Is X equal to zero? She needs to know why he's sorry. Michael lays his head down on the pillow. He doesn't lift his head, he talks into the pillow. He's talking to the pillow but she can hear what he says. His head so sweet, the blond curls a bit longer now, right on the pillow beside her.

"Sarah," he says, "I have to tell you, you have to know what happened there. In the deli." He closes his eyes, opens them, but he's not looking at her. "A grenade, they say it was a grenade that was thrown in the window. These two men," he swallows, "came in and fired machine guns. They, they shot people. Six people have died already. And five are really badly injured, we don't know if they'll make it. We don't know." He closes his eyes again and his face is wet, there are tears on his face. "They're saying, the authorities, that it was Palestinian gunmen. And, Sarah, you almost died. That's what the doctors told us. And now they're telling us that you're a bit better and, and they're telling us that there's hope, you're so strong, you're young. But you're not out of danger. That's what they're saying. So I have to let you know what happened. I need you to know what I did. What I didn't do." His eyes are open now and he's looking at her, his face close to hers.

What did Michael do, what didn't he do? Sarah is watching his face, all the features, nose, eyes, cheeks, adding up to him, Michael. And he's not gone, he's here, right beside her. Here when she needs him.

"When the men," Michael is saying, "when they came, I was standing right beside you. What I should have done, I should have grabbed hold of you, pulled you down to the floor. Right away. I should have known something was wrong. But I didn't protect you. I did nothing. I didn't do anything. The blast from the grenade, it must have knocked me out, thrown me onto the counter. Because, it's just – when I came to, I was there, on the floor, behind the counter. Safe. Behind that heavy wooden barricade. It must have protected me. The explosion, the shrapnel, the bullets, Sarah, they didn't go through. There's hardly a scratch on me. And look at you, Sarah. Look at you."

His eyes are closed again. Is he tired? Is he too tired to talk? Sarah's tired now, Michael's words are so soft she can hardly hear them, but there he is, he's talking again.

"I just lay there, Sarah. When I came to. I don't think I knew who I was, where I was. And I didn't do anything. I didn't do anything to save you. I don't understand. If I didn't look after you, if I didn't protect you, I don't know who I am."

Michael didn't save her. That's why he's sad. And sorry. He's afraid of who he is if he didn't save her.

But isn't she saved?

❧

It can't be right. The bright nightmares are back, things are thicker now, she was in a different room for a while, her eyes were closed most of the time, it was hard to open them. And she thought Rose was in the room, Rose standing right beside Pat, who was crying, why was Pat crying if Rose was in the room? Rose really in the room, singing to her. It can't be right. The doctors explained in English, there was an infection, they had to operate again, to

222

clear out the infection, a mop-up job, clearing her insides, they didn't get all the shrapnel the first time, and now she has a fever. The operation was successful, they removed all the significant shrapnel, they stitched her back together. But it's still touch-and-go. Sarah has a fever and in that fever she dreams. Dreams are terrible things, but now she's dreaming Laura in a red scoop-neck dress singing about sifting sand. She's dreaming Gail knitting the bright red thread of a scarf. And now Rose is here, Rose is reading her something, words about dancing, a little family dancing, it's 1945 in Pittsburgh, there's a radio, and broken furniture. The family is dancing *as if we were dying*. The Nazis didn't win, that's why they're dancing. Sometimes dancing is the right thing to do, Rose says. Because we're still here. *Oh God of mercy, oh wild God.* That's what Rose is telling her about in the dream, or is it Gail? Her sisters aren't angry with her.

Now the dream Rose is gone. Sarah is talking but the fever makes her not make sense. The fever is talking and she doesn't know what to think, how to solve the problem. About Michael, who didn't save her. Even though he was saved. Isn't it good, that he's saved? But he doesn't think it's good. And even though he's trying to fix her now, she isn't fixed. Gail is here, so maybe Gail can fix her. Maybe Gail can knit her back together. And here's Pat, she can smell her mother's fresh soap smell, touch the soft fabric of her shirt.

Sarah can't stop talking. The fever is telling her she's the one who has to solve the problem, it's her, not Michael, she has to fix things and she has to fix them with numbers. "– and six and then seven, no five and four, two then, and two, makes seven, no five –"

It's Gail beside her now. "Hey, Sarah, listen to me. The doctors are saying that you're still fighting the infection, and this babbling, it's from the delirium the infection is causing. What you're saying doesn't make any sense. But I think maybe you can hear and understand me, so I'm going to keep talking to you. I want you to know I'm here. I'm not going anywhere."

Gail is not going anywhere and Rose can't be here, she can't be here singing. Sarah has to figure it out. Two sisters. Three sisters now. "– and four and then two, six and four, eight now, and three, that must make twelve –"

"This counting you're doing, that's you trying to figure things out like this, put it all together, right?"

Nine then three, six makes eight now, plus five. *Mene, mene.* Michael and Pat and Laura and Gail and Rose. A dizzy circle of faces. Where is Abe? Did they take him away in his striped pajamas? Who's missing? Is Sarah missing?

"You're trying to keep track, keep things in balance, aren't you? The way you always do? What did they call it in Hebrew school – a *kheshbon,* a reckoning?"

Four and then seven.

"Listen to me. I don't care what they said in Hebrew school, you have to know, I told you before, that's not how it works. It's not how God works, if you're thinking about God for some reason. And it's not how the world works, how people work. I know I can be like that too, counting things up, taking sides all the time. But it's not sums and subtraction, a line of numbers in one column to the right and another to the left so that what's added to one column has to be subtracted from the other – it's not that kind of ledger."

Take away ten, plus three, makes twelve, then seven, six. Where did Michael go? Who can he be if he didn't take care of her?

"Okay, Sarah. You rest now." Gail touches her good hand.

Rat-a-tat-tat. Attentat. Sarah has to solve for those men with the grenade, with the guns, she has to add them up. What did they want that added up to so much more than the lives they took away? She can't work it out. She has to.

She has to solve for Michael. And Rose. She's been dreaming Rose. And Gail.

She has to sleep.

NI LE MAL, NI LE BIEN

A STRANGER. A THIN YOUNG WOMAN, someone who looks like her. Someone she doesn't know, though something about her is familiar. Sarah blinks for a moment, that face in the mirror.

"So, what do you think?" Gail asks.

Sarah turns around. There's a young woman in uniform leaving the room, one of the cleaners.

"Sarah? What d'you say?" Gail is holding the mirror for her.

She turns back to the reflection.

It's not the stranger, it's her own face, pale and still drawn, thinner even than usual, but her.

She looks at Gail. "Good. It looks good," she says. Gail has helped her comb her hair. Michael and Gail managed to get her into the shower, she's doing that well. She's doing so well that Michael has gone back to their apartment, is actually catching up on some work. And now Sarah is sitting in a chair by the bed with freshly washed hair. Gail tries to get the part straight, then swears and puts the comb down.

"Don't worry," Sarah says. "It doesn't matter." She takes the mirror out of Gail's hand, puts it into a drawer in the bedside table. "Did you see that woman?"

"Who?"

"One of the cleaners, I think." A woman who looked like her, who looked familiar.

Gail shakes her head.

"So," Sarah says, "you got to visit me in Paris."

225

"I did." Gail doesn't smile. "Rose too. Her first time."

"I can barely remember her being here, I thought I was dreaming." But Rose wasn't a fever dream, she was here, in Paris, for four days. She was here because they were afraid Sarah was going to die. Rose has gone back now, but she was here. And Laura was visiting Sarah at the hospital almost every day until they finally convinced her she was wearing herself out, working full time and spending evenings at the hospital. She needed to get back to her own life, her work. But she still comes two or three times a week, always bearing gifts, tidbits to tempt Sarah's appetite, flowers, funny old-fashioned postcards from the *bouquinistes* near the Pont Marie. She and Michael conferring on what treats, what flowers Sarah will like best.

"David called yesterday, just checking in. You were asleep. He says Rose really does seem to be better these days."

"Gail, I remember Rose reading me something, a poem maybe? Can that be right?"

"I think so. She was reading you all sorts of stuff. I think there was a poem. I'll ask David the next time he calls."

"Your two crazy sisters."

"Huh? What do you mean? Being crazy didn't get you here. It didn't get you these scars." Gail gingerly touches the rough scar on Sarah's hand, runs light fingers over her belly.

That woman, the stranger, she had a scar on her left cheek. Something familiar. Sarah remembers the pale scars on Rose's wrists, remembers seeing Rose's hands in the fever dreams.

"No. But I'm remembering how nuts I was after the abortion."

"You were a kid. A dumb scared kid. And on top of it, that creep dumped you." Gail's picked up her knitting, a green scarf now.

"I didn't know you knitted."

"Stress relief. I need to do something with my hands."

It's a simple pattern, knit, purl. "I don't know, Gail." There has to be a pattern, even for a simple scarf. "Maybe there's something wrong with me, some flaw that made me weak, made me crack that easily."

"Well, you didn't stay cracked," Gail says.

"I don't know."

"Maybe half-cracked?" The rhythm of Gail's hands is soothing.

"Maybe." Adding things up all the time, letting the penny decide.

"You'll be fine." The rhythm becomes fierce. "You're getting better, and you'll get home, and you'll pick up the pieces."

If she can. She's not sure what pieces to pick up. "Poor Mom and Dad," Sarah says, "two out of three kids crazy."

"Hey, what about me? I'm crazy too. In my own special way." Gail is grinning now. She sets down the knitting. "Ranting ideologues are their own kind of crazy." She picks up the knitting, looks down. "You know I came because I love you. Cracked or half-cracked or whole."

"Of course you do. You have to." She has to. They have to love each other, that's how it works. "I can't believe Rose was well enough to come."

"It was all right." Gail puts the knitting aside. "She wanted to come. And Mom did a great job of bossing her around, making sure she took her meds, all that Mom stuff. You know, I think it did her good. Being needed. Helping out."

Sarah shakes her head. "I don't know how to put our big sister, the one who looks after us… I don't know how to put that person together with the crazy person who tried to kill herself."

"She still is that big sister. She came because you needed her."

"I did. I needed her to be here." With Rose, with Gail, she can slip back into herself, can be more than the partial self she has to be without them. But she let Rose down when Rose was so sick. *You're not here and I need you.* "When she needed me I didn't come."

"You did come," Gail says. "You went to Winnipeg. And you helped. Rose told me. See this?" She holds up her right hand.

"You've got the puzzle ring I gave her."

"Yeah, she left it with me. She told me to give it to you, to wear till you

227

get better. Here." Gail is working it off her finger. "Here."

"Careful. Keep it on your finger," Sarah says, "you don't want it falling apart."

"I can put it back together," Gail tells her.

"You figured it out?"

"Rose showed me." She puts it carefully onto Sarah's finger. "It's too big on you. It used to fit, didn't it? I can put it on your middle finger."

"You keep it. For now."

Gail fits the ring back on her own finger. "That crap I said to you about not being a help, when we had the fight, the Chinese food, it wasn't true. I was drunk. It was bullshit."

Sarah nods. "Yeah. It was." She's watching Gail's hands at rest for the moment. "I lost my lucky penny."

"Huh? Oh, that penny you were always fiddling with?"

"Yeah. I had it during the attack and it's gone."

"Okay. It's gone. We'll get you another penny." She looks at Sarah. "Listen, do you want to get back into bed, have a nap?"

"No, I'm okay for now."

Sarah's doing better. That's what the doctors say: infection's gone, fever's gone, incisions are pretty much healed now. She's *out of the woods*. It's not just what the doctors say, it's what her body is telling her. It was the abdominal injury that almost did her in, shrapnel from the grenade that, lucky for her, ricocheted off the counter before it got to her. Plus the bullet wound in her left arm, it was pretty straight-forward, through and through. The physio explained in her faulty English that Sarah could expect a full range of motion in the arm eventually, though she'd need months more of rehab at home. They are amazed at how fast she healed once the infection was licked. And the docs told her the small shrapnel bits, those dots and little lumps she can spot on her arm, her side, will keep emerging, probably over years. She needs to keep an eye on them, because they can migrate, but at that size they likely won't do any harm.

"Okay. Good," Gail says. "Listen, I finally got my hands on a proper dictionary and looked up *attentat*. You kept asking for a definition, even when you were babbling. *Attempt* is one definition. Criminal attempt. But *attack* is better, I think."

Sarah shivers. *Rat-a-tat-tat. Attentat.* The light of that day. Someone kneeling.

"You cold? You want a blanket?" Gail gets up, reaches into the cupboard.

"No, I'm fine."

"You don't look so fine."

"*Atrocity*," Sarah says.

"What?"

"*Atrocity* would be a better definition."

Now that Sarah is officially *out of the woods*, they've filled her in on what is known about the attack. Gail and Laura mostly, Michael and Pat can't seem to stand to talk about it. It's still anything but clear what happened, who is responsible. What is clear is that the killers meant to cause the maximum harm – they attacked the deli at one of the busiest times of day, used the grenade first and then the machine guns. They sprayed the street with machine-gun fire as they ran off. More people were injured in the street.

They still haven't caught anyone, but since the first day after the attack, the French government has claimed that the Abu Nidal group, a pro-Iraqi Palestinian extremist faction, is responsible. The attackers used a special machine gun that was the same type Abu Nidal used in the London attack on the Israeli ambassador in June, and in an Abu Nidal attack against a Vienna synagogue a year ago August.

"Listen, Sarah, if you need cheering up, I have some good news for you," Gail says. "You kept worrying about that older woman in the deli, the one you thought was a Holocaust survivor? Laura sweet-talked one of the doctors into looking into it for us. The docs found out who she was. And she survived. She was at another hospital but she might be out now. She was injured, but not badly."

The woman survived. Again. The ledger balances this one time. Because you want your death to bear some relationship to your life and you want some sort of justice, or at least causality. Let the woman not die in an assault on Jews after she's lived through the largest assault on Jews in their long sad history. And she didn't. She's alive.

And so is Sarah. And Rose. And Michael.

"The doctor said she kept talking about you, or at least it sounds like you, a thin young woman who threw herself on top of her, saved her. Do you remember anything about that? Do you remember doing something?"

There was something she could do. That she did. Her body twisted itself to cover the woman, her white silk blouse a banner in a strange wind. Sarah crouched over the woman, looking into her eyes. "Yeah. Maybe. I'm not sure. I think I may have tried to protect her just as the grenade was thrown, before I got hit. I can't really remember."

Gail nods. "You can't expect to remember. Hey, maybe they'll let her visit once you're a bit better. You can piece it together with her. The nurses told me Mitterrand came to the hospital to see you and the other people who were injured here. I guess you don't remember that either?"

Sarah shakes her head.

"You remember when you were still fighting the infection, you were delirious, talking in numbers?"

"I remember a little of it. I also remember you talking to me, saying something about how counting wouldn't work, the world couldn't be figured out with simple addition and subtraction."

"I'm surprised you remember. You were so out of it, Sarah. You scared us so much."

"But the medics, the doctors, they saved me."

"No." Gail is playing with the puzzle ring.

"What do you mean?"

"Nobody saved you. You saved yourself." She pulls the ring off, puts it back on her finger. "You weren't supposed to live. I don't know if you knew that, that it was touch-and-go for so long. You weren't supposed to live but you wanted to."

"Like Rose."

"Rose?" Gail is playing with the ring, slipping it up and down below the knuckle. "Does Rose want to live?"

"Yes! She does. She has to. Or at least, she does now."

"Okay. Okay. And it sounds like you not only saved yourself, you saved that woman."

The gaunt, animated woman, the banner of her silk blouse. Her little spaniel with the hints of grey in its white fur. "The dog wasn't there," Sarah says.

"What?"

"I saw that woman in the neighbourhood a couple of times before the deli and she always had a little dog with her. Floppy ears, white-and-grey coat.".

"Why are you fixated on the dog?"

"I think the dog's okay."

"Oh Jesus. When we get you two together you can ask her about the dog."

"You remember calculus, Gail? You were so good at maths."

"We were both good at maths. Rose was the one who couldn't add two and two. Still can't, as far as I know. Calculus. It's been a while."

"I've been thinking about what you said when I was babbling with the fever. About how if there *are* calculations that can be made to understand what our lives are, it has to be a different kind of mathematics, a higher mathematics. If we want the calculations to make sense." *Mene, mene.*

"First floppy-eared dogs and now calculus. Are you sure you don't want to lie down?"

"It's okay. I'm okay. I've been thinking about this. Do you remember limits in calculus?"

Gail nods. "Yeah. Funny how clear it still is."

"So," Sarah looks up at Gail. "I figure now it's better for me to think not just about numbers but about limits among people. About how hard it may be to understand that something that made perfect sense can stop making sense. At a critical point, a singular moment, everything goes haywire, the relationship blows up and it doesn't make any sense any more."

"Zero divided by zero, infinity divided by infinity." Gail has stopped fiddling with the ring.

"Babel," Sarah says. "Nonsense. But if you figure it out just right, weigh the loss on both sides, you can see past the nonsense and hold onto the value."

"Yeah. But it's not easy."

"No. It isn't. Look, what I'm trying to say – I'm not sure I understand what the limit is of the value of a human life. With the abortion, there was a life inside me that I stopped, a life I didn't let start. And I still don't know what the value of my life was against that possible life. I can try a more complicated way of looking at things, some kind of proof, a higher math. But I'm not sure I know the value of my own life now. The abortion was a kind of subtraction, wasn't it?" A woman's right to choose. What's Gail going to say now?

"Oh Christ, Sarah."

"But there was a loss, wasn't there?"

Gail looks up at her. "Yeah. Yeah, there was a loss. But you know it was also right."

"I know. I know. It was –"

"And then you saved that woman –"

"Yeah. But it's not as though that evens it out. And I still don't know these limits, don't know in some ways if I was right to value my own life like that. Or why I valued the woman in the deli's life. And what about the killers, at the deli, how do they figure into everything? I want to work it out and I still can't."

"Listen, Mom will be here soon. She'll flip out if she hears you like this, if you haven't rested up. You don't need to work all this stuff out. Not right now. Take it easy."

"But I need to figure it out somehow at some point."

"Right now what you need is to get all the way better."

Sarah rubs at her face, her eyes. "I should get back into bed."

"Yeah, do that."

She wants to sleep.

∽

Sarah is at the window. She's wearing her own clothes, jeans and a t-shirt. No penny in her pocket, nothing to turn, nothing to turn to. But it's all right. She doesn't need it. She's watching clouds move purposefully across a grey sky, and it seems possible that it might snow in Paris. Not the snow of Winnipeg, of course, and not even the snow of Toronto, where Sarah will soon be heading, since she's mostly healed, almost ready to leave. But it does look like snow, and Sarah pictures the profiles of the lions' heads on the fountains at Place des Vosges thickened with a layer of snow that heightens rather than veils their features. Maybe Paris will become even more itself under snow. Another week, the doctors say, ten days at the most, and they'll be ready to discharge her, let her go back into her life, whatever life she's willing to try.

She feels a touch at her shoulder, Michael, then his lips light against her neck. Every gesture now feels like a gesture of apology. She's tried to send him home, back to his work, which is waiting for him in Toronto. But he doesn't want to leave until she does. Gail left for Winnipeg three weeks ago.

He asks her how she is, and she tells him better, always better. He's brought and distributed a bag full of warm croissants and pains au chocolat for the nursing staff, a ritual now, he brings one almost every day, everyone has been so good to them. Mostly croissants, sometimes the perfect little tarts and other fancy pastries the pâtisseries sell.

"Michael," she says.

"Yes?"

"I want to ask you something, you have to promise to answer, okay?"

His mouth tenses, then slowly relaxes. "Promise," he says. "Go ahead."

"If it had been me," she says, looking out on the impossible Paris sky, "how would you feel?"

"What?"

"If it had been me," Sarah says it again, "if I'd been lucky and wasn't hurt, and if it were *you* who were hurt but still survived, how would you feel?" The sky readying itself.

"I can't think about that. That's not how it happened."

"But I want you to tell me how you'd feel. If it were you sitting right here right now, in hospital, like me almost better. And if I had hardly been hurt at all. What would that feel like?"

He stands beside her at the window. "Looks like snow," he says.

"It does. Michael, answer."

He turns and touches her arm, runs his hand along the healed scars. Puts a hand gently on her belly where more scars have closed themselves. "I don't know," he says at last.

"You do. Imagine that I had lain there behind the counter without knowing who I was or where I was, without being of any help to you, so it was me and not you. Me standing here just fine, not having been through all this, all these weeks, months."

"I'd like to imagine that."

"All right then. So tell me, how would you feel?"

"If you'd been lucky and I'd been hurt?"

"Yes!"

Michael hurt and treated and recovering. Michael in the hospital bed, hurt so badly and then getting better, and Sarah almost untouched, Sarah watching over him, sleepless, worried, helping.

"I'd be happy," he says at last. "Of course I'd be glad you weren't hurt."

"So why shouldn't it be the same for me? Why can't I feel like that for you, glad? Because I do. I am glad."

"But that's not right."

"Why? Why isn't it right? It isn't wrong. It was up to me to save myself. Not you."

He shakes his head. One snowflake coming down from the dark sky, then another.

"You didn't have to save me, Michael. It wasn't your job. It isn't. I had to save myself. My life isn't any less mine than yours is yours."

He shakes his head again. "Was it your job to save Rachel? Rachel Bernstein is here twice a week with books, flowers, chocolates. She'd bring that dog with her if they'd let her. And every time she visits, she tells you how grateful she is. Why was that your instinct? Why wasn't it mine?"

And it's true she turns it over and over in her mind, the thing she did, the good thing. Her body thinking for her. At last doing something that was unequivocally good. But she doesn't know why. "I don't know. But I'm asking you to see how I feel."

"I can't. I can't see it like that. I was supposed to put your life ahead of mine."

"You didn't have to. Look, I'm alive. I'm okay. I came through."

❧

Sarah's asleep that night in the hospital room she'll soon be leaving, a week, ten days at the most, but something wakes her, and it's not the usual pain, dull now, occasional. It's dark outside, but the bits of snow that drifted from the sky didn't amount to anything, the city glistens damp out the window, not white. What woke her? Not one of her waking dreams, she doesn't dream those now. Something else. She looks around the room and the stranger she keeps seeing, the young woman in uniform with the scar, one of the cleaners, she's there, armed with a mop and pail. She's standing in the dim doorway, looking at Sarah, her dark eyes serious. The woman Sarah's seen in the mirror, at the doorway, in the halls, not always working, sometimes just standing, watching Sarah. And now she's there at the threshold of the room in the middle of the night, an odd sort of stance, patient and anxious at the same time.

This thin young woman in the night who still seems familiar. The face in the mirror.

Sarah closes her eyes, maybe she's dreaming, but when she opens them again the woman is standing right beside her bed, her face intent, her hands clasped against her chest almost as if she were at prayer in some way.

"Do I know you?" Sarah asks.

The woman doesn't answer, smiles a hesitant smile.

"Do I know you?" Sarah asks again, in French.

"No," the woman says.

"I think I know you from somewhere."

The woman touches her hand to her own cheek, the scar there.

"No," the woman says, her voice soft. "You don't. It's all right. Go back to sleep."

Laila

You think this is your story, don't you? But it's mine.

You think this is your story, Sarah.

I know your name, *Sarah*, I read it on your chart.

I know your name but you don't know mine. Laila. It's from the Arabic word for *night*. Someone once told me that it means the same in Hebrew. They're in the same family, Hebrew and Arabic. Sister languages. A way we should understand each other, though Khalil said it was gibberish, Hebrew, a corrupt language, a language that was stolen from us.

I was here when they brought you in, I saw what the bullet, what the shrapnel did to you. You were taken apart and they've put you back together. You put yourself back together. You wanted to live.

You asked me in French if you knew me. You don't. There's just this little bit of my life touching yours, our lives bumping into each other, a brief collision. You'll think of me this once and not again.

Even though you don't know me, I'll tell you my story. So far.

I never saw my country, the country my parents want me to know. I never saw my country because the Jews took it away. I was born in a country that wasn't mine, I grew up there. That's where my family is, the fresh smell of washing on the line, the cigarette smell of my father. My mother setting grapes on the table in a wooden bowl, cheese and bread on a white plate set on an embroidered cloth. It was in the country that wasn't mine that my brother's friend raped me and cut my cheek.

I want to tell you it wasn't the Jews, it was my brother's friend. It was him.

I came to Paris with a boy. It was here in Paris that I found out what he loved: that clean gun in his arms.

And I cleaned, that's what I did in Paris, that's what I do. I cleaned for Mme Dupont and for Mme LeBlanc. Mme LeBlanc wanted to help. You work so hard, she told me, and you're clever. Your French is getting better. You should have steady work, a better job. She told me all these things.

I'm still washing Paris clean of its sins, but Mme LeBlanc found me a job here at the hospital. Now I work eight hours a day, five days a week, every week. And twice a month they give me my paycheque in a white envelope. Nobody tucks bills into my pocket with their dirty clean hands. I live in a room that's mine, a room that has a lock that I have the key to.

Mort aux juifs. It might as well have been me who wrote that. I'd never met a Jew. And I'd never met the man under the blanket I saw on the TV, his arm loose, the man whose face I didn't see, the one the newscaster said died in Beirut. Can I not mourn him? Can I not hate you? I can't, I will. I can't, I won't. I won't hate you, don't hate you, but not for your sake, for mine.

It might as well have been me who wrote *mort aux juifs*, because it was me who watched the boy write it, who was happy he wrote it. But it's not him I'm telling my stories to now, not the boy who loves a gun. He's gone, and I want him gone.

But I do want to tell you, I don't think it was him.

There was a picture in the newspaper of the gun they used in the *attentat*. It doesn't look like his. I know that gun and it wasn't his. I want to tell you this. I don't know what other business he has, but I don't think it was him who hurt you.

I wish I could wish you well. I wish I could tell you *assalamu alaikum*. Peace be with you. But the war between us hasn't ended. I don't know if it will. I don't know how long we have to be patient, how long we have to wait for justice.

This is my story, Sarah. So far. The Jews took my country. I live in a new one. And even if you think this is your story, it's mine too. If the war between us ends, maybe we'll both read our stories backwards, the right way, read them right to left.

Toronto

GIFT

1984

THE ROOM IS EMPTY, THE WHOLE APARTMENT VACANT, its white walls blanks now, so it's only the shape of an apartment. Everything that was hers has been emptied out, so that the space has gone back into possibility. Her life in these rooms is done. And now after two years the apartment is about to be filled with someone else's life. Sarah herself is about to be filled with someone else's life. She goes to the living room window, puts her hand against the screen, the scars faded but still there. It's August, the Japanese quince bush has long lost its flowers. The window's open to a heavy Toronto day, the air thick with humidity. There's hardly any breeze, but she can smell cut grass, someone has just mowed one of the miniature front lawns. She takes a breath, takes in the life she took back, the life that's starting.

The movers have dismantled and removed the little city of cardboard boxes she constructed, its rampart walls and ziggurat heaps, what she owned condensed into beige squares and rectangles. The mop and pail, broom and dustpan are stacked by the door. She's done her last cleanup here. The new place is bigger, room for the baby, which is due in December. Michael's baby, theirs. For two years, she's lived here with Michael, slept beside him. Slept beside him and not once has she dreamt the old terrible waking dreams.

So how is it that she's here, in this empty, open space, this summer – the attack a winter she lived through, a fig tree buried in soil, a tree pollarded to its stump, pruned to its core.

When Sarah and Michael left Paris, Gail was waiting at the Toronto airport.

And now, two years later, as Sarah looks out through the screen, the dense Toronto air, she still isn't sure whether Michael has forgiven himself. Despite the baby they decided on, the pearl that's forming from that seed of grit between them. Despite the way their lives have gained momentum as they change course, Michael's work, hers.

They'll have their own garden in the new place. Sarah won't plant a fig tree, she doesn't want anything forced. Before she decides on what to plant, she'll need to understand the yard, its light, its soil, what is possible. To learn her own terroir.

Her hand with its scars, the dots of shrapnel rising like memory to its surface, rests against the screen. But soon she'll go out into the yard, wade through the thick air to look it over one last time.

And one day she'll go back to Paris, because it's the city that took her apart and put her back together. She'll watch their daughter, a small and defiant child, eat her first Parisian croissant on the Boulevard Saint-Michel, she'll watch her at the Luxembourg Gardens, afraid to ride the ponies but content to be pulled along behind them in the little cart. Sarah will go back to a changed Paris, a Paris where a glass pyramid has landed suddenly in the centre of the courtyard of the Louvre; where the Impressionist collection has left the Jeu de Paume and been translated to the new Musée d'Orsay; where striped barber poles stand impudently in the cour d'honneur at the Palais-Royal. A Paris Sarah will at first refute, the Paris that is an accumulation of times rather than a place out of time, that can contain as many overlapping layers of time as is necessary: the roundups of the Vélodrome d'Hiver and the medieval ghetto, the Terror of the guillotine and the terror of 1982, which Sarah survived.

She won't tremble as she walks up rue François Miron, where the doorway to her favourite *pâtisserie* is still flanked by portraits of a dainty male sower and female reaper, each posing within the delicate gilt scrolls of their painted frames. She won't tremble as she walks the quick blocks up rue Ferdinand

Duval, past Bazar Miriam. She'll stop where the street ends, at that non-descript triangle, the arbitrary intersection of irregular streets which is not a place at all. Which is the place where the light changed, a shift in time, a hiccup. She'll stand steady in the place where something splashed into the room and the light was sharp. Because it was here that her body decided to save another woman who deserved more of life. But here also stood the sad man in green scrubs, his hands asking a question that couldn't be answered, that hasn't been answered yet.

She won't understand.

Her daughter will begin to cry, a wail that will trail behind them as they pull her away from what happened there. A long howl.

Sarah will come back and come back, with Michael and by herself, she will come from a life that is strangely rich, one she didn't expect to have in those brief and narrow days. She will come back to Paris as an excursion from this changed life, a visit tucked into the interstices of her work, Michael's work. She'll come back and show off first their daughter and then their son to Laura. She'll come back with Gail and then with Rose, with her nieces and nephews, Gail and Rose's children, with Pat and Abe. She'll come back to read the plaque set into the façade, which reads in French 'Anti-Semitic Attack' and gives the names of the dead, calls them 'victims of terrorism.' An attack with certain victims but with no certainty, because there is a continuing vital doubt about who was to blame. Justice is confused.

She will come back to the city that undid her, that took her apart and where she put herself together. But Sarah will not be in Paris when, as 2015 begins, in the wake of the murder of twelve people on staff at a Paris satirical magazine, a gunman will enter a kosher supermarket in the suburbs of Paris, and he will take hostages, helter-skelter, and kill four of them before French security troops free the rest. She will watch these images dribble and spill onto the screen of her TV and her computer, and time will be held briefly as she watches a blonde woman, freed, throw herself into the arms of a policeman helmeted in black, cloaked in black like a messenger of Hades, a man who is in fact, for the woman, an angel not of death but of life. She will not be there in fall of the same year, when a nightclub, a stadium, cafés are the targets, and she will watch briefly the surveillance video in one café, where five are killed by a gunman who looks, on the video, like a blur, like a white ghost. Five are killed at the café, but not the server who hides behind the bar where the camera has just shown her shrugging in conversation with a co-worker, where she has been polishing glasses. She is not killed and the woman who was sitting at a sidewalk table who runs to shelter with her is not killed. Behind the bar they hold one another like sisters, they hold hands, these strangers, and the server strokes the woman's head, *it's all right, it's all right.*

Sarah will come back in a mild and sunny fall with her grown son, who will be angry because no one is reading the words on the plaque, the tourists with their gleeful shopping bags, the street with its signs in Hebrew, its Kosher Pizza and Authentic Falafel, the butchers with their kosher foie gras, the stores with their 350€ handbags. None of the passersby will read the plaque and none will know what happened here just as no one can know all that hap-pened in this place in the many days before, the many days after the attack. On the street Sarah and her son will hear people speaking in French, German, English, Hebrew, Spanish, Yiddish, Japanese. A young man in full Chassidic garb, black hat with thick beard, *tzit-tzit* fringes dangling below his jacket, will go up and down the street, accosting tourists: *You Jewish?* he will ask in English. *You Jewish?* In English, in French. A question he will ask boldly on a public street. And *yes. Yes,* Sarah will answer in her head.

What is a Jew? How would Prof. Koenig answer the man?

You Jewish? the man will ask her son sternly, *tefillin* in his hands, offering her son instructions on how to properly wrap the little black boxes with their black straps around his forearms, and her son will watch and learn, or re-member.

And among the proselytizing Chassid keen on his mission and the bands of ignorant tourists there will be other, more subtle, Jews dressed in their Shabbat finest. *Lekhah dodi likrat kallah.* Oh beloved bride of Sabbath. Jews will be filtering among the crowds through the Pletzl, the place where they belong, the place as much theirs as it ever was. *Vivent les juifs.* Leaning against a wall will be a young man in a hoodie, his *kippah* jaunty on his head, scrolling through his cell phone.

Sarah and her son will leave rue des Rosiers, taking the old route down rue des Barres, then down the little pedestrian road to Pont Louis Philippe and across to Île Saint-Louis, where Sarah will buy them salted caramel ice cream cones from Berthillon, and then they'll walk across the footbridge that connects Île Saint-Louis to Île de la Cité, drawn by music that seems both familiar and unfamiliar.

There will be a trio of young people dressed in porkpie hats and tailored vests who are playing a music that is a mix of reggae and roots and klezmer, and while they speak to their audience in good English and French, quietly to each other they speak some other language that is theirs. The woman in the group will break into a solo soprano, her voice sweet and unearthly, and that voice will take Sarah apart, take her out of herself and then back in, will remind her she has been given a life, she gave herself a life.

Then a tune will begin on one of the young men's balalaika, a Yiddish song whose name Sarah can't remember, but one that she knows is about exile and hunger and displacement and longing. A gift that will move through the light, alive.

AUTHOR'S NOTES

The attack described in this novel is based on historical events which occurred on August 9, 1982 at Goldenberg's Deli on rue des Rosiers in Paris. Six people were killed and many injured in the attack. My hope is that this book acts as a memorial to the six people who died in the attack: Mohamed Benemmon, André Hezkia Niego, Grace Cuter, Anne Van Zanien, Denise Guerche Rossignol and Georges Demeter.

In the photograph of Elie Wiesel mentioned on page 63, the Yad Vashem on-line archive has the following information: The naked man standing on the right is probably Chaim Dovid Halberstam who was born in Nowy Sacz, Poland. He was the business partner of Gershon Blonder Kleinman. He survived and after the war he settled in America. *Bottom bunk level*: There is contradictory identification of several of the individuals in this photo, including the man furthest left on the bottom bunk level. He may be Gershon Blonder Kleinman, born on 06/05/1928 or 05/06/1928 in Nowy Sacz, Poland, who was an inmate in Bergen-Belsen, Auschwitz and Buchenwald concentration camps, who settled in America after the war (identified by his son Hudson Manor Terrace). However the Holocaust Museum in Washington identifies him as Michael Nikolas Gruner. A third source identifies him as Joseph Reich and the man beside him as his brother Isaac Reich. The man fourth from the left has been identified as Max Hamburger. *Second from the bottom bunk level*: The man third from left has been identified as Losh Wertenberg, later known as Yehuda Doron. However, according to other sources (Yaakov Marton) this man is Jeno Marton. The man fourth from the left has been identified as Abraham Hipler or as Berek Rosencajg from Lodz. The man seventh on the left is indeed Elie Wiesel. *Third from the bottom bunk level*: The man third from the left has been identified as either Ignacz (Isaac) Berkovicz or as Abraham Baruch. The man fifth from the left is Naftali G.

Furst. *Top bunk level*: Mel Mermelstein has been identified as the person at the far right. The man second from the left has been identified as Perry Shulman from Klimitov, Poland.

Max Jacob, whose identity is disputed in the scene on page 131 at the Closerie des Lilas restaurant, was in fact a French poet, painter, writer, and critic. A roommate and close friend of Picasso, he was part of the coterie of artists which included Apollinaire, Braque, Cocteau and Modigliani. Despite having converted to Catholicism in 1909, because of his Jewish origins he was arrested by the Gestapo in February, 1944. He died in the Drancy internment camp of pneumonia before he could be deported to Auschwitz, where most of his family had already been killed.

The unnamed curator of the Jeu de Paume during the Occupation, referred to on page 146 is Rose Antonia Maria Valland, a French art historian and member of the French Resistance.

While the photograph referred to on page 191, which Sarah finds of the family in the Vélodrome d'Hiver can be easily found online, I have been unable to find any more information about the individuals' names and fate.

The poem Rose reads to Sarah in hospital is "The Dancing," by Gerald Stern, from *Paradise Poems*, University of Pittsburgh Press. Copyright © 1982.

ACKNOWLEDGEMENTS

Once again I owe so much to the magnificent Warren Cariou for his edit of this book. He saved me from myself in instances large and small, and it is thanks to his wisdom, expertise and talent, that this novel is so much better than it would otherwise have been.

I am especially grateful to Haifa Staiti, Founder and Executive Director, Empathy for Peace, and Philanthropy Solutions Advisor for Grantbook, for her insightful input on the Laila sections of this book.

My thanks to Nancy Richler (z"l), Sam Znaimer, Sima Godfrey, Billie Livingston, Lee Anne Block, Jeanette Block, first readers. Special thanks to Leslie Walker Williams for her expert eye and invaluable advice on revising very early, and very tedious, drafts of this book. Thanks also to Sam Znaimer for his assistance with the section on calculus.

Thanks also to Dr. Catherine Chatterley, Founding Director, Canadian Institute for the Study of Anti-Semitism (CISA), for her information on the first Holocaust Studies course at the University of Manitoba, which was taught by Lionel Steiman in 1987/88. (The course Sarah takes precedes the actual date.)

ABOUT THE AUTHOR

Rhea Tregebov's first novel, *The Knife Sharpener's Bell*, published by Coteau Books, won the J.I. Segal Award for fiction, was shortlisted for the Kobzar Award, and was listed in the *Globe and Mail's* top 100 books. An award-winning poet and celebrated author of children's picture books, Tregebov has also edited numerous anthologies.

Born in Saskatoon and raised in Winnipeg, she did postgraduate studies at Cornell and Boston Universities, worked for many years as a freelance writer and editor in Toronto, and from 2004 to 2017 was a professor in the Creative Writing Program at the University of British Columbia (UBC). Now an Associate Professor Emerita at UBC, Tregebov continues to live and write in Vancouver.

MIX
Paper from
responsible sources
FSC® C100212

Printed by Imprimerie Gauvin
Gatineau, Québec